PRAISE FOR

SOUND

"Simpson has achieved a magical balance of superb characters, a spectacular setting with breathtaking scenery, and a compelling plot. She describes ships and the sea with the eloquence and clarity of C. S. Forester or Tony Gibbs, and she combines carefully delineated procedural detail with fascinating material on whales and marine fisheries. . . . Mysteries don't get much better than this one."   —*Booklist* (starred review)

PRAISE FOR

CROW IN STOLEN COLORS

"As many unexpected turns and thrills as the wild Alaskan coastline where it unfolds. A stunning debut."
                              —Margaret Coel, author of *The Lost Bird*

"Great characterizations . . . a captivating plot . . . strongly recommended."   —*Library Journal*

"Simpson illuminates two little-known societies—the watery isolation of the modern San Juan Islanders and the spiritual animism of the native Northwest tribes. And all in the middle of a nifty murder mystery . . . Quite a feat."
                              —Stephen Greenleaf, author of *Strawberry Sunday*

"Exciting . . . describes the beauty and danger that is Alaska."
                                                —*Midwest Book Review*

ROGUE'S YARN

MARCIA SIMPSON

BERKLEY BOOKS, NEW YORK

B

A Berkley Book
Published by The Berkley Publishing Group
A division of Penguin Group (USA) Inc.
375 Hudson Street
New York, New York 10014

This book is an original publication of The Berkley Publishing Group.

Copyright © 2003 by Marcia Simpson.
Cover illustration by Marc Yankus.
Cover design by Steven Ferlauto.
Text design by Julie Rogers.

PRINTING HISTORY
Berkley trade paperback edition / December 2003

Library of Congress Cataloging-in-Publication Data

Simpson, Marcia.
Rogue's yarn / Marcia Simpson—Berkley trade pbk. ed.
p. cm.
ISBN 0-425-19198-2
1. Women—Alaska—Fiction. 2. Single mothers—Fiction.
3. Alaska—Fiction. I. Title.
PS3569.I51165R64 2003
813'.54—dc22
2003055811

PRINTED IN THE UNITED STATES OF AMERICA

10 9 8 7 6 5 4 3 2 1

rogue's yarn: (naut.) a brightly colored strand woven contrary to the braid of a rope to show the strength or purpose of the rope.

ROGUE'S YARN

PART ONE

TOM

1

It's hard to say when it all began, maybe when my dad drowned and Mom got a lot of troubles, or when Matt came, and then Toby, or when Mom decided we'd grow up dumb in such a dinky doo town where nothing ever happened. But I think the real trouble started last fall on the afternoon our Permanent Fund checks came.

I was ten, then, and I think I must have had a blank tape inside my head instead of a brain. Now, all of a sudden, the tape has started playing back. The minute I get in bed at night I hear that whispering radio voice, "We know where you are . . . we're right behind you," and when I shut my eyes, I see black tide rips screaming past, empty where somebody should be swimming.

But the blank tape didn't see the trouble coming on that afternoon mail plane. All it saw was oil money dividends, $800 for each of us, just for being alive in Alaska. When we got home from school that day, Mom had spread the checks out on the table. Bo grabbed his and held it above his face and made kissing noises, but Mom stood on tiptoe and grabbed it back.

"No, you don't," she said, "this is it. We're going south—Disneyland—Mexico—see the world!" She pushed all the checks together in a pile on the table and put her fist on them.

"You crazy?" Bo said. "We gotta eat, right? You got a few more of these hidden away somewhere?"

Bo never believed anything Mom said. "That's mine," he said. "You can't cash it unless I say."

"Since when are you of age, my little downy chick?" she said.

Bo was fifteen and not little, I can tell you. He was already six feet tall and on the wrestling team, even though he was bone skinny.

Bo reached over and grabbed all the checks off the table and stuffed them up under his sweatshirt.

"You want a sponge for a brain?" Mom said. "The moon drowns this place twice a day. The skin of your mind mildews."

She started dancing around him, chanting, "Moonman, moonman . . ." Then she put her arms around him and slid her fingers up under his shirt and came out with the checks.

Bo went slamming off to his girlfriend's house and Mom stood at the window staring out like she did a lot, even though there was never much to see, just the Boat Works with the crane and travel lift and all the boats sitting up on blocks. Boats up on blocks always look to me like they're dead, like it's a boat graveyard. It was raining, mist really, the sort you can't see falling but gets everything soaked, anyway.

"This darkness . . ." she said, "it's an epidemic. The moon just imagines this place."

Mom had started talking to herself quite a bit, more than to us, actually. She'd change voices, sometimes talking like herself, sometimes like somebody else. It sounded funny, and I'd laugh and then she'd see me and laugh and say, "Well, hell-o-o-o, Tom Rohlik." I just thought it was kind of a joke between us. Bo would look disgusted, though, if she did it when he was around. It made him feel embarrassed, I guess. I think everyone in the family embarrassed Bo for even existing.

After Mom said that about the moon imagining us, she started tracing circles on the window glass with her finger. Inside the circles she printed, "YOU ARE HERE," in big letters, and there wasn't anything there at all, just glass and mist and dead boats on blocks. That did give me the creeps. I mean it was pretty freaky, watching her write, "YOU ARE HERE," and nothing there at all.

THE NEXT DAY, the trouble had already started when I got home from school. Usually when I got home, Mom would be listening to a Praise-the-Lord guy on the radio and some talk show on TV at the same time. I once asked her why she always listened to them.

"Because they do indeed know where they are going. Listen to this . . ."

She made her voice deep, sort of phony announcer-sounding— "*Please tell our audience, Audrey Bickle, how did you feel when you went to the police?*"

She started to laugh. "Audrey, do tell us, how did you feel?" she said. "How did you feel when your husband broke your arm?"

"So how does that tell where she's going?" I asked.

"She went to the police so she knew where she was going, didn't she?" Mom said. "It isn't Audrey who has all the answers, though. Listen now—this is the guy who knows—here it comes: *Let's get our audience reaction, Audrey.*

"Hear him? Poking at the silence? Building fences out of questions? Mapping his territory? It's the talk show hosts that know exactly where they are, Tom, the talk show hosts and the news anchors and the evangelists. Just listen to them."

I didn't hang around to listen. I didn't even think "crazy woman," in my little blank-tape brain. The trouble is, when you start noticing stuff, it's always too late. Have you noticed that? (Joke.)

WELL, ANYWAY, WHEN I got home the day after the checks came, Mom was at the door talking to a lady I'd seen around town a few times. The lady was fat and she had brown hair cut very very short, practically shaved off her head, so she looked weird next to Mom.

My mother was exactly the opposite, tall and thin. She had long blond hair and green eyes and a little scar under her chin where a fish hook got her, but you couldn't really see it, hardly at all. She was very pretty, especially her eyes, even though she thought she was way too skinny.

Mom was leaning against the door while the lady talked. She had her arms folded the way she did when we were too slow coming home after she'd told us a bunch of times. Like she was counting. I waited to see if the lady was going in or leaving, but they didn't move. I could hear Toby crying in the bedroom, so I squeezed past and went in to get her. When Mom moved to let me get past her, the lady pushed in, too. She looked around with her eyes going quick over the pile of laundry and the dishes in the sink, then back at Mom, pretending she wasn't really looking.

Toby was standing in her crib in the bedroom where us kids slept. Mom slept on the living room couch so she could stay up and watch TV or have her friends over and it wouldn't keep us awake. Toby started tramping up and down and laughing when she saw me. Of course she was sopping wet. I hung her overalls and shirt on the crib to dry out because we'd done the laundry just a couple days before. Then I put the dress on her with cute clowns on the front that was Leslie Sue Anderson's before she outgrew it.

Toby turned three on Halloween, the week after I turned ten. She was just our half-sister because her dad was Matt Abernathy, and ours was Boone Rohlik. Matt only lived here about a year. He left the day Mom went to town to have the baby. She was going to call the baby Matthew or Jessica, but it rained every single day the whole month, and then Matt went away, so she named her October Rain. I like October Rain better anyway. I babysat her a lot, since Bo was always out for wrestling and basketball, and Mom worked.

Toby was very small—only the size of Lynn Danof, who was just a year old. She had light-colored eyes you could almost see through, and a face like a little old man, or like one of those leprechauns on St. Patrick's Day. She didn't talk, but when she saw me coming home she'd squeal and duck her head down laughing.

People sometimes whispered mean things about Toby because of her strange looks and her not talking, but I just ignored them. I figured she'd talk when she'd thought about everything and knew what to say. Sometimes I even wondered if she was just very sad because her dad went away without waiting to find out who she was.

When the fat lady saw Toby in her cute dress, she swooped down like an eagle and grabbed her up, and said, "Oh my, oh my." Toby went all stiff backward and screamed as loud as she could and hit with her hands. Mom and I rushed to get her. The lady stood there looking like Toby had bitten her. She couldn't give her over to me fast enough, just shoved her into my arms.

Mom was furious. "Look at how you scared her," she shouted. "Take her in your room, Tom," so we went back and I shut the door. I sat on my bed and rocked her till she got quiet. Then we got out my cars and I let her play with them, even though I didn't usually, because she threw them instead of rolling them on the floor.

While I was rocking her, I heard the lady ask Mom where her husband was.

Mom said, "Dead."

The lady said, "Well, my records show that Mr. Matthew Abernathy is living at 2305 Sprouse Street, Anchorage."

Mom said, "So?"

"Well, then he's not dead, is he?"

Mom said, "I never said Mr. Matthew Abernathy was dead."

"Well, isn't he your husband, then?"

"No. He is not my husband, then."

"Are you divorced, then?"

"Are you the FBI, then?"

"Mrs. Abernathy, I'm only trying to get you some help with these children, especially the little one."

"You've got the wrong address. No Mrs. Abernathy here."

We started playing with the cars and Toby laughing, so I didn't hear any more until the door slammed. Mom came in looking pissed at everyone and said, "If that social worker snoop comes around again, don't let her in, or say one word to her, Tom. I'm going to work."

THE NIGHT AFTER that fat woman came to the house, Mom got home very late. I was asleep when she came in, but I woke up when I heard a voice out in the living room. When I got really awake I recognized it was Mom talking, going on and on, shouting like she was angry, and then laughing. I kept waiting for somebody else to say something, but nobody spoke. I could tell Bo was awake by the way he was breathing and lying on his back with his arms folded under his head.

"Bo," I whispered. "Hey, who is Mom talking to?"

"Shhhhhh, it's no one," he said, rolling over against the wall. "Shut up, Tom, go to sleep."

Well, of course I was going right back to sleep, my mom hollering away in the living room, laughing out loud and maybe nobody else there. So I lay as still as I could and listened.

"Mrs. Abernathy?" she said, and laughed in a funny way. "Mrs. Abernathy? What did you say *your* name was?"

She made her voice different. *"Call me Gail . . ."*

"Oh yes, Call Me Gail. Well, listen up, Gail. Let me tell you a little story."

"Bo, who's in there?" I said. "Is it that social worker lady?"

Bo hissed at me, and kicked his foot backward off his bed to make me be quiet.

"You know what Matt's doing now, up there in Anchorage?" Mom said. "Leeching some woman dry. Sitting around in some back room waiting for her to get off work so he can get enough for a six-pack, lace it with a little gut-burner. Let's imagine Matt a father.

"*Impossible.*

"I agree. He spawns, not fathers. There are better things than staying with such a man. No doubt I'll discover them.

"I thought Matt knew something I needed to know, that his organ voice would boom out You Are Here, but no. We will never be anywhere, not this child of ours with her pickled brain, not Matt waiting for the woman to bring him her fear, not I, Jess Rohlik, lost while sitting on the couch listening to all the Good News."

For a second I thought she'd started to cry, but then she went on talking.

"Matt was so present, like unforgivable words. Laughing all the time, a voice like a string bass, melody for those words, whatever they were. His fingers—seaweed drifting across my legs, oiling my thighs and breasts fat with his presence. You can see how it was, can't you, Gail? We were real at the tips of our fingers."

She kept saying, "you"—there had to be somebody—"Bo, who's there?"

"Shut up," he said, "just listen. I'll tell you later."

I tried to be quiet even though I knew he wouldn't tell me later. He promised that all the time and then when I wanted to know, he'd just say, "Ahhhh, quit bugging me, Tom."

"If you lifted up a stone in a tide pool you would see something like that man," she said. "It would be white and fat. Some of its insides would show through. You would feel sorry for its loneliness, but you wouldn't touch it.

"When I found out I was pregnant, I tried to get my head clear, tried to quit the booze cold turkey, but I slipped some. Everyone made me so mad with their knowing 'Get rid of that kid,' 'Matt will pay for the doctor,' what a laugh, he couldn't work long enough to pay for his own six-pack."

Mom stopped talking and laughed very loud, but not the way she laughed when she teased us or when we told her something funny. It sounded more like the kind of laughter you hear in a horror movie.

I rolled over on my side and propped myself up on my elbow so I could hear better. "Bo, what's wrong with her—why does she keep talking and talking like somebody's there?" It didn't seem like a joke between Mom and me anymore, her talking to herself. I mean, I wasn't even there, so how could it be anything between her and me?

"Stoned," he said. "Wasted, strung out, whatever—just shut up and listen or shut up and go to sleep, dammit."

"Have I told you how my friends hijacked me? Listen, now, Gail. They took me out on the *Lucy Jo* to dry out. Diane and Mark and Toni, my old friends from high school, put the snatch on me, and we floated around out in the Strait for a week on Mark's Bayliner, drinking club soda and milk and listening to soothing tapes, me throwing up when I got the chance.

"I loved them for it—they cared—they were like pure water after the twentieth filter. I've filtered out my friends, family, husband, lovers, nothing left but pure springwater. Diane, Toni, Mark. And my sons. And my scallop-shell child.

"Four months along in my pregnancy, I was, too far along to do the job, and anyway, I'd already decided not to. Decided by default, I guess, but it was my choice. I knew—don't for a minute think I didn't know I'd made the choice.

"Look at her, Gail. She's the one you really came about, isn't she? Well, there she is, sweetheart. October Rain. Wrong. All wrong. Can you imagine what her life will cost the world? Send them to me to talk about it, to look at her. Suffer the little children, and the mothers of them, the mothers of them, to come and look."

Mom was shouting like she was furious. Toby started sucking her thumb and scuffling around in her crib and I thought for sure she'd wake up and start crying, but she turned over and went back to sleep.

Mom's voice fell to a whisper so I could barely hear her at all.

"Did you change your ways?

"This is the truth, Gail. I was better. But not strong. Matt, you see, was still there on shore, the Siren on the reef, not the Warning."

All of a sudden Mom's voice got louder and sort of bogus, like she was holding her nose or talking into a tin can.

"I'd like to address my question to Audrey: Audrey, didn't you feel disloyal when you turned him in to the police?"

She laughed again, that creepy horror laugh. There was silence for a while, and then I heard her drag the guitar case out from behind the couch. She strummed a few chords, tuning the strings, and then sang, the first lines of "Mrs. Robinson."

"Gail, listen, I want to tell you about a night, six weeks before Toby was due. We went to the bunkhouse. Matt had a bottle of Everclear he won off Bert Anderson, and he got so drunk his eyes were fixed and his breathing made his whole body rock. Then he started, in a whiny, singsong voice I'd never heard before, to tell me exactly what he'd do if I brought the baby back to Tern Bay. When I argued, he slammed me against the wall. I could have screamed, but I didn't want anyone else to know. I waited.

"Matt paced and muttered like something caged, finally sat on the bed, rocking side to side. I thought if I pushed him down he'd pass out before he could get me again, but I waited.

"He sat there, legs apart to brace himself, belly sitting in his lap, hands working between his legs to loosen his jeans where they cut him. His mouth sagged at one corner, lips all shiny spit, hairs from his beard stuck to them. His whole face looked like it was tattooed on old scar tissue. I waited.

"He jerked his head up to look at me, but I was invisible to both of us. He toppled over on his side. His breathing lifted his belly above his half-open fly, let it down, lifted, dropped. I should have put a pillow over his head and then his belly would have stayed down covering his fly, covered it for good. I waited.

"He breathed and I waited . . .

"He breathed, and I opened the door and went out. I went along the hall, stepped around the cans and old newspapers and someone's laundry basket of T-shirts gray with fish slime, opened the door, went out to the road. The cold air slashed my skin, rain spun the streetlight into rope. I walked home very slowly, lay down on the couch without opening it, and waited for the black dream."

She played a few notes on the guitar, and sang another line from the Simon and Garfunkel tune.

"I woke late, long after the boys had left for school. The couch cushions were wringing wet and smeared with blood. I called Nancy at Mountainair and told her I had to catch the mail plane. I put some sweat pants and a shirt, my brush and comb and toothbrush in a plastic shopping bag, and sat down at the table to write a note for Bo.

"I was just finishing it when Matt arrived. He poured some coffee into a mug and threw himself down on the couch, not even noticing its condition. He'd had a shower and combed his hair across the bald spot; his eyes were open wide enough to show the blood-streaked whites. He was glad to see me and didn't remember slamming me into the wall. I fixed that."

Mom laughed then, like something was really funny, even though I didn't see how she could ever laugh again after what Matt did to her.

I'd never known all that junk about Matt. Nothing. Well, I was only six the year he was around, so what would I have known? I was glad she thought there was anything funny—I was thinking how I'd kill him for what he did to her, me being ten years old and very very brave and smart as you can tell.

When Mom finished laughing, she said again, "I fixed that. 'Know that thirty-eight you keep in the case under the bed, Matt?' I said. 'Well, last night, I got that gun out of the case, and I looked to see if it was loaded, and then I held it against your head, Matt, flat against it. Reach your hand up—I'll bet there's a ring there, right above your ear. I sat there a long time, a super long time, Matt. And then I thought, no, not worth it. The State would support me all right, but who'd look after the kids?

" 'Know what, Matt? You aren't even worth the bullet it'd take to spread what little brain you have around the mattress. So I put the gun back and came home. Next time, kaboom.' "

She laughed, and said it some more—"kaboom, kaboom, kaboom." Then she sang the last line of the song.

"Those frayed buttonhole eyes—he just sat there, staring at me with those eyes. Then he shoved himself to his feet, set his cup in the sink, and shut the door . . . very quietly. When he passed the window, he was holding his hand to the side of his head above his ear. I never saw him again."

Her voice got that bogus, tin-can sound again.

"Good news, good news! We're winners with Jesus!

"Today, the President said he will veto the bill—there are no guarantees . . .

"*And so please, Mr. President, veto bills that have no guarantees, hee, hee, hee . . .*" she sang, like it was another verse of "Mrs. Robinson."

"*Please tell our audience, Audrey, what were you thinking as you ran out the door?*"

Then she started playing, "The Sounds of Silence." "*Hello, darkness . . .*" she said, winding the words into the tune without singing them.

She'd played the guitar since she was pretty young, taught herself to play. She usually played sixties stuff—Bo said, "That's so old, man, why don't you grab a few new tunes?" but I liked those songs, even though most of them were sad. "Blowin' in the Wind," "Scarborough Fair," even "Puff the Magic Dragon" was a little bit sad—when I was little I'd cry because the dragon was so lonely at the end.

She started to sing "The Sounds of Silence," but then silenced the strings with her hand.

"I must have gotten lost again," she said, "I can't quite see where I am.

"But what good are they? Do they tell you where you're going? Where you are?"

The rest of "The Sounds of Silence" came twisting off the strings, and then there really was silence. After a while, I heard her put the case away, and then the couch springs creaked, and then nothing.

RIGHT THEN, HER talking to herself, nobody around, not even me, seemed like something dangerous. Like something I didn't want to think about at all. I don't think I actually thought "dangerous," but I know I was scared. Finally I said, "Bo, can I come over there a sec?"

Bo pretended like I'd woken him up—he said, "Unnnh." I knew he must mean, "Come right on over and get warm," so I got in under his blanket and he actually scooched over toward the wall to make room. Maybe he didn't even mind a little company himself, though naturally he'd have rather died than admit it.

I lay there soaking up the warmth where he'd been lying, and pretty soon I stopped shaking as much, but I kept thinking about what Mom had said about Toby: "Look at her . . . All wrong . . . Send them . . . to look at her . . . the mothers of them . . ."

But I didn't want to think about it, not any of it. So I lay there next to Bo, getting warm and not, not, not thinking about Toby or Matt or my mother. About my mother who was stoned, wasted, strung out.

OF COURSE, IT must have made Mom furious to be called Mrs. Abernathy. Her real name was Jessica Sjogren Rohlik, but everyone called her Jess. The only man she was ever married to was my dad, Boone Rohlik. Mom had lived in Alaska her whole life. She was born out on Little Spit Island, on the path to the beach, because my grandma, Bekah Sjogren, waited too long to go to town, and decided she'd rather have her baby on a bed of pine needles than on the floor of the skiff. Anyway, that's what Grandma always said.

Grandma wanted my mom to go away to college and turn into somebody. Mom said she tried—she went for a year and a half to a college in Seattle, Washington, but she wasn't turning into somebody after all that time, so she came back and married

Boone Rohlik. My grandma was quite a bit disgusted and washed her hands of it.

My dad, Boone Rohlik, was a Tlingit Indian from Iyukeen. Everyone liked him. People were always telling me about what a neat guy my dad was, how he made everyone laugh. He moved to Tern Bay after he got out of the Army, and bought a troller named *Defiant*. I was only three when the *Defiant* sank in a storm, and my dad and Del Janofsky drowned. Bo was eight so he remembered him pretty well, because my dad took him everywhere, especially fishing weekends and summers.

Of course I've heard about that storm a million times. Sometimes it seems like I remember when Mom found out about Dad drowning, a lot of people coming and Grandma carrying me down to the dock and putting a blanket around me when we got in her skiff. Maybe I don't actually remember it, though, because I heard so many times about Jerry and Sam coming to the door and saying, "The *Defiant*'s down, Jess, they're gone," and Mom not talking for about a year after, that I can't tell what I remember and what I've just heard so often.

Mom was still very sad and sometimes she'd stay in bed all day crying. She had this drawer that had broken things in it, cups with broken handles and bent spoons, stuff like that, broken necklaces, and sometimes she'd sit on the floor and look at those things, picking them up and turning them around.

MOM WORKED AT a lot of different jobs when she could, in the winter checkout at the Trader or the hardware, and in summer, the slime line setting up fish at the cannery, which is when she made the most money. The slime line is very hard work though, splitting, heading—her hands would be too sore sometimes to lift Toby or cut up her meat for her. In the winter, her jobs didn't pay enough to get a babysitter for Toby so she just worked a few nights after I got home from school.

She teased us a lot, and mostly she was a pretty good sport, but sometimes she'd get pretty tired working late, and then she'd be crabby. But mostly OK. She didn't yell at us about school grades like a lot of moms, she'd just say, "Up to you, kid—you stay in this dinky doo place it's nothing to me—you want to get out you gotta work for it."

So Bo and I tried to do well—Bo was actually on the Honor Roll every year, and lettered in three sports. I wasn't ever that good, especially not in sports. Mom always said I'd be good when I caught up to my height, but I still can't get the ball through the hoop, only for a once-a-game hallelujah play.

Once Bo started high school he was way too important to be alive even. He never spoke words, only noises. He kept his Walkman headset on all the time and sort of jived around the house if he was off the sofa, which he wasn't much, since he also watched TV and listened to his Walkman at the same time, how could he?

He never did the dishes or looked after Toby. When I told Mom it wasn't fair she'd say, "You know the rule about fair: It ain't always," and I'd wonder how that could be a rule.

Bo was also a drummer—"Percussionist, dumbo," he'd say if I said drummer—and he spent a lot of time drumming with anything and on anything he could lay his hands on, especially the top of my head, which drove me cuckoo. He played in the high school band—he'd sit there through the whole piece going *gonk, gonk, gonk* now and then, only sometimes there'd be a place where he could dizzy it up and hit on all the clangers and then everyone would clap. He had a rock group, too, a couple guys with guitars, and sometimes they got Bo's girlfriend, Sara Inslee, to sing with them. She had a cool voice, very low for a girl.

Sara was quite a cool girl, in fact. Sometimes she'd walk home with me if she was going to the store or somewhere after school, and Bo had to stay for practice. She always talked to me like I was her age, like I wasn't just blank brain dumbo. She'd ask what I thought of some teacher, or tell me she'd heard that the cannery workers were thinking of striking, or something like that. I liked Sara a lot, even though I hated most girls. The ones in my class were pretty snotty, whispering and giggling behind their hands whenever you walked by them.

Bo and Sara spent a lot of time on the couch, supposedly watching TV, Sara's red-polished toenails teasing up the edges of Bo's cutoffs, and Bo rubbing his hands up and down her bare arms.

Watching them, I'd get this prickly feeling, like something trickling all the way from the back of my throat to my knees. It wasn't a feeling I could name, exactly, but the TV was nothing compared with watching them, and Bo knew it. He'd tease me, running his hands up and down her arms, or he'd wind her shiny brown hair around his neck, and lick the tips of it with his tongue.

She was just absolutely beautiful. Last year, I thought I'd die of Sara.

TERN BAY, ALASKA, where we lived, had around five hundred people in the winter—Mom always said counting dogs, don't even mention cats. In the summer, a lot of people from down south came to work in the cannery and lodge, or to go sport fishing.

There weren't any roads to Tern Bay so you had to get there on the ferry or the floatplanes. I mean, it was so isolated we could just about have been living on the moon. Well, actually we were in a way, because, like Mom said, the moon drowned the place twice a day. Trees grew practically as high as the moon, too, and the plants' names kinnikinnik and devil's club and British soldier moss, told you who was around there before us.

"Watch the waves," Mom kept telling us, only she didn't mean the ocean waves—she'd make a list: "gold-seekers, trappers, loggers, fishermen, oil drillers, land developers, trophy hunters . . ." She'd shudder, like all those waves could drown her.

"Watch those tugs, now," she'd tell us, "see that—the *Fred Archibald* and the *Anna Paget*—those barges—the crane unloading all those cars and refrigerators and steel beams and carpet and bags of cement? Hunh! Positively civilized, ain't it?

"So the land's already carpeted in mold, and salt air rusts the engines and waves tear out the docks. So what? The oil money lubricates everything, doesn't it? A family of five can travel to Disneyland, or buy enough alcohol to lift the lid right off the world, right?"

Well, Mom was right about one thing—the dividends from the Permanent Fund paid a big price.

2

My best friend was Andy Millins. He was practically the smallest kid in the class, and since I was second tallest next to Debbie Cunningham who was huge and also very snotty, Andy and I must have been kind of funny-looking always hanging out together, but he was full of ideas and pretty fun most of the time, and to tell the truth, most of the other kids treated me like I was kind of freaky, mostly because I had to drag Toby around with me all the time after school.

Andy and I had some pretty good hideouts. One was under the boardwalk where it went out to the breakwater, and another was an old shipping container Trader grocery left out back, and we hauled up the hill to a place we knew, past old Simon Kaminsky's shack.

We stopped going to the boardwalk hideout though, because a few days after that social worker lady came, we got in trouble there. Andy got sent to his room for sassing back, and he sneaked out, and we took a bag of potato chips my mom had hidden under the couch, and went to the hideout under the boardwalk. We lay on our stomachs and pretended we were snipers.

We could see them unloading a long-liner at the cannery dock. One of those halibut was so big it looked like they were lifting up a huge white rug. Those things weigh two or three hundred pounds, some of them. Man, would I like to catch one. I'd take a hundred, even.

I was getting cold and also pretty wet from the gravel under the walk, but Andy said don't go back for dinner, then they'll be sorry. So after dinner, everyone started looking for Andy—we could hear them over our heads, his mom yelling for him, and saying how she knew it was my idea to run away, and when she found us she'd put an end to this once and for all. I thought she meant me. An end to me once and for all.

We kept real quiet under there and I didn't dare look at Andy. Then I did look and he wasn't there. All of a sudden, his mom reached in and grabbed me. She yanked me out and pushed her face right in mine, and my sweatshirt was sliding up over my head because she had her hands holding the neck of it way too high. She was screaming, "You little bastard, where is he? What'd you do with him?"

Then somebody yanked my shirt backward so I nearly strangled, and Andy's mom let go. I fell back, and there was my mom, right behind me. Her sweater smelled just like it always did—beer and perfume, I think, but always the same.

Mom yelled, "Get your hands off my kid," but Andy's mom already had got her hands off which is why I fell backward.

They had a big screaming fight right there under the boardwalk, with the rain dripping between the boards, and the stones all slippery from the stuff growing on them. Andy's mom was panting like some big old fat dog, and talking about Mom drinking, "and now look at that baby . . . Keep your filthy kids away from mine or I'll turn you in . . . When they see that baby . . . hunh!"

I didn't know what she was hollering about, but it sure made Mom furious. Mom reached across my head and slapped Mrs. Millins right across the face as hard as she could. Mrs. Millins took both hands and shoved me backward into Mom so we both fell against the piling under the boardwalk. I knew we must have gotten tar on our clothes, and it probably couldn't get washed out.

All the way home, Mom was whispering, "Terrorist, bomb squad, look out for the tripwire," and walking so fast I was running to keep up. I didn't have the slightest idea what she was talking about. Sometimes it seemed to me she didn't even use the same words as other people, like she talked some other language, Japanese or something.

A LITTLE WHILE after Mom's fight with Mrs. Millins, Andy and I got in more trouble. I collected cans and glass to sell to the recycling barge that came around to pick up. Once I had almost twenty dollars saved up, but somebody found it and took it. I'd already saved up $8.73 again, but I had it hidden where nobody would ever find it. One thing I'd learned, at least, was about hiding stuff. I may have been dumb about some things, but not that dumb.

Anyway, one day Andy and I were coming down the hill from our hideout, and we found this huge pile of bottles out behind Simon Kaminsky's shack, under some bushes. We went on down to my house and got a bunch of grocery bags and went back up and filled the bags with bottles. We tried to be quiet and hurry because old Simon was mean as a she-bear. We thought he might come charging out his back door with his thirty-ought-six and blow us out of there, bottles and all.

We sat out behind my house in the bushes and started dividing them so we'd each get the same number of bottles. We were arguing because Andy wanted to trade one large wine bottle for two small ones. He showed me that the labels said the amount in them was the same. But I knew there was way more glass in two small bottles than one big one, so he'd get a lot more from the barge for two than one. He got mad, because he thought he was smarter. Well, he may have been smarter, but he wasn't as good on glass.

When Andy got mad he talked real loud and fast. I guess he thought you'd give up because he was saying so many words loud, he must be right. His mom was going by and heard Andy talking loud and fast and recognized his voice. She came around back and pushed her way through the bushes like an Army tank. She stood there with her hands on her hips, her face purple-red, and her eyes blind mad like a brown bear ready to charge.

She said, "Andrew Millins, put that bottle down and march straight home. I'll see about this."

She grabbed me by my shirt again and said, "When I get through with your mom, you kids won't be living here one more day."

Then she let go of my shirt, so I fell back and tripped in the bottles. They went clashing and clanging down all around her feet. One bottle had some beer in it still, and the foam spilled all over her sneaker. She said, "Ooook yuck uuuck," and she was limping on her other foot when she went around the house, like the beer made her foot hurt. Was that funny!

I showed Mom the bottles when she got home. She said, "Hey, good work, Tomtom," and poked them around with her toe. I told her about Andy's mom. I showed how she limped when the beer spilled all over her shoe, and Mom sat down on the kitchen chair laughing to hard she had to wipe her eyes.

I asked her what Andy's mom meant, "You kids won't be living here when I get through with your mom."

Mom's eyes got squinchy and she said, "Say that again."

So I did, and she said, "You keep away from Andy awhile. An underground explosives specialist, that woman. A tunnel expert."

I asked her if Mrs. Millins could make us live somewhere else.

Mom said nobody on earth could take her kids away. "Believe you me," she said.

I did, actually. Sometimes she made up stories to tell us, but we knew they were pretends. When she said, "Believe you me," and her eyes were squinched up, I did.

3

One afternoon Toby and I were walking around on the dock and there came my grandma in her skiff, wearing her knitted Indian cap under her yellow rain hat like she always does. She had long gray hair she braided and pushed up under all those hats, so they sat up on top of her head like a tower.

Grandma used to come and see us almost every day, but then she and Mom started fighting a lot, especially about Matt and Mom's drinking. After Toby was born, Grandma hardly came over anymore. It seemed to me she didn't like my mother anymore, but I knew that couldn't be, because my mother was her kid, and Mom said that mothers always love their kids no matter what. "You just take what you get and love it," she said. So I knew my grandma loved her, but I thought maybe she just got tired of coming over because of being old, or some-thing.

After my grandpa died, my grandma went on living out there on Little Spit Island all by herself, fishing and setting some crab traps. My mother always said it was stupid for her to live like that, all by herself, because what if something happened, and Grandma always said, "Like what?"

Grandma wrote these notes to herself so when her mind went she could go on living out there. Grandma said her mother's mind went, and she wasn't going to wind up helpless like that. So she wrote little yellow stick-ons and pasted them up on everything. They said things like, *Run the generator once a week—it's a stubborn starter,* or *Matches here!*

Even though she wrote herself all those directions, she got in trouble now and then. For example, she went out fishing one morning, and one of the planks in the skiff just opened right up. Grandma said she guessed she hadn't been paying attention.

Well, Butch Jim happened to be going by in the *Moodoo*—he said he named it that because it was nothing but a cow pie float-ing on the water—and he looked over and thought Grandma was standing on the water, the skiff was so far under he couldn't even see it till he got right up to her. No way she was going to get aboard the *Moodoo*, he said. All she'd do was let him tie the skiff fore and aft along his beam, and she sat there in a foot of water all the way to town.

People in town really laughed when they heard, and they talked about "that crazy Bekah," but everyone liked my grandma. My mother was pretty mad. "I keep telling you you're too old to live out there all by yourself," she told Grandma for about the one millionth time. "You don't even read those crazy memos. Something's bound to happen."

"Like what?" Grandma said.

I think Mom washed her hands of it.

THAT DAY WE were down on the dock, I tied the skiff up for Grandma while she got out and hugged Toby. She hugged me, then, and I told her we were going to take the dividend checks and go down south. She listened very carefully.

"Listen, Tom," she said, bending right into my face so I had to look at her. "Listen now. I'm going right up to talk to Jess about this, but I already know what she's going to say. You make sure she buys round-trip tickets everywhere, you hear? Not one-way— round-trip. You look at what she buys every time she gets tickets, OK? I'll tell Bo, too, but I know you look out for things, so you check on that."

She put her hand on her back and straightened up like it hurt a little, and tipped my head back so I had to look up at her.

"Remember, Tom," she said. "Only round-trip."

I nodded and I was going to ask her why only round-trip, but Toby was pulling on her leash and getting ready to sit down on the wet planks. I fastened an old dog leash to the loop on her life jacket so she could look around and not have to reach so high up to hold my hand.

I told Grandma that Mom was at work so she couldn't see her right then. Grandma said, "Well, that's a good sign at least." She said we could go to the store with her, which we liked to do because she always bought us something.

WHEN WE GOT back down to the dock, there was Sam Nagyak just tying up the *Tykan*. He climbed over the rail and gave my grandma a huge hug which lifted her right up in the air.

"Bekah Sjogren you taken up the swimming I hear," he said, laughing the way he did so his whole face was one humongous smile. "Don't you know to nail up them planks 'fore they fall off?"

Sam shook my shoulder, teasing, and grabbed Toby up and kissed her all over her face so she squirmed and pushed and laughed at the same time.

In the summers, I fished with Sam on the *Tykan*. Bo fished with Jim Donner on his gill netter, the *Sunny Belle*. The *Sunny Belle* was a very excellent boat with all fancy electronics that Bo was crazy over. Jim was a great fisherman, a real high-liner, and they cleaned up most summers, if the price wasn't in the cellar. Sam was pretty old, though, so he only went out for day trips, trolling. That way I got home in time to look after Toby so Mom could go to work.

The *Tykan* was an old boat, no fancy gear on it, but we did OK. Sam taught me to run it so he could tend the lines. Also how to clean the fish, unhook the shakers easy so they didn't get hurt, stuff like that. If there was a shaker too far gone to make it, Sam always gave it to me to take home. Or sometimes, if they all went back OK, he even gave me one of the keepers, which was pretty excellent of him, I thought.

Sam grew up out on the tundra, and came down to the Southeast with his mom and dad when he was twelve years old. Sam's son, Joseph, got killed in Vietnam like my uncle, the one I'm named after. Sam and my grandpa were best friends. Sometimes Sam told me stories about fishing with my grandpa, and Joseph and my Uncle Tom. He always told the stories laughing so hard the tears ran down his face.

I once asked Sam about my uncle and Joseph, how they died. I was thinking bombs or torpedoes or airplanes getting shot down, but Sam said, "Ehhhh, Tom, was lies killed them. That war, it made everybody lie."

He shook his head and shrugged. "You're better not to think about it," he said. "It's over—won't be no more like that, everybody lying to each other that they could trust before. Won't happen like that no more."

I wondered how a lie could kill you. Just go off like a big bomb or something? I didn't believe lies could actually kill somebody. I thought Sam probably was just talking. He was pretty old, actually, older even than my grandma.

THE THING OF it was, everybody treated me like I was a little kid. Even when I got to be ten years old and I wasn't so dumb anymore. I mean, if you're ten years old, you know about most of the stuff that they think you don't know, right? And so they might as well talk about it. But it's like, "Oh, no, he's such a young little child, we don't want him to feel bad that his dad and uncle and grandpa died, and his mom had a baby and didn't get married to its dad, so we'll just whisper when he's around."

It drove me cuckoo, they way everybody acted.

Once, when Andy was mad at me, he told me my grandpa had gotten shot by a crazy man, and our whole family was weird because of it. Well, I thought, if somebody in your family was shot by a crazy man you'd for sure know it. I mean, everyone would tell you about it. So the next morning, I asked my mom how my grandpa died.

"He went away in the dark," she said. "Torn on the dotted line."

Well, that sure made a lot of sense, but she wouldn't say anything else, just "Don't ask me right now, please, Tom? Some other time."

At least I figured out from that that he didn't just die of his heart being old like I'd always thought. So when I saw Sam getting in his skiff at the dock, I asked him.

"What did your mother tell you?" he said.

I told him that Mom said, "He went away in the dark. Torn on the dotted line."

"What does that mean, though? A lot of the time I don't know what Mom's talking about, do you?"

"Shouldn't bother over it, Tom—Jess's head's full up of old blue reef-rock sorrow."

"But what got torn up?"

"I guess that's what Jess felt like that day—the whole world tore up. You sure could say that. Yes indeed you sure could say that."

Well, I wasn't saying, I was asking, but Sam just nodded his head and went right off telling me about one time when he and my grandpa caught this huge halibut and they couldn't get it in the boat, like he'd already forgotten what I asked.

I told Bo what Andy said.

"Yeah, it's true," Bo said, "he did get shot by a crazy man. Grandma told me. Now, off my back, buddy."

"So why won't anyone tell me about it? I've asked everybody and it's like, hey, you're just a little kid, you're too little to know stuff like that."

Bo picked up a couple spoons from the table and started

drumming away on the edge of the table. He looked over at me and I ducked because I figured he was getting ready to drum on my head, but he just threw the spoons down and shrugged, not looking at me anymore.

"So why me?" he said. "I always gotta be the one, right? In your face, kid."

"Nobody else talks to me. I'm not kidding, everybody in the whole world treats me like I'm two years old."

He picked up the spoons again and did a few fast riffs.

"Well, so this is all I know, OK? Lenny Carter was some fucked-up weirdo, right? Didn't have either oar in the water? He was head sawyer at the sawmill and he had a really bad temper—Grandpa fired him for beating up a logger. So Lenny went up and shot the trumpeter swans that Grandpa used to feed in the winter. Mom went up there with Grandpa and they found the swans lying in the snow, all bloody and blown apart.

"Then, a couple days later, Lenny went screaming into the harbor in his skiff and leveled everything in sight with his AK-47, three guys dead, five wounded, the whole dock covered in blood like it was Vietnam right there."

"You mean Mom saw him do it?"

"Nahhh, I think she was in school when he did it—I mean, she was only sixteen then, hardly any older than me. It must have been harsh, though, like the worst? But now, it's like it never happened."

"She couldn't just forget it, though—I know you couldn't just forget something like that."

"See, bad stuff like that makes you do things so you won't think about it, like her getting stoned all the time and talking out loud to herself."

"But you gotta feel sorry for her, even if she does do stuff like that? I mean, she must be very very sad inside."

"Listen, Tom, she drinks. She fucks around with guys and drugs—haven't you seen her around here with that new guy lately? They're in the bar every time I walk by—she's fucking up our lives, Tombo."

He started drumming with the spoons, whirling around, clinking them on the edge of the sink, clack on the counter, rat-a-tat on the tabletop.

"Wake up!" he said—*bam bam bam*. "That's why nobody tells you bad news..." *Clinkety clink*—"You keep hoping." *Slam. Bash. Clack. Clack.* "You don't listen." *Rattaty rattaty, bam, bam...*

Well, I was listening. Believe me, I was listening.

1

Listen to me. I was caught in Boone's net from the minute I saw him crouched there on the dock, untangling the bird's nest of fish line in a little boy's reel.

"Well, Joey, it's a damn 'ol mess, hey?" he said, and looked up at me, laughter spouting from every line in his face, never looking anywhere else again the rest of his days, my breath gone from his looking, from our eyes locked up so tight there wasn't any air to breathe between us. You have to hear this, how it happened to us, how he locked up my life like that and carried it down with him, deeper than the moon ever uncovers, far below that eighteen feet of world the moon draws up each day.

He was an Indian fisherman with hands like alder,

pliable and knotted and strong as whips, dear god, you have to understand the way all my senses drowned twice, in his voice, his smell, the taste of salt on his arms and thighs, how I followed his fingertips until I lost my way, drowned again in the sea, the waves taking my life down in a little wooden boat.

Do you know how much we wanted each other, right from the minute we met, wanted everything? But we didn't know how to get there. Boone was so polite, and I was so young. We didn't know how to get past those two things, as if we were wearing survival suits that kept anything from touching.

We would have stayed like that, even when I started crewing for him, except I got sick. Oh, was I sick! Boone had all these wonderful ideas: stay on deck, focus your eyes on a distant object, breathe deep. I did all those things when I could stand up, but mostly I just hung over the rail and threw up everything but my skin. There was nothing, not one thing, left inside my skin, and I just couldn't stop.

When I was so exhausted throwing up I could hardly get to the rail anymore, he came up behind me and balled his fist up and plunged it between my ribs right where my muscles were so sore, shoved his fist so hard into me I couldn't breathe.

I wrenched around and bit his shoulder right through his flannel shirt. He picked me up and dropped me down the ladder, and we were down there on the bunk, half wrestling, half working at our clothes, waves on the hull thumping, poles clanking, tin tub on a nail sliding back and forth, back and forth, tin tub, tin tub, decks awash . . .

We didn't ever have much except each other—it was hard, paying for the boat and two kids, one season OK, the next no fish, or so many the price wasn't enough to make the boat payment. Even then I worked at the cannery and the grocery, but we

could barely make it, food costing so much, shoes for the boys—
they seemed to grow through them before I got the laces tied.

I thought we should go into town in the winter where I
could get a better job, and Boone could maybe work in con-
struction or something, but he wouldn't even talk about it.

"No way I'll ever live like that, some dump in town, nine to
five, somebody bossing me, all those loggers crowding in."

Boone hated loggers—I don't know what would have happened if my father had been around when Boone and I linked
up—Boone hated loggers and he hated the mill. Logging's messy,
slash and bark in the streams, booms breaking up in the ocean
so the logs get into the fish nets, or break a propeller, or hole the
boat in the dark.

Boone sometimes tangled with the loggers in the Grizzly Saloon, got himself cut up several times when everybody'd had a
few too many, those fights when there's a sudden silence, then a
stool knocked over when somebody's ready to make his point
with his fists. EJ, the bartender, was good, she'd see it coming,
and hold the door open after one warning, and with her size and
the sudden quiet of her voice when she got serious, not many ignored her.

We'd be asleep at home, the boys and I, the heavy footsteps
in our dreams thumping us awake. Boone hung from the men's
arms like seaweed from the cliffs at low tide, one eye already
shut, two Band-Aids pulling the cut on his jaw together around
the black blood dried at the corner of his mouth. I'd feel Bo's
gasp jolt my hip hiding him. Boone's face turned to clown mask,
his effort to smile breaking loose the Band-Aids, breaking up my
horror into rage, the two men desperate to leave, to shuck themselves of the limp body leeched to their arms.

The second time I saw Boone brought home all bashed up and the other guy getting flown out by the medics, I was sick of it.

"Cut it out," I told him, "or I'm headed for town where I can make a living from something besides fish. Listen, Boone Rohlik, I was raised on lumber money by a prince of the earth you'd have worshipped yourself."

His temper would be gone by then and he'd cry from the booze and tell me it was over, he didn't hate loggers, just that one.

He didn't often drink too much, but when he did he saw someone coming at him with a whole forest dragging into his trolling lines, saw them chopping down every tree in the Southeast, the salmon never coming back, the bears homeless, the deer dead on the beach. Booze, the great exaggerator. When we're sober, of course we know these things could never happen.

BOONE DECIDED HE'D go long-lining for halibut, those crazy two-day openings regardless of weather. I threatened him, told him this time I would leave him, take the kids: "You don't care about us—don't think what we'll do when that stupid boat sinks!"

He promised. He promised me. He could still make his boat payments if he missed one opening, so he wouldn't go unless the weather was OK. He said so. That's exactly what he said: "I won't go if the weather's brewing up, Jess." Remember how he said it? He didn't have to long-line to make his boat payments.

But he went anyway. All because Del Janofsky, who was crewing for him, was broke and needed money because his wife was pregnant and not doing too well. You remember that, don't you? That Boone only went because of Del?

The spring storm that took Boone was the worst storm on

record, the worst ever. Nine boats lost, five men. The Coast Guard helicopters got as many as they could, dropped their ladders and rings, stayed up even when their fuel gauges read near empty. But the *Defiant* was heavily loaded—she iced up and the load shifted— she went down so fast the guys on the next boat couldn't believe it.

"One crest we saw them, the next one, nothing. You wouldn't believe it!" they kept telling me.

"Boone plugged his boat before we were half-full," they said. "Too good, that guy. Went down like a stone."

"You had to see it. Just whoosh—nothing left. Gone."

They couldn't stop talking, just saying it over and over. "Whoosh, nothing left."

I shut out their words. Because there's always a chance, always a space somewhere, if it isn't filled up with words. Voices burning me up like wine. "Whoosh, nothing left." I wish that were true.

Look. See that boat coming in at dusk, running lights on, winking green, rounding the outer marker, winking red, slowing to no wake? No wake. Look at the boat turning into the slip, engine dead slow, dead slow, roaring and grinding to stern, bow swinging, straight with the slip now; he'll jump across the gap, knot the doubled line, back to the deck, switch the engine off, flip the panel switches, run the bilge pump one more time and switch it to Auto.

Come home, Boone, the kids are ready for bed, Tom shuffling around in his blanket sleeper, Bo propping up the sail again on the boat he's building for you. First, though, you have to shovel out the old ice, hose the hold, stack the buckets. We're waiting. It takes you so long.

Why does it take you so long? Don't you know I'm down to zero from holding it in so hard, waiting till you've thrown Tom in the air and bounced him a thousand times on his bed till he's too sleepy to laugh anymore, till you've checked the rigging on the sailboat that's only pieces of driftwood and string, till you've showered and wrapped a towel at your waist long enough to get from the bathroom to bed, till you've flung your wet leg across me, your fingers starting at the beginning and finishing what I can't hold in anymore? Our skin grafts, makes a sucking protest when you move to sleep.

You know all this, and still you have to stack the buckets first, scrub the deck clean, leave the boat a monument. In the net at the bottom of the sea. My whole life.

I SHOULD HAVE left Alaska years ago. I tried. I tried. I went south, found a room, walked that ironclad checkerboard of city streets. But my head wasn't right. You know that, don't you? That Jess Rohlik's head has never been right?

I got lost. Everything looked the same, the corners where four streets came together, the sidewalks and the glass, cement buildings with doors that ratchet you through, people all alike. How can anyone tell where they are? Not me.

There are never enough arrows. "You are Here." Maps should show people's faces, how their hands look, the shape of their bare necks coming up above their collars and meeting their ears. How else can we know where we are?

Once I saw a man who had no neck—his head sat directly on his shoulders. How do I forget him? That's the trouble, you know. Never forgetting what you don't care to remember, just because of some look or smell or feel—the inside of someone's arm raised to hold the bus strap on the way downtown. You look at the arm, and you think, nothing special, why look, so you look away, and there's that arm, the skin of it like an old potato, a little powdery with time, leather strap over it, gray Brillo head pressed to the arm's own sadness for help. And you never forget that, the man with no neck, the faded brown scrubbiness of someone weary.

But do they tell you where you're going? Where you are? "You Are Here at the neckless man; at the straphanger."

Some people know everything. Preachers, TV anchors, talk show hosts—their voices brush my oyster brain and leak across the membrane raw as iodine.

—*Jesus is holding his arms out to you!*

—*Today, the President vetoed the urban reclamation bill . . .*

—*How could you come so quickly to that decision, Audrey?*

These people know everything, but you can't touch them. Have you noticed that? You can't touch the backs of their hands.

I THINK WE'D better talk about the social worker. Call Me Gail. She has been here three times. She is very sorry about us. What, I wonder, is she sorry about us about? The children, she says. Bo, in particular, he seems angry, silent; his teachers say he is silent and angry. He's fifteen, I told her, and not stupid. Why would that make him angry? she asked. He doesn't know where he is, I told her. It runs in the family.

The little one, she said, Toby. She should be getting therapy—socializing play experience, speech instruction. She has no brain, I said, she is a black hole—everything goes in, nothing out. We have to maximize her abilities, she said. I think it is restful in there, I told her, she is at peace in there why disturb her? I'll let you think this over, she said, and I'll come back in a few weeks to discuss a program for the children.

She came again. We think Tom is hungry, are they getting

enough to eat, he doesn't seem to eat before he gets to school. Of course he's hungry, I told her, it is part of the hunt, being hungry.

"Can anyone help?" she asked.

"That *is* the question, isn't it," I said. "The axle of the universe, that question."

She stared at me a long time with her eel eyes. She was nodding when she left.

This social worker knows everything that matters, knows in exactly the same way that talk show hosts know. They build fences out of questions until you see that the boundaries are not ones you can live with. You take up flying, and the words for flight carry you over the fences, but there you are again, lost in midair. Arrow pointing Up. She knows how to use questions for answers. Tombs made of Lincoln Logs. Well, they're never going to get them. Not my kids. My two sons and my chambered nautilus with no one home.

Bo is sometimes an old man who hasn't believed anything for a long time, sometimes a boy called up on stage, his eyes shielded from the sudden spotlight and the cruel assuming faces. He commands my utmost tenderness. You recognize that, of course, from the way I address him. Have you ever tried to transmit tenderness to a fifteen-year-old male?

Tom's still all child, with his father's capacity for love, and the sweetness, the innocence, of my brother, the artist-dreamer who carried the gun and tramped on the mine. Give my child a Geiger counter, a white cane, to feel his way along the path. If I must, I'll beat him first myself to save him from the world. Who lays a hand on Tom has me . . .

All right, all right, I hear you drumming on the tabletop in mighty irritation . . . Such shameless word games, Jess!

2

You know my mother, don't you? Bekah Sjogren? Thick gray hair braided around a sea urchin shell. Prickly as they come. Let me tell you, she is mad. Do you know what she's doing? Little yellow notes pasted up on every object, every wall of the house. At first I thought she must be getting ready to sell the island—everyone's been after her to do it, living out there all alone, seventy years old, using a chain saw and axe, hauling crab traps, taking the skiff over to town. But no, the memos are for her. For her to read when her mind goes, so she can go on living there, know how to run the saw and the generator, find the matches. Jesus god, do you get that? When her mind goes!

The note pasted above the sink faucet:

If the faucet doesn't run, there may be needles in the hose. Unfasten the hose clamp and run the wire up the hose.

Do you believe this? She says it's hard to know what directions to leave herself. When her mind goes, will she know what a hose clamp is?

A while after she wrote that, she added: *You have to use the screwdriver to loosen the hose clamp. The toolbox is under the window seat.*

Will she understand that the needles are from the spruce that hangs over the roof, not the cedar?

So then of course she has to add that to the note: *In the fall, get up on the ladder and rake the cedar leaves off the screen covering the rain barrel.*

But now she's worried. Will she understand rain barrel? Will she know where the ladder is?

The kids die laughing—they make up silly notes to themselves—Bo wrote a big sign the other day for the bathroom door, *Pee Here*, and Tom almost peed before he could get the door open, he was laughing so hard. So then I have to yell at them, because I don't want them to hurt her feelings. But my god, when her mind goes? Goes where, you have to wonder.

Besides this catalog of survival, Mom's writing down her history so when her mind goes she'll know who she is, even if she can't remember who she is. Now, I ask you. If you can't remember who you are, what is the point?

She's using the back of Dad's account book from the sawmill, but she's going to run out of pages soon. She says if her mind doesn't go soon, she'll have a buy another notebook. Jesus god. She calls it *Self Operating Instructions*.

Your name is Rebekah Mary Macdonald Sjogren. You were

*born in Iron Oak, Wisconsin, in 1919. Your parents were Ellen
and George Macdonald. They loved you, but you let them down.*

*You live in Alaska, now, on Little Spit Island. Your husband,
Gus Sjogren, named it when you came here with him to homestead. You were married to him for 33 years. He was very stubborn.*

For a while, that was the end of it. But she said that for some
reason it made her sad. She decided it was because "he" could
be anyone, of no particular importance, when "he" had been
her husband for thirty-three years. So she crossed out "He" and
wrote "You." Then the note said, *You were very stubborn.* But
that wasn't right, because *she* certainly wasn't very stubborn. So
finally she wrote, *You were very stubborn, Gus.*

"REMEMBER YOUR GRANDMOTHER, Jess," she keeps saying, as though I could forget her. My grandmother's ghost sits
on my shoulder. She sits stiffly, rocking forward from her hips—
forward, straight—forward, straight. Her hands wash themselves
and her eyes look through the window, but whatever she sees is
behind them. Her hair is all herringboned gray and white, her scalp
pink where someone has raked some of the hair into a knot at the
back of her head. She looks like a woman of ninety. Fifty-four.
Ellen MacDonald is a decrepit, senile, old, old woman at fifty-four.

The refrigerator motor hums into life and my grandmother
picks up the sound. The humming fills the whole kitchen, a
counterpoint between the refrigerator and the old woman in the
corner. She sits, rocking and lost, on my shoulder. My mother
has set her there.

Of course you remember my dad, Gus Sjogren. No words.
He never had words for bridges. He was a toucher. Not bad, I

don't mean the kind of horror you hear about all the time, the
secret, cruel "gimme, gimme" touching. Just the "how are you,
your arm feels thin with worry" touching.

By his hands we knew him, the first joint of his left ring and
middle fingers left under a blade, the lifelines buried in whorls
like knotty yellow cedar. I can still smell the work of them, the
outboard oil, the crabpot he pulled on his way from the mill, bit-
tersweet odor of black logs ripped into sudden orange lengths,
wet wood smoking in the stove.

His hands knew everything: the span of a tree, the length of
a plank, the pulse of twenty fathoms on the crab trap line, the
axe handle, the filet blade, the scribe he used to carve the heart-
wood into loons. The splinters of my brother's bones.

His hands knew my mother. They thought I didn't know, but
I'd watch them touch. They brushed each other, secret codes,
love, irritation, laughter in their fingers. I saw it. I learned it early,
touching. They knew every surface, in and out, it showed in their
passage, in their presence in a room, every surface, hot and wet,
smelling of sawdust and bread, stretched and tuned and exhausted, they knew it all.

My mother's body lives inside a vacuum now. I know exactly where she is. We are the same in space, but we are not *in*
the same space. Can that be true? There is something here I
don't understand.

What? Something you don't understand? Oh, surely not, Jess.

When I was three, Dad took me fishing and let me hold the
pole myself, at least he said he did. I caught a huge lingcod—
could I have held a thirty-pound lingcod by myself? He'd smile
when he told it, "Jess caught a thirty-pound lingcod all by herself."

But he wasn't the only one smiling. That fish smiled an
enormous toothy grin, lips flapping thick as a clown's, "Hi, Jess,

guess where I've been?"—a sort of huge Hobbit creature leaping in front of me, and Dad hit it on the head. Not once, but over and over till it stopped leaping and asking me riddles. I screamed for hours.

Out there on the island, death was all around me—eaglets blown from the nest, deer hung for venison, their brown marble eyes watching me from the rafters of the woodshed, crabs writhing into the boiling water. But every single day the tides renewed the land, lifted the island again, spread the table with life. And nobody so relished that renewal as Gus Sjogren.

I never saw anyone like my dad for keeping track of all the little changes, the light coming and going—"Watch now," he'd say, "how fast it goes—in December, never even a halo back of Comfrey."

By February he'd have us watching for the sun to clear Comfrey Peak in the cut before Quarter Round. "Just like that yellow ball that bounced over songs at the movies—watch for it now—Comfrey to Quarter Round, then up over Elder Jim, then out to Gnome Rock."

Three days later there it was, bumping along Hopewell and Littleman Ridge, then the whole sky. "See, Jess, an anthem, now, not a song."

I loved to go to the sawmill with him, stand next to him with my hands jammed over my ears to keep out the pain of the saw's scream. The sawmill's closed now, sawdust burner tilting like the Tower of Pisa, rollers rusting in their tracks, but I can still see those huge trees coming down the rollers, sawyer signaling, setter nodding. Bandsaw sidles, sets, there's the squeal of the first rip into a hundred years, orange peel planks marching through side by side.

"Watch the sawyer's hands, Jess. See? 'Turn ninety degrees,' 'taper,' see how he talks with his hands?"

Dad would hum under his breath—how could I hear such a sound beneath all that whining scream of blades? I know I couldn't have heard it, but it's in my bones, those tuneless words, ". . . *Praise the Lord, and pass the ammunition. Praise the Lord, and pass the ammunition . . . and we'll allll be free.*"

The words would build up in the back of his jaw till they burst out without the tune at all. Those big old trees like mortars slamming into place, carriage kicked back, planks exploding out of the gang saw like arrows, the dust of their passage filling the air. Sometimes his feet stamped while he marched on that saw-dust road, ammunition rammed home.

Dad hardly ever lost his cool, but I remember how mad he was when I told him he was raping the earth by sawing up those trees.

"Me?" he said, like I was talking to the moon. "Raping the earth? Listen, young lady, you get your dinner and your fancy-dancy blue jeans from those saw logs. And it's a two-bit opera-tion at that. You want to complain, you go after Louisiana Pacific, and leave a little food on your plate."

I told him I wouldn't touch a bite if it was bought with log money. I even went out and caught some rockfish to eat while he and Mom ate steak she'd bought at the store with his log money. He asked me very politely if I was concerned that the supply of rockfish might be impaired if my crusade against logging caught on. He didn't laugh out loud, of course.

There were troubles besides his daughter's rebellion. It seems to me that trouble at the mill was as much a part of Dad's work as the account book and the log booms swinging into shore. In-juries, labor. Fingers lost, heads split open, strikes. Sometimes it was ugly, people in town divided, not speaking to each other, not speaking to us, the owner's family. Fisherman, logger; Indian, white.

The price per board foot fell, bids from bigger mills went too low to match, the setter quit, the foreman went to Ketchikan, the sawyer drank. Blades tore out, machinery balked, the old steam wheel was replaced by hydroelectricity and the power plant burned down. People in town blamed the mill for overloading the lines and starting the fire.

Every night a new trouble to tell at the table. Mom always had a solution, especially for the labor problems.

"You're weaseling, Gus. Why don't you just lock them out?"

"There are two sides to it, Bekah. The men have families just like us."

"You ought to make them sign a contract. You're too soft on them."

"We have to be calm, talk calmly with them, Bekah, try to keep things from getting stirred up."

"Why don't you fire that sawyer, Gus, Lenny Carter's a troublemaker like I can't believe. You ought to fire him."

Fatal words. Jesus god, what fatal words those were.

You remember my brother, don't you? Tom Sjogren, the dead one? The magic boy blown to confetti in celebration of elephant grass on the Mekong delta. Jesus god. Do you think he saw it? What he stepped on? Did his eye ever miss an eagle, a tube worm, the motion of stones?

Listen. He took me under the water, surface like asphalt, "Look deep, Jess, will your way down, turn it clear. Fish like straw shadows, see them? Do you see them? Watch now. The stones on the bottom rise toward you."

He saw through every disguise—he knew how to live in a country imagined by the moon. But over there in Vietnam he had no camouflage.

Tom and I were wild things growing up out there on the island, as much at home in hollow trees and rock caves as in the
house our father made.

"You be the eagle, I'll be the bear."

"You be the tree, Jess, I'll be the rock."

"Lie perfectly still, Jess. Listen, now. Do you hear it?"

I would try to be the rock or the tree waiting for the eagle to
return to its nest, or I'd try to feel the thud of surf on the other
side of the island through my body pressed to the sand. Tom
could lie there for hours, inhaling the bitter yellow tracheal smell
of salt marsh, till the tide touched the soles of his boots. My legs
twitched, though, and my chin rested on gravel. I had to turn my
head to see if Tom was still there, and seeing him I had to touch
him, and in order to touch him I had to dig the toes of my boots
into the sand and arch my body like an inchworm and creep my
fingers secretly across the space between us, disturbing the gulls
and starting the eagle perched in the snag above its nest.

"Lie still, Jess. Can't you be still?" Tom would complain. But
even in those days I had to ruin the silence.

ONE SUMMER, A cousin who lived in Seattle asked to send
her son, Dennis, for a "wilderness experience," meaning a few
weeks with Tom and me on Little Spit Island. We all went over
and met him at the ferry dock, Tom and I wary; an intruder, this
sandy-haired, chubby kid, not anyone we needed. Tom was
twelve, that summer, and I was seven.

Dennis was a year younger than Tom, but he had all the joke-
talk we'd never encountered, and I was constantly bewildered by
his winking remarks to Tom. "Yoooou know," he'd say, grinning
at Tom, poking him, and shrugging his shoulder at me. I think

Tom often was puzzled, too, but he played the game, and I spent a lot of time kicking over stones on the beach and complaining to Mom who insisted I leave the boys alone some of the time—"They're older than you, and boys like to do things on their own some. You can't always play with Tom, you know. Come on, we'll take the skiff and go over to the store, and maybe Diane will be around."

Two days before he went home, Dennis took a washtub out of the tool shed and carried it down to the beach. He wanted to make a tide pool in it, "rocks, crabs, stuff like that," and we helped him. We worked away all that day making it exactly right, rocks with barnacles tasting the sea with frilled tongues, hermit crabs, sea urchins, snails, gumboots which Dennis insisted on calling chitons, rocks with flowery anemones fastened to them.

We rushed back after lunch and searched the growing tideland for more treasures—a sea cucumber, the smallest jellyfish we could scoop up gingerly with a tin can, mussels, and the greatest find of all, a baby halibut rippling across the inshore edge of the tide, so young its eyes had not yet migrated to the same side of its head.

When Mom called us for dinner, Tom said, "Time to dump it back in. You take one side, Denny. Jess, stay back, it's heavy and we don't want anything to slop over before we get to the water."

Dennis stared. "Nothing doing," he said. "I'm taking this home—I'll put them all in Aunt Bekah's canning jars and take a box on the ferry. I'm going to show them at school—write a report for extra credit."

Tom and I looked at each other. Tom shook his head, baffled. "They can't live in jars, they have to have saltwater," he said. "And oxygen."

"And waves," I said.

"Oh, well, I know they won't live very long," Dennis said, "but our science teacher knows how to pickle them. He can make them into specimens for the lab. I'll get an A+ for bringing everything for science."

Mom started hollering for real then, "I mean it, you get in here right now," so we ran, Tom not saying anything more, not even looking at me all the time till bed. But I was ready when I felt his hand shaking my shoulder, had my jeans and sweatshirt on under the blanket, ready.

We stopped on the back porch and pulled our boots on, looking up through the cedar at the smoked glass sky, the August night like a solar eclipse. The path had no shadow to warn of roots and rocks, but our feet knew every obstacle, and we ran, the muffled thud of our boots shaking the earth itself.

The tub showed paler than the beach it sat on, and we stood a moment looking down at the shining surface. A stream of bubbles erupted like bullets in a mirror, and Tom bent close to look, but the sky reflected too brightly to see into the tub. He straightened, holding the handle on his side.

"Try it, Jess," he said, "but if it's too heavy we'll have to try to drag it across the sand."

I lifted with both hands, facing the tub so that the bottom edge carved both my shins as it rose, and Tom turned and put his other hand on the handle, so we were facing each other, leaning away, straining to keep the bottom up off the gravel. The moon had kindly brought the water back for us, covering the afternoon acres of mudflat and seaweed, so we hadn't far to go. When we got to the edge, I started to tip my side over but Tom stopped me and set his side down so that my hands slipped and I let it down with a jolt.

"Be gentle," he said. "First we have to lift out all the rocks, so they don't fall over on the halibut or the hermit crabs or anything. Don't be in such a hurry, Jess. Reach in carefully, and lift the rocks out first."

It was too dark to see down into the tub, and everything was slippery and scurried so there was constant grating of shell on sand and metal, and a couple of times Tom snatched his hand back. I was scared to reach in and feel around and I remembered the jellyfish. I waded the ends of my fingers. Everything felt slippery. Slimy. Sharp, too. Everything was sharp.

Tom's face was in the shadow because he was bent over, so I couldn't tell how he was thinking about what he was doing, but I could hear him breathing, sort of quick, uneven, like maybe he was scared, too, reaching in, thinking about the jellyfish, listening to the scuffling.

"Come on, Jess, hurry up, we're getting soaked," he said.

I did it, then, put my hand in, felt around, picked up a rock, listened to the slip slip of the water licking the gravel, and set my rock right there in the edge, reached in and got another, back for more, why had we collected so many? I could hear Tom stirring his hand around, the sand gritting against the bottom of the tub; we must have gotten all the rocks.

"OK," he said, "I think we got them all, we can pour it out, but go slow, we don't want anything to get hurt."

We stood up and grasped the handles and the back edge of the tub and poured, slowly slowly, until we had the tub clear over on its side. Then Tom said, "Hold it like that and I'll rinse it out."

He waded forward a step, reached down and slapped water into the tub, tilting it and turning it around carefully to be certain no resident was still lurking. "Step back away from it before you turn around," he said, "so you don't step on anyone."

He stepped backward himself, then stretched out and lifted the tub high and carried it back up the beach. We left it on the rise where the tree roots curled down to the beach, and went back to the house, shucking our boots from our feet on the porch. We tiptoed across the plank floor, right turn at the wood-stove, left around the kitchen table, right through the living room, dogleg into the back hall, not even breathing past Mom and Dad's door. Tom's hand on my shoulder steered me, a little squeeze and a push at my door, then on to his own room, his bedsprings complaining as he sat on the edge, Dennis muttering in his sleep.

In the morning, we were silent when Dennis asked Mom for some jars and a box. We followed him along the path, stumbling far more frequently than we had in quarter light. He took it all in in an instant. We should have left the tub at the water's edge, told him the tide must have covered it and washed everything out. Our experience with crime was too limited. The tub was enthroned above the beach, framed by ferns and salal. Our footprints were everywhere. Dennis turned and brushed past us, lurching along the rocky entrance to the woods, running as his feet found the path. We followed slowly, in silence. By the time we got to the house, Mom had heard the story and was ready for us.

"Did you empty the tub?" she asked. We nodded.

Then she asked, "Did those things belong to him?"

Fierce, isn't it, a very very serious question with only one possible answer, if only one knew it.

We failed. It wasn't the first time Tom and I were rendered speechless in our own defense, nor the last. In silence we went to our rooms and spent the day alone considering our sin. Dennis was imprisoned in the great outdoors, companionless, too nervous about stings and bites and pinches to collect more "specimens." He had the consolation, though, of being able to answer the question.

OFTEN WE'D SEE the humpback whales between the island and the shore where they feed every summer. We'd go to sleep hearing the forced sigh of their breath like wave over rock, or we'd go out in the skiff, and suddenly those barnacled jaws would rise like the pipe wrench of God. They'd roll up alongside us and their ancient eyes asked questions, gathering verse for their songs. They sing a language I learned long ago, the only one I *ever* learned, the only one . . .

I remember one fall morning when my brother and I rowed the skiff across to the mouth of Karen Creek and hiked up Littleman Ridge to the muskeg to pick wild cranberries. Clouds overlapped each other like fish scales, and the sun behind them teased every color.

We clapped our hands and shouted, "Hey, bears, ho, bears," while we climbed. Tom had to drag me up the steep rocky outcroppings, and wait while I sat at the top to catch my breath. How old were we, then? Five and ten, I'd guess. Not very old. Not very old, at all.

You know how the muskeg looks in fall—all purple and orange embroidery, trees huddled over pools of water, searching for a taste of soil. We moved in circles away from each other, following our own water-filled footprints, feeling for berries under leaves, singing to warn the bears.

After a while, we came together on opposite sides of a pool, our faces perfectly mirrored. I could see Tom's upside-down lips move silently. He said, "Hi, Jess, I've got more cranberries than yoooou do."

We stood there, laughing and arguing silently, "No you don't," "Yes I do," until my foot slipped at the edge. Then our faces splintered into tortured tree branches and birds flying overhead. When the ripples stopped, the pool had no bottom at all.

WHEN MY BROTHER was thirteen, he and Dad discovered a pond halfway up Quarter Round, right at the edge of the muskeg. A flock of trumpeter swans were using the pond for a layover, eating the stuff on the bottom, poking their heads down through the thin film of ice that formed at night. Swans have to eat under-water—they can't just pick food up off the ground like chickens.

Every year after that, Dad and Tom would go back at the same time, and sure enough, the swans would be there. One year, though, we had a very cold winter, tons of snow, everything frozen up, avalanches thundering down whenever there was a warmer day. That year they found the swans starving because the water was frozen solid, except for one little place where a stream ran in and kept a few feet open. They came down and got some of the men, Sam Nagyak and Arnie Mark and some of the others, and packed grain up through all that snow to the creek mouth.

Mom didn't want them to go. "The bears," she said. "They're so dangerous in winter if they wake up hungry. You'll have all that grain on your backs."

"We'll be together, Bekah," Dad said. "Don't worry, we all have guns."

So of course she didn't worry.

—*Don't worry, Jess. I won't go if the weather's brewing up.*

The men poured the grain into the water, and broke up some more of the ice around the edges. Dad and Tom went back up every few days for weeks to break the ice until the swans left on their journey north.

After Tom died, Dad asked me to go up with him. It was slow, the snow in the gulleys soft and the sides steep, our feet sinking into slush and bog. Dad waited patiently when I stopped to empty the water from my boots, never urged me faster, though he and Tom would have been home again before we even reached the pond.

The swans were there, so clumsy on land you couldn't believe they were the same guided missiles we saw over the Strait. Dad watched them just a minute, and then took my hand and pulled me back along the trail without a word. The next year, I think he went alone, if he went at all. I didn't ask to go. Only once. Only one more time to see the swans.

Call the social worker; silence and anger are here. These swans are so hungry they're dead!

Am I running on? I do that when I go back to the island, wander around its edges in my mind, watch the mist fingering the hemlock, stand under the cedar braiding the shaggy bark, listen to the rain ticking onto the salal. Listen to the waves folding over the land, a winter wren whirring in the brush. Listen to the vacuum in the universe after the loon wails. We weren't crazy and lost in those days. We were at the *center* of the universe.

Yes, I am running on. Where was I? My parents.

Their worries and arguments carried through the chinked walls with the flare of the lamp and the settling of the fire, fueling my dreams.

Dad was always for letting things alone. "Why don't we just leave them be, Bekah?" he'd say.

Mom was all action. When she made up her mind that Tom had to go to "real" school, that he needed companions and sports and currying, she dug in her heels.

"He's growing up wild, doesn't know a farewell from a 'How do you do.' He never wants to stay in town with the other boys, wants to get right back out here, hunker over that drawing paper, lie on the beach and turn over rocks like he'd find some answer under them. I don't mind it, Gus, he's good, he's smart and he's learned well everything we've taught, but it's time he knew what's out there. He can't live here on seven acres floating in the ocean the rest of his life."

Mom had taught us herself. Tom was fourteen; he'd finished the second-year algebra book and much of the high school program in history and English. He could have taught biology himself. Dad gave in, and since Tom would be taking the skiff over to school every day, why not send me with him?

There were few places to hide on Little Spit Island, but that year I was nine I wore them all out. The safest was on the steep west bank of the island, a cave visible only at low tide, when eighteen feet of cliff appeared each day, trees clinging desperately until the tide gathered them. The moon, the moon—it giveth and it taketh away.

Day after day I crouched in dark spaces while angry voices passed overhead. I think I knew, even then, nine years old, that I would never find my way along a sidewalk or know where I was in a cement corridor. There's no way to learn their rhythms. Jesus god.

Tom finally persuaded me to try. "It's not so bad, Jess—we got way ahead of the other kids, so the teachers give you time to do what you want. Like drawing. There's a great art teacher, Jess, you'll like her."

"I can't draw," I said, "and there's all those stupid boys always pushing around and making fun."

"I won't let them," he said. "Promise."

I went, and I hated most of it, but there were a few friends even then, Diane I'd known since earliest days, Toni who came in seventh grade and was scareder than I. A few others. But after school I'd go straight to the bar. EJ, bartender and my mother's best friend, was always there, safe as tree trunks, waiting to yell at me and give me a cloth to dust with, a towel to dry glasses, and a ten-ton shoulder to scare away the day's horrors.

Mom, of course, has EJ recorded: *You had a friend, Ella Jane Ratkys, sometime Havlicek. She was planning to outlive you. You old turkey vulture, EJ. Pity.*

You remember EJ, don't you? The Paul Bunyan of women, so strangely shaped, like a child's stacking toy put together wrong. The layered look: a bunch of plaid shirts on top of a knee-length sweater, under that skirt of some burlap material flapping over giant rubber boots, an old watch cap on top of her head.

EJ lived in the red shack right at the top of the ramp to the dock, so none of us ever got away with a thing. She'd corral the unwary and invite them in for tea, some herb stuff she favored to punish those who had failed in some way, which was every one of us.

"Tastes like shark's piss, don't it?" she'd snort, watching to be sure you drained your cup. "Reams out the evil."

Good lord, it was awful, nauseating glop EJ made—it left a thick smelly residue like tar at the bottom of the cup. You'd feel so relieved when you got down to that, and then EJ would hand you a spoon. Not one whit of human kindness in that woman.

EJ made her living tending bar at the Grizzly, and later bought out the owner when her tips exceeded his take-home.

Maybe it's hard to see how this could have happened, but EJ said yes indeed it could if you always kept Number One in mind.

EJ had three children, Jonathan, Sandra and James, but when Mom first met her, EJ told her they were abroad. In fact, it turned out that EJ's husband, Charlie, had put them aboard his old junker boat and headed north. He'd left a note for EJ which she found when she got home from closing the bar at 2 A.M:

You arnt fit to raze these kids, drunk all the time. Dont try to get them back—I got them where you wont see them no more.

EJ kept a thirty-ought-six mounted on a tripod in the front window, aimed right at the end of the dock.

"Loaded?" people would ask her. "Isn't that kind of dangerous?"

"Danger, babe, is what I have in mind. Murder. That man sets one foot on that dock and I'll blow his whatsis right off."

One morning, EJ looked down on the dock and there were her three kids standing there, shivering like scared deer, no sign of Charlie. She went down there and got them and spent the next fifteen years getting those kids back in shape as she saw it, hounding and hollering till they all finally finished school and went off and turned out fine. That little one, James, is a lawyer, even.

EJ claimed that parents should have a "statue of limits," as she called it, absolving them of further blame when any child reached thirty. "Goes with the no-fault insurance policy you get when a kid comes packaged without directions," she said. No wonder James turned out to be a lawyer.

Ella Jane Ratkys, sliding cans the length of the bar to "that old fart, Elmer, down there at the end," is one reason bars are home to me.

■   ■   ■

LATER I JOINED the gymnastics team, traded one bar for an-other, and I was actually pretty good—tall and much too skinny even then. But the year I was thirteen, my career came to a quick end. I first saw the emptiness from the balance beam. I was nearly through the routine, poised for a back walkover, when I knew it was there. Right behind me, waiting for me to hurl my-self into it and disappear forever. I couldn't turn and look, couldn't breathe. I froze there until Margaret, the coach, came and took my hands and helped me down.

I tried a few more times, but it never left me alone again. How can I describe it so you can understand the terrible attraction? Something wanting me, some light-forsaken loneliness wanting me to share it, enter it forever. If I moved, I would be part of it, never again able to touch anyone or hear their voices. "Never" seemed so long. "Never" was what was out there in the center of the floor.

Of course there was an argument.

—Leave her be, Bekah, she feels terrible enough as it is.

—Gus, we can't ignore this—what is it she sees, anyway? Didn't you ask her? On the way home, didn't you say, "What is it that makes you freeze up like that?"

—She said, "Did you see it, Dad, could you see it?" and I said, "I couldn't see it, Jess, but I know it was there."

—Gus, for pity's sake, you "know it was there"? What does that mean?

—Well, if she sees something so scary she can't move, it's there somewhere, isn't it?

—But what does it mean, Gus? She needs help. We don't know what it means.

—It's just the way she is, Bekah. We better just leave her be.

My mother nails up the hard ones—have you noticed? "What does it mean?"

. . .

MY BROTHER WAS a fine basketball player. Sometimes I
went on the team trips when my parents were chaperones. We'd
take the ferry and arrive in other towns in the middle of the
night, sleep on gym floors and the basements of churches. In
Tom's senior year, the team won the Small Schools District
Championship in Ketchikan, and went to the state playoffs in
Anchorage. They were eliminated immediately by a team from
Shishmaref, but the excitement of being in Anchorage far out-
weighed the loss. All we wanted to do was ride around on the
buses. Buses and cars were thrilling modes of transportation to
those limited to ferries and floatplanes.

Things were gaining on us, though. Everyone at school began to talk war and protest, draft and draft evasion—"Would
you go—run—go to Canada—go to *college*?"

A couple of the older ones signed up—a couple of them
went off when they got their notices. They were rumored to be
in Prince Rupert, fishing; in Guadalajara, sunning; in a Mexican
jail. Some new fishermen appeared now and then, no addresses,
no mail. They'd hang around in the bars and fish enough to buy
booze. A lot of the time they just sat around on one boat or another, passing a joint, and listening to the Stones and Joan Baez.
Eventually they'd drift off without saying goodbye.

My parents had always assumed Tom would go to college—
by the time he finished, the stupid, meaningless war would be
over, they thought. But the year that Tom was a senior, college
stopped being an option. Everybody had the same chance of going—all the birthdates were put in a bowl and drawn out one at
a time—a lottery.

When Tom's number came out of the fishbowl so early, a

war broke out on Little Spit Island and my parents changed sides. Dad, the pacifist, took up arms for responsibility. Dad's brother had died on the beach at Normandy. Tom would go. His country had called him.

Mom's drive for action turned to Peace. She brought out the heavy artillery. "Killing's wrong!" she shouted. "Anything, anywhere." Then she strapped the bayonet to her words. "Better *die* than kill!"

She rode the ferry to Seattle and joined the marchers. Most of the protesters seemed crazy to her, though, an army which used flowers and pop cans like weapons. She said her hair was wrong—braided and coiled. She let it loose and an icy wind beat it to a mat she couldn't part.

She saw that she was wasting the days that were left, that nothing there was worthy of Tom. None of that rage and screaming had anything to do with *her* child carrying a gun.

When my mother came back from the protests, her eyes were bruises in the bones of her skull. "We're sending our *children* to Vietnam," she said. And when those who lost their childhood there came home, a whole generation died another death.

Is that when we all went crazy? When the loon stopped calling and the universe filled up with noise? Because that was when we started listening to the radio voices.

—*Today, the White House said the American response was directed solely to patrol craft . . .*

—*Air power now used north of the twentieth parallel can be used in Laos . . .*

—*If peace does not come through negotiations, it will come when Hanoi understands our resolve . . .*

—*Accordingly, I shall not seek, and I will not accept, the nomination of my party . . .*

■   ■   ■

WE WENT OVER to the dock to see Tom off. Over the whine
of the plane taxiing up the inlet, Mom shouted at Dad, "You've
sent him off to die!"

Dad shouted back, "You've ensured it."

Did they forgive those words? That is some of what I do not
know. But not the sum of it.

Tom wrote to them but his letters were all about nothing,
about the jungle and rice paddies and rivers, children, water buf-
falo . . . nothing at all about real things like killing people.
You'd have thought he was a tourist.

Tom was an artist, though; his drawings told another story.
The pictures he sent me . . . clawed wounds, backlit by bursts of
white space. The last one showed the surface of water splintered, as though a film of ice had cracked and layered across itself. Beneath the ice was a face. One eye was large and staring,
the other drooping and filled with sorrow. Only a corner of the
nose and mouth showed, distorted by the movement of water
under the ice. There were other shadows below the face, flying
people, the head of a bird, bent over, the body invisible.

He didn't want to upset Mom or Dad, so he made me promise I wouldn't tell them what he sent me. My folks taught us you
never break a promise, or else no one in your whole life will ever
believe you. "In your whole life." Do you have any idea how
long that is?

You've promised, you see, but you're burning. You burn
down to ashes. Cold, gray, blowing in the wind ashes.

In my whole life I can never tell about Tom's last letter, because I promised.

Dear Jess, I killed a little girl. She was going to shoot Billy. I wanted to save them both but I couldn't. Mom was right. Better die than kill. Tell Dad and Mom I love them. I love you too. Tom.

Mom was right? Words like trip wires. Now she says that everyone should receive a once-only lifetime exemption on words. How would she ever choose?

The Army cable came only three days after his letter. *Regret to inform you . . . result of enemy action . . . line of duty . . .*

And then the letter from his buddy.

Dear Jess, Tom was the best point man so they didn't never leave him off. He never missed only the one time. He got too far ahead, I tried to stay on him, but I couldn't. They should leave him alone some. I don't know why he did it, why did he? I wish it was me. Your friend, Billy Garcia.

Did Tom see that trip wire that he stepped on? Did his eye ever miss the motion of stones?

—She's out there in the woods like a wild animal, Gus—look at the scars on her legs from thorns. She's doing it on purpose.

—Leave her be, Bekah. She's missing him, that's all. She's trying to see what it's like to hurt that much.

—She's crazy, that's what. We have to get some help before she tries to find out what it's like to be dead!

—She has to get through this herself, Bekah. Just leave her be.

Magic boy, look deep; the stones on the bottom rise toward you.

TOM

All of a sudden, Andy's mother got very friendly to me. I didn't know why, but she started asking me over after school and Saturdays. I couldn't go after school, usually, because of taking care of Toby. Mrs. Millins would say, "Oh, Tom, what a shame, couldn't your mom get a sitter?" so I'd have to tell her that Mom didn't make enough in the winter to pay a sitter out of what she got at the grocery checkout.

Mrs. Millins would pat my head, but then I'd see she'd always wipe her hand off when she turned around, like maybe I had something catching like that beer foam. I really didn't like her—I didn't in a way trust her since she'd always yelled at me up till then, but I was glad to play with Andy.

I didn't bother to tell Mom about it, how I was going to his house some—she might have said, "That terrorist, you keep away from Andy awhile like I told you," something like that.

Mrs. Millins let us set up the car racetrack and play right there in the living room. She had this friend that sat there on the sofa most of the time, and this friend and Mrs. Millins would talk and talk but sometimes ask me questions like did I get to do the laundry.

"Boy," Mrs. Millins would say, "I sure would love to have a boy like you that wanted to do all the chores, wouldn't that be great, Melba?"

Then Melba would say something about she wished she had a helper, all right, she could sure use somebody to cook at her house, did I do the cooking, too? And I'd say, well, not always, and they'd laugh and nod and say oh, wouldn't it be nice, Andy and Jason and Jennifer just never lifted a finger to help their poor old mothers.

It seemed as if all they talked about was what I did at home. Once Melba asked if that nice Matthew man was still living at our house, and I said no, he hadn't ever lived there, really, and they just looked at each other and Melba said, "Oh, I see."

I guess I didn't want to think about why they asked me so many questions, because I liked playing with Andy inside. It was raining all the time, and cold, and the hideout wasn't too great. So I tried to be polite, but not tell them much, even though they kept asking.

I was with Bo one time going home, walking behind him, of course, and Melba passed us, so I caught him up and asked if he knew her. He said, "Melba Dingdong Diller—she's the one on the school board that's always trying to get them to cut out all the sports programs to save money. She's an asshole."

I told him she was always at Andy's house when I was there and she'd ask me all this snoopy stuff about me and what Mom did. Bo about croaked.

"Wha'j'ya tell her?" he said loud under his breath, digging my arm so it about came off.

"Nothing," I said, "only that Matt doesn't live there anymore because he didn't ever live there, me sometimes babysitting, stuff like that."

"No lie? She asked you stuff like about Matt and you babysitting?"

"Yeah, she asks stuff, and Mrs. Millins all the time does, too, but I don't ever tell them anything, only those things I said."

Bo stopped right smack in the middle of the road and grabbed both my shoulders like he had pliers in his hands. He said, "Tom, you tell them one more word and I'll hold you under the dock till your head's froze to your butt. Got it?"

He made me so mad. Why did he get to shove me around and tell me what I could say just because he was bigger and older. I wouldn't say OK so he started twisting my arm back like he did so I finally said, "OK, just leave me alone." Sometimes I just totally hated Bo. I hoped he'd hurry up and get his boat and go out fishing forever and never come back to Tern Bay.

OF COURSE IT was Andy's mom that made the trouble at school, then. Another of those times when I noticed stuff too late.

Bo and I got these white envelopes with Mom's name on the outside, just when the bell rang for us to go home. They were sealed up, but Bo tore his open anyway. He read it out loud, about Mom giving permission for Bo to talk to Ms. Alexander, the school district social worker. I asked Bo what a social worker was. He said, "A party animal. You know, somebody that works at socializing—partying, drinking—that stuff."

"That's the dumbest thing I ever heard. Nobody would get a job with the school just to party," I said.

Bo said if I thought that was so dumb wait till Mom read this. Would I ever get my ear blasted then. He crumpled his paper and envelope up, stuffed it in his back pocket, and went off to the locker room to dress for basketball.

WHEN I GOT home, Toby was out in front with Mom waiting to go to work, so I forgot the letter. It wasn't till late, when Mom got home and we were watching *L.A. Law,* that she got the letters. I remembered it, because I was looking for some report I was supposed to be working on, and there was the letter in my pocket. I gave it to Mom. She read it and said something under her breath. She read it again, and then asked Bo if he got one.

Bo was pretending he didn't notice any of it because he was so busy paying attention to *L.A. Law,* but when Mom asked him again, he stood up and got his out of his back pocket and threw the crumpled ball on the table. She spread it flat and didn't even say anything about his being already open. She stared at them awhile and then she took each one and tore it down the middle, and then each piece into little pieces, like she enjoyed tearing.

I was glad I wouldn't have to hand anything back to Mrs. Harper. Mom told me not to worry about it, she'd take care of it, by god she sure would take care of it. So I went to bed because I believed her. She'd for sure take care of it.

■   ■   ■

AT SCHOOL, I got picked to go with Mr. Raymond and get the Christmas tree. Andy was mad that I got chosen, so at afternoon recess he started saying stuff on the playground like "You only got picked because they feel sorry for you."

I said, "Why would they feel sorry for me? What're you talking about?" and Andy said, "Everybody knows about your mom, that's why they let you do everything."

I just pushed him away and told him to shut up, "There's nothing about my mom so just shut up," but he kept going, saying Mom was a boozer and sleeping around, everybody knew it, she was super crazy, too, couldn't even talk like normal people, all the time laughing by herself or saying stuff out loud that nobody understood.

He kept getting in my face and he'd pretend he was whispering and then shout it out so the other kids could hear it. A lot of the guys started hanging around listening but pretending they weren't, and the girls were all standing together watching with their heads turned sideways.

I pushed Andy a little and walked away from him but he kept following me, so I finally told him, "Fuck off or I'll knock the shit out of you."

My mom would have killed me for saying words like that, but Andy kept going, going, about Mom being crazy and boozing and sleeping around so I did. Knocked the shit out of him, I mean. I just whammed him in the jaw so hard he fell over screaming and yelling and rolling around.

The playground lady, Mrs. Arnott, came running over and grabbed my arm and told me to go straight in to the principal's office and sit on the bench till she got there. Then she started cuddling Andy and saying, "Oh you poor thing, where does it hurt?" even though anybody could see his jaw was all swollen up.

I waited in the office and the secretary was pretty nice and told me I could go get a drink of water, and a couple teachers came in to use the copy machine and said, "Hi, Tom," so I got to feeling not so scared but I was still mad, man, was I mad for Andy saying all that rotten stuff that wasn't true.

Pretty soon Mrs. Arnott came in and she had Andy with her and one of those blue ice things that he was holding on his jaw that covered up most of his face so he didn't have to look at me.

The secretary rang the phone on Mr. Walker's desk and told him we were all waiting out there. He came out of his office and looked at us and said, "Come in, come in," and held the door open for us and then shut it. He pulled chairs around in front of his desk and he sat in one of them, too, not behind his desk, so that seemed not so scary either. He was a short man, with a mostly bald head and horn-rimmed glasses. He was usually laughing and cheerful, but he could get very serious when he wanted, and even the older kids were always very polite to him. There was something about him that made you respect what he said, or at least listen to him and not argue.

"Whose turn first?" he asked, and Mrs. Arnott started right in about how I'd punched Andy, and I was much bigger than he was and she thought I was turning into some bully and getting very asocial because I was either hanging around by myself or fighting, which wasn't true since I'd never been fighting one single time till that day.

Mr. Walker said, "Well, Tom, it sounds like it's your turn next."

So I told him it wasn't true I was asocial because of hanging around by myself and fighting because I never had fought in my whole life but Andy was saying these things about someone I happened to know pretty well and they weren't true, they were lies, and he kept on saying them and shouting them so everyone could hear, and I asked him to stop and told him to shut up and warned him if he didn't I'd hit him and he kept on going so I did.

So Mr. Walker said, "Andrew?" and Andy said, "I didn't say any lies, it was all true, because my mother says somebody ought to take those Rohlik kids away from their mom and look after them, that's what she says, and I was only telling him so maybe he could look around for somebody to look after him."

Mrs. Arnott was looking first at Andy and then at Mr. Walker like she was really surprised, and Mr. Walker kind of shook his head at her a little, like he didn't want her to say anything.

Then Mr. Walker said to Andy, "I think we'll let your mother speak for herself, Andrew. You don't seem to have been a very successful messenger."

He reached over and picked up the phone and asked the secretary to call Mrs. Millins and ask if she would come into the office. Then he said to Andy, "You owe Tom an apology for cruel and careless words, Andrew."

Then he looked at me and said, "Tom, you're big and strong, and you can punch your way through life, but there are better ways. By three o'clock tomorrow I want you to come up with a way you could have handled the situation with your hands in your pockets and your feet on the ground and your head in the air."

Then he stood up and put his hand on Mrs. Arnott's arm. He opened the door of the office. "We'll leave you two to apologize and shake on it," he said. "You may leave when both of you are satisfied."

I sat back down and folded my arms and stared out the window like I'd be there all day, because I knew I'd never be satisfied, not till that creep had eaten every word, even if I had to rub his nose in them and cram them down his throat.

We just sat there a long time, now and then the secretary looking in the window from her office to see if we were still there. I was getting not so mad but still not going anywhere. Pretty soon I looked at Andy and he still had that blue thing over his face but he had it down a little so he was looking at me with one eye. I put my arm over my face and looked at him with one eye and we started to laugh and then we were laughing so hard we couldn't sit still anymore. We were banging into the walls and all bent over holding our sides, and Andy dropped the blue ice thing and I stepped on it accidentally and it burst right on the rug and that made us laugh harder. So the secretary came in and said, "You boys get." We went running out, bumping into each other because we were still laughing so hard.

When we got on the road, Andy grabbed my arm and said, "Don't tell my mom, but I don't really believe all that junk about your mom. I didn't really want to say it, OK?"

So I said, "OK because it's just lies, but your mom better not make trouble, is all."

So Andy said Mr. Walker would tell her that it wasn't true, what she thought, so everything would be all right then, except she'd be so mad at Andy for telling that he'd probably get grounded for a year.

I told him never mind, we'd run away and live in our hideout and fish and sneak food from home when nobody was around. We started talking about it, planning what we'd do, so we didn't hear Mrs. Millins coming up behind us until she grabbed Andy by the back of his neck and half lifted him up by it and just kept walking super fast, Andy sort of tiptoe stretching from her hand with his feet barely touching the road. That was some mad woman. I knew I wouldn't be seeing Andy for a long time.

JESS

I tell you there are things I cannot tell you. You want to know facts, but the facts are fog-shrouded shadows now, the colors leached out by the flames before us.

My mother is writing down facts so she will remember this dream when she wakes—do you think she *will* remember it? Our first lives turn into shadows on the cave wall, the flames in front of us consuming even those shapes. We will wake from our dreams remembering nothing.

AFTER BOONE DIED, I tried to live in the forest again. I took the kids and moved to Tino Ramirez's float house that he'd skidded up the beach into the woods on Vonney Island. Tino abandoned it after he won some lottery land up on Prince William Sound. It was a pretty good house, except the floor tilted badly where one of the roller logs had slipped out, and Tino had never jacked it up and blocked it, so the stove side of the kitchen was about two feet higher than the bed side of the other room. An uphill existence, you might say. The boys entertained themselves racing cars down the slope, laughing and rolling after them.

I wanted them to grow up knowing the woods the way Tom and I had, mourning branches, mountains of snow sliding off the spruces onto the roof like clods of earth on a coffin. The way the light pokes a scalpel into your veins, dissects your mind into isotopes. This is important. This is connection. Elastic moss like a winding sheet around trees that fell before white man came, mummy trunks humped beneath those standing now, new roots arched over the lost parent. Family ties. It's all here.

See how I learned my way by touch and smell and taste? But it doesn't work that way, the world. I've groped my way through, had some blind luck, like Boone, the rest smelling like shit. Touch doesn't tell you enough, I guess. The smell of ink in the woods, the taste of salt on a man's back, they're not keys to the world, in case that's what you think. It all went wrong.

We couldn't stay out there in the float house. I taught Bo with the correspondence program the first year—he's quick, he learned, and I learned more. But the sorrow took hold, darkness seeped like a plague on our souls and drove us out. Bring out your dead. They had to take us all.

I went back to the house Boone and I bought when the fish company sold their employee housing cheap so they wouldn't have to look after it anymore. Wouldn't have to fix the sinks or patch the roofs.

I went to work, watched to see how to join up. It wasn't so hard. I went back to the bar, still home that year, with EJ still there. I should explain about the drinking. This town is soaked, pickled, preserved in alcohol—it is impossible to separate which liquid substance percolates down from the mountain, muddies the minds and the roads, carries off the children and the wet leaves and the detritus of civilization.

Let me tell you about alcohol. Follow the swallow: brush the scent glands with a hint of autumn oak leaves drying in the sun, quick chill to the molars, spreading to the base of the eustachian tubes so no one hears as well as smells its passage; beginning now to burn the soft tissues, raking the esophagus and plunging hot as dragon's spit into the vial of acid, vaporizing to char the ribs, warming the arterial flow like sun burning fog from the valley. Overnight the fog will come again, but tomorrow and tomorrow and tomorrow we can warm the air around it.

Perhaps you've forgotten the Grizzly Saloon, the men and women gathered around the pool table under the Tiffany lamp, the people pressed three deep against the bar, a dozen crammed in every booth, the pie auction and the spaghetti feed to raise money for Al Crenshaw's kids while he's in detox, to pay Mary Joe's medical bills, to buy a motorized wheelchair for Butch Jim's mother who's had a stroke but still smokes her own halibut. More myths have been born of the Grizzly Saloon than ever of Indian legend.

ACROSS FROM ME, Nellie James gets up from the booth where she's been sleeping and starts slow-dancing around the pool table, steering past the guys hunched over their cues. She weaves her own music around the hard beat from the jukebox, and with great delicacy conjures her T-shirt over her head, wafting it about her like the seven veils.

Mark, the new bartender, says, "Hey, Nell, not tonight, all right?"

She keeps on dancing, though, and brushes against Billy Denny's arm just as he's lining up. Billy gives her a shove and she falls against the corner of the table. Nellie's pretty creative with her swearing and a lot of people start to laugh. She turns and swears at them, too, her arms stretched forward and her fingers casting a spell.

Mark comes out from behind the bar, takes her by the arm and tenderly pulls her T-shirt back over her head, all the time talking quietly to her like you might gentle a terrified horse. She tries to jerk away from him, kicks him a couple of times, but he just keeps talking to her and holding her up. Behind her back he crooks his finger at Randy Martin, who comes over and gets his arm around Nellie, nods yeah, he'll get her home.

My brother, Tom, fell in love with Nellie their last year in high school. She was so beautiful, to see her now you wouldn't believe how beautiful she was—solemn eyes, her face sweet-polished present tense, scarce smile like a moonrise. After Tom went to Vietnam, she went off for a while, and Tom kept writing to her. She didn't answer, so he wrote to me and told me, "Look out for Nell—I think she might be in trouble and I could get leave and come home and we could get married."

Nellie didn't want to have anything to do with me, though, when she came back. She was always a cool customer, just a little nod, nothing to say. She wound up married to Joey Blackburn who knocked her front teeth out. Three kids, and spends her welfare checks at the Grizzly.

. . .

NOW AND THEN a new face shows up, which is about the most that can be said for Grizzly entertainment.

"Kozloff," the man says, sliding into the booth beside me, "I'm Rick Kozloff. This is Don, and that woman over there, who just left Don forever, is Lanny." He waves at Mark. "Keep it coming, man," he says. "What's that slop in your glass?" he asks me. "Bring her another, here."

Mark slams everything down on the table and glares at the man named Kozloff.

"On a tab," Kozloff says.

Mark shakes his head and pats the tabletop. "No deficit financing," he snarls in his rudest possible voice, and I think Kozloff might have noticed his eyes, because he gets his wallet out pretty fast.

Lanny comes back, then, and slides in next to Kozloff so he has to shove over against me, and we all sit there across from Don who has a whole side of the booth to himself. He reaches out and tries to lay his hand on top of Lanny's, but she jerks it away, grabs her purse from under the table, and marches off to the rest room.

"What's with her, now?" Kozloff says.

"Ahh, shit, Koz. Who cares? She's always got ants up her puss. She'll cool. Needs a little refresher course, is all."

Koz turns to look at me. "Where you from?"

"You wouldn't believe it if I told you."

"Try me."

"Tern Bay."

"You're shitting me. Nobody's from Tern Bay. You mean you lived here a long time?"

"Beginning of time. Universe was still smoking."

"You're shitting me," he says again, with more certainty.

He waves at Mark and has his wallet out even before the drinks slop onto the table.

"Soooo long, it's been good to know ya," Mark says, while he counts out the change. "*Jess,*" he says, fiercely. He stares at me over his shoulder as he walks away, his eyes dancing across my face.

I turn my head toward the wall so he'll get the message. "Every bartender in this damned bar thinks he's my mother. Just because I've lived here forever, they think they can treat me like some juvenile nut case. Ignore all remarks made by the help."

"Unfriendly Native?" Koz says. "No trust White Man?"

"Ignore him. He's just on one of his kicks."

"Speaking of . . ." Don says, "I'll catch you later."

He slides out of the booth, and a second later I see Lanny come out of the alcove where the rest rooms are, walk behind the pool table and through the bar. I don't see either of them again all evening, which turns out to be quite a long one, what with Koz slipping his wallet out to wave at Mark, and Mark slamming our drinks down as ugly as he can be without punching anyone.

In spite of Mark's ridiculous attitude, I enjoy meeting somebody new for a change. Do you know how often outsiders come to the Grizzly in December? We just sit, comfortable and easy, talking a little about ourselves, mostly about him, of course, since what can you say about mildewed brain cells and salt-rotted veins?

Koz grew up out east, south of Chicago. His mother raised him after his dad left them. He had an older brother, Kenneth, who was in the Army, stationed in Anchorage. Koz said Kenneth saw dollar signs posted at every corner up there, so as soon as he got out of the Army he went back and started working on the pipeline. Wrote to Koz and told him, "This is where it's at—money flowing like oil, plenty of time off to blow it in town."

So Koz went up and made a bundle, but Kenneth got laid off for drinking on the job, then he got to hanging out with a group of junkies and wound up stabbed to death over some woman. Koz says he never got on with Kenneth, only went up there because of the money. Then one day a loader cable snapped and nearly cut his head off.

"Right then," he says, "I'd had enough tundra and arctic express to last a lifetime."

So when he got out of the hospital, he took the money he'd made, came south and bought a purse seiner with Don Lockwood, a friend from the pipeline days.

He and Don must have done well on that boat, because in a couple years they bought a second one. They always fish together, hit the towns together, that kind of thing.

"Only thing is," Koz says, "Don picked up that bitchy sniper-type last year and now she hangs out with him all the time, which cuts me out. Maybe something'll turn up, though. For me, I mean. If I play my cards right," he says, turning his head and looking straight at me.

He takes his Tern Bay Seafoods cap off and rubs his hand over the bald top of his head. The right side of his face is tattooed in purple animal tracks from the loader cable accident, and the neon of the Budweiser sign gouges the scars deeper.

"I'll be hanging around here awhile. We're trying to work it out with the fish plant to pack for them next summer."

"Can't you do better fishing for yourselves?"

"For the money, yes, for the muscle, no," he says. "It's a hell of a way to make a living, dragging net."

Mark starts shouting, "Last round," and Koz waves his wallet, but I shake my head.

"I gotta work in the morning." I slide over and push him to let me out. "Thanks for the drinks. My round some other time."

"How about tomorrow night?"

I'm about to say, "Well, we'll see," but Mark comes bumping past me, muttering under his breath for my ears only, so I say, loud, "Sure, Koz, I'll be here per usual." Mark is so rude.

Two years ago, when EJ finally got to coughing too hard, she sold the Grizzly to Mark. I've known Mark Banning since the year I started at the Tern Bay school. He was one of those friends who hijacked me on the *Lucy Jo*.

Second only to EJ, Mark's the perfect bartender. He has something wrong with his eyes—they jiggle—there's a name for it in medical books. They seem independent of Mark himself, twittering away when he looks at you. Drunks are blown away when he gives them a stare—no one ready to stand and fight after looking at those eyes, like watching water coming to a boil. If they're from Outside, they think he does it on purpose, and they're outa'here.

Mark bought the bar to collect deaths. He has a stenographer's notebook—he learned shorthand in the Army—and he keeps each death on a separate page.

A few years ago, I found Mark sitting on one of the gravestones in the cemetery up there above town. He was reading out of one of his notebooks. I knew right off what he was doing, reading there, seemingly all by himself. He was introducing people to his wife.

Annie, Mark's wife, died one morning when she went out to hang the laundry and a blood vessel burst, an aneurism they called it, just as she was pinning up the bottom sheet from their bed. She was six months pregnant with their first child; they'd waited so long for it.

Two deaths at once, Mark comforted only because Annie had the baby with her. But he thought it wouldn't be enough, a woman all alone with such a tiny infant, having to care for it for eternity, so he started collecting others and introducing them to her so she'd have company, someone around when she got tired of the crying and nursing.

People learned what he was doing and brought him deaths from all the way north to Yakutat. Not me. I told him, "Mark, I don't have a single death for you, not one."

He stared at me, eyes atwitter, and laughed like he does. "Sure, Jess," he said, "I know there ain't no one knows less about death. Just please don't lean on the bar in case blood should run out of your ear, OK?"

Most people get very serious with Mark after a few beers, line up to tell him about their uncle who was buried in that avalanche over at the nickel mine, or their cousin Eleanor who got caught by darkness when she was out hunting and went over a cliff, didn't find her for three weeks.

Mark leans on the bar and jots down squiggles that mean cliff and avalanche, and then the next morning he sits in a booth while Billy Denny mops the floor, and he writes the whole thing out exactly the way he's going to read it to Annie. But he won't take just any death. I've seen him turn some down—Mark's particular who Annie knows.

HERE'S ALL THIS stuff from the school again—why don't I come to parent conferences, they'll be happy to set a different time to accommodate my schedule—report card conference, Meet-the-Teacher Night, Open House. Well, I don't go because it isn't anything to do with school they want to talk about. They're into happiness.

Bo doesn't seem happy, Tom's such a sweetie, we love him but he does tease, doesn't he—especially the girls—is there some reason, do you think, that Tom teases the girls so much?

Probably. How about his math?

Oh, he tries so hard, sometimes, but other times, well, it seems as though he's just thinking about something else altogether. Sometimes he seems tired, doesn't pay attention—is he getting plenty of sleep—exercise? Sometimes he looks so sad, would it be missing his father do you think?

What about long division?

Is he under any stress that you know of?

Fractions? Decimals?

This is the way to stop teasing, avoid stress, borrow and carry and regroup. Regrouping is very important.

I never go to the conferences anymore. They know so much about happiness at school.

RICK KOZLOFF IS around a lot these days. He seems to take an interest in the place—maybe he'll move up here, he says, Ketchikan being pretty tame. Ketchikan is a cosmopolitan center of civilization compared to Tern Bay, I tell him. He says Tern Bay has a certain attraction that Ketchikan lacks. Now, who could argue with a nice comment like that?

Rick Kozloff is a good man.

Do you believe that?

Would *this* Jess lie?

That Jess—that Jess is tough as sealskin; swears and drinks, drops acid, shoots up, dares anyone to trip the wire. "Step on it, go on, step on it. 'Put your little foot right there . . .' Multiply your single company into millions. Yeah, man."

That Jess is not this Jess, this one peering out through cedar branches at snowdust on granite headstones.

Well, let me whisper in your ear. *This* Jess doesn't like Rick Kozloff, or Lanny either, or Don, but you know what—they're the original weathermen. Specialty: cloud effects. They can conjure silver linings right out of their pockets.

Watch the sun rise, baby, lean back, watch that silver mirror, like the sea at dawn, isn't it, all promises?

Yes, ma'am, this is how it is, this is how it can be, this is how it will be. Slip along the surface, dive down, watch yourself in the silver mirror.

My brother taught me to start a fire with a mirror. He'd take a mirror and aim the sun's arrow at a mound of dry moss until the sweet smoke rose. In my enthusiasm, I'd smother the flame in damp needles, and he'd scatter it and start over.

Remember those days? Those were the days of sweet smoke and mirrors and kindness and silence, when we knew nothing. When we were reflected in the pool. Then the ripples stopped and the pool had no bottom at all. Were we drowning then?

BO

I never thought my mother was actually crazy. You know what I mean? Like, she bugged the hell out of me, sure, but I just thought mothers were designed that way. That they'd always have a war on with someone my age, and also that family members always embarrass each other because of wanting the other person to act different from how they act.

Take my grandmother? My mother thought she was crazy because she wrote all those notes to herself to tell herself how to do things she'd been doing all her life. But not Grandma. She wasn't crazy, she was tough as a horse clam. She was just determined to hang on because she thought my mother was crazy, and somebody would have to look after *her*. See what I mean about family members embarrassing each other?

Once Mom started hanging out with those dudes from Ketchikan, though, I knew, I knew absolutely, that she was nuts. N-u-t-s, more than a dollar short.

To begin with, those geeks were not too darling. Right away you thought of switchblades and screams in dark alleys. So that's one thing.

And another . . . before they came, maybe she did jazz around and hang out at the bar some, but there was like, a routine? She went to work, came home, fixed meals (sometimes), talked to herself—yeah, I mean, weird, but she was there, at least. Now what? We couldn't exactly drag her home, right? All I knew was that it would be better if one, she didn't know those alley rats, and two, we weren't related.

I'd glance in the bar when I walked past, and Mom and the dame with the frizzy hair would be sitting with their backs to me and those dudes facing me. The one Mom hung out with, Koz she called him, had this scar up the side of his face like he'd been a prisoner of war tortured by men with flaming pokers. If you asked me, they never should have let him go. Sheeeh—what an ugly dude. What she saw in that guy could only be snow, hash, whatever sent her.

Look, I know she'd had like, major trauma. I mean, no kidding, most people would probably jump off a bridge or something if their brother blew himself to powder and their father got mowed down by a madman and their husband drowned on his boat. Really. How could one person stand all that and still be one person, if you see what I mean.

So I could understand her getting snowed, strung out, turning into more than one person, which is sort of what she did when she did one of her talk-to-herself numbers. Hey, I understood it, all right? But it was like the sequence was wrong, or something.

What I mean is, first all those horror stories happened, then us. With three kids to raise by herself, she needed to concentrate, but it seemed like the horror stories just kept leaking in. Like shadows moving just beyond the door? You know those scenes, camera zooms on a gnarled tree through an open door, shadow crosses the threshold, pauses, curtain on the window flaps, shadow brushes past the window—see, I knew that kind of creepy thing was going on in her head. But the order that things had happened to her was wrong, because there was us, Tom and me, and afterwards Toby, and she needed to be a little more like, together?

So how likely was it she'd pull it out? I'd say, maybe one chance in fifty million? I mean, no kidding, we were trashed the very second she met those guys.

ACTUALLY, I FELT sorriest for Tom, except he was always in my face about everything. But I mean, it was like he was in a trap because he was still a little kid so he had to do what people told him, but he also had to do a lot of things that little kids shouldn't have to do. And he was the type that felt guilty about everything, you know what I mean? Like, if he got mad at Mom or got sick of Toby and yelled at her, he felt so bad he had to do everything perfectly for about a year.

No kidding, he had a tough life. I wouldn't have traded with him for a million-dollar recording contract, even though naturally I was certain that was right around the corner.

Seriously, I felt sorry for him. He didn't have anyone, if you know what I mean, no one to rap with, let it all hang out. Well, there was Andy, but Andy was sort of your basic dumb little kid.

And of course, Mr. My-Door-Is-Always-Open Walker. I could just hear Tom telling Mr. W. that his mother made him babysit all the time, cook and do the laundry and he was just "Well I'm just plumb weary of it, Mr. Walker, sir." Right.

What Tom needed was his own Sara. Well, he was maybe a little young, but actually I'd been going with Sara ever since I found her on the beach when we were ten years old, the same as Tom. I'd gone down there to get a bucket of seawater for Mr. Raymond so we could measure specific gravity in science, and there she was, huddled on the rocks, crying her eyes out.

First I pretended I didn't see her, but then she got up and started walking away and she looked so sad I just followed her and finally caught up to her. It turned out she'd just moved to Tern Bay because her dad was going to be head mechanic at the cannery, and she was scared to go to school, so she left before the bell rang, and went down to the beach.

I didn't know what to say to her, so I started showing her the hermit crabs in the tide pools, and the anemones, things she'd never seen, coming from Missouri, and she got interested, started turning over rocks and looking at everything, laughing at the way a shell would skitter sideways because a hermit crab was inside.

We kept moving along from one tide pool to the next, and then I looked up and there was Mr. Raymond.

I said, "It's Sara Inslee and she's scared to come in the school," and Sara just stood there, staring at her feet.

So Mr. Raymond put his arm around her shoulders and said, "We missed you, Sara. Would you help Bo carry that water back now? That bucket gets pretty heavy."

So we carried the bucket back together, trying not to slop it on each other, Mr. Raymond miles ahead of us and not looking back, so Sara wasn't scared by him. And she's been mine ever since, only a few wars and a few window shoppers.

A LOT OF the problems our family was having were from all those authority types that kept coming down on us. I mean, it wasn't just on Mom, even. Sure she took it up the kazoo—and she was very cool, too, you know? You should have heard her telling off that social worker—"Axle of the universe, that question," she said, when the woman asked her if anyone could help.

You could see the woman was too dumb to get it, though. She thought it was just Mom's crazy talk, but hell, Mom was right. Everyone's always running around trying to help and it's like "Hey, you gotta do it this way because then everything'll get better," but all they do is mess up your life which would be OK, maybe not the greatest, but OK, if people just left you alone. But that social worker, she was programmed for interference big time, worse than static. I mean, there was no squelch knob for that social worker bitch.

They came after me, too, and even tried to get at Tom, if you can believe it. A lot of very grungy stuff happened after that social worker started snooping around. Not intentional stuff, just like, events?

For example, Sara and I were walking home after a basketball game against Haines which naturally we'd lost, us having only a quarter their bench, and when we passed the Grizzly this drunk came lurching through the door. He threw his arms around Sara, maybe just to steady himself, but whatever . . . he kept swaying forward and back, and Sara tried to unlock his arms from around her and steer him over where he could lean on the porch rail in front of the bar. He wouldn't let go, though, and he was trying to kiss her and he smelled like something left over at the bottom of the fish hold.

I grabbed his shoulders and pulled him backward off her. Well, I maybe underestimated how drunk he was when I pulled him off, because his knees gave way and he fell and hit his head on the cement step to the porch. He was bleeding from his forehead pretty bad. I tried to straighten him out on the walk, and Sara went in and told Mark, the bartender.

Mark came out and bent over the guy, his eyes going a mile a minute like they do—I don't know how he can see like that—it must have looked like the blood was spraying all over when it was actually just snaking down one side of the guy's face.

Anyway, Mark went back in and called the Village Public Safety Officer and the guy that runs the clinic, and they came and asked a lot of dumb questions. Ben, the clinic guy, pinched the cut together with his fingers till it stopped bleeding, and then they loaded him in the back of the V.P.S.O. van and took him away. A couple days later, I saw him sitting down on the dock with a filthy bandage on his forehead. Like, if he'd died, it would have been bacteria, not encounters with cement steps?

Well, the next thing was, I got called to the office at school and Mr. Walker wanted to know what happened, so I told him.

He said he understood, he certainly understood that I was just trying to protect Sara and the rest was accidental.

Only, how he said it, it sounded like he thought it wasn't accidental that it had happened to *me*. You know what I mean? I mean, he kept bringing up all this crap about my family, like maybe running into drunks outside bars was in our genes, for god's sake. Like, how was my mother doing—what a shame about the baby but the school had such splendid special programs now for children like that—did I think Tom was doing all right because he'd been fighting with Andy.

"You know, Bo," he said, "I want you to know you don't have to carry everything on your own shoulders. My door is always open—I encourage you to come in and talk, any time you feel like it. There are so many ways the school can help, you know, and I want you to get yourself right in here any time things get ahead of you."

He stood up behind his desk, so I stood up, too, so he came around and put his arm around my shoulders. He smelled like this Irish Spring soap that's supposed to smell like grass or mint or something, but maybe I was allergic to it, the grass, or the soap or whatever, because I couldn't inhale, and I pulled away from him. He turned around facing me, so I couldn't really go on holding my breath, and when I inhaled I made a snorting noise so he probably thought I was being sarcastic or whatever.

He said, "I mean, we all get angry, right—but you've got some extra heavy burdens, and it's always better to talk about your feelings, get things right out on the table, than just seal them up until they explode."

Do you get it? He thought I'd hit the guy and knocked him down and maybe given him a concussion or whatever, because I was mad. No kidding, he really thought that, I know it.

After that, they tried to get me to see the school counselor every week, but Mom wrote a letter and said that "Bo will keep his own counsel, if you please," very nasty polite. And they can't force you to talk, actually, without legal action. But with that social worker hounding Mom, and Mr. Walker thinking that any minute I might turn into Lenny Carter and mow down half the student body, I figured the next thing would be the officer at the door with some legal order.

So, yeah, after that I was pretty much thinking it maybe wouldn't hurt to get out of town for a little, but not the way Mom had it planned, some unknown destination with three goons, two little kids, and a wasted, blown-out mother.

TOM

Grandma came over on the weekend and had it out with Mom like she used to do before Toby was born, hollering about Mom's drinking and running with "that crowd from down south."

Mom hollered right back, of course, and they got all red-faced, both of them, and Toby cried from the yelling, so it was pretty noisy.

"Am I supposed to take advice from someone who has to write down how to find the matches?" Mom said.

She told Grandma it was none of her business how she used the dividend checks, and she wasn't having us stuck forever in this dinky doo town.

"It's time they see there's more to life than rotted boot liners and moss up your nose," she said.

"So how come you didn't get out when you saw there was more to life?" Grandma asked her.

"That's none of your business, either," Mom said. "And anyway, you know why."

Grandma said, "Jess, I worry, that's all. These kids . . . listen . . . the other day, down there on the dock, I thought, dammit, these children aren't neglected—this requires some type of planning. Tom had on huge pants rolled up over his boots, a jacket with the filling exploding from a rip in the side, and that enormous life jacket Toby wears makes her waddle like a robot. Don't you ever look at them, Jess?"

"Write it down," Mom said. "Post it on the fridge. That way, maybe I can get Tom into his Brooks Brothers before you come next time."

"Jess, I worry . . ." Grandma didn't finish what she was going to say, just shook her head.

Mom put her arm around Grandma then, and said, "They're OK, Mom. It'll be OK. Don't worry so much," like she felt sort of bad yelling at her own mother that way.

Grandma sat down a little while, then. Toby sat in her lap, and I showed her my writing notebook which was all A's because I was pretty good at writing and drawing, not math, not at all!

I WOKE UP that night after Mom came home from work because Bo was yelling at her just like Grandma about "that crowd from down south—don't lie—I see you all the time with those two dudes and that frizzy dame with the big boobs."

Mom said, "Listen, Primrose, those guys have seiners down in Ketchikan. They're fixing things so they can pack for the fish plant here next summer. They've promised to take us to Mexico if you can touch down for half a second, Moonman."

Bo shouted, "Unh hunnnh, I'm sure! On their boats? Mexico on some floating disaster in midwinter? Not me, buddy, no way!"

"Well, we wouldn't go on their boats, I'm sure. We'll just go together. And Lanny's not some 'frizzy dame'—she happens to be a friend of mine, Bo—she's very nice when you get to know her, and she's been with Don a long time."

"Steady income, hunh?" Bo said, nasty, and I think Mom might have slapped him, because a second later he came in our room like there wasn't even a door shut—I don't know why there was even any door left the way he came in there.

WHEN OUR ALARM went off, I took Toby out in the living room to change her, because Bo always stayed in bed until almost time for the bell at school, and he got mad if Toby woke him up. I just fixed Toby up and put her in the high chair and gave her her cereal.

Mom wasn't there, though and the couch wasn't open. Then the front door opened and Mom walked in, right past Toby and me, like she didn't even see us. She pushed past Bo, who was coming out of the bathroom, and went into the bathroom and turned the water on hard in the sink.

Bo just stood there. Then he said, "Jesus Christ, not again!" He went crashing around the bedroom grabbing his stuff, shoved past Toby and me, and out the door.

Pretty soon Mom came out. She was walking all shaky with her hand on the wall. She went and got in my bed, rolled up in the blankets, and said something I couldn't hear. I asked her if she was sick. The back of her head went up and down, so I thought I'd better stay home with Toby. I shut the door so she wouldn't be bothered, and turned on cartoons.

Bo didn't come home at lunch. I made a can of soup and we had bread. I was tired of keeping Toby in the living room because there wasn't much for her to do. She got fussy, because she could only do one thing for a minute at a time, then it was something else, then she was bored with that.

I sneaked in and got diapers so Toby could take her nap on the sofa. Mom seemed like she hadn't moved at all, but she heard me and said, "You all right, Tom?" through the blanket. When I said yes, she said, "Good kid." She sounded like she'd been crying.

When Toby woke up, the rain wasn't so hard and the wind blowing so much, so I took her down on the dock. There were a couple of otters whistling to each other under the dock. Jim Donner's dog, Barney, was chasing up and down, sticking his nose in the cracks, just about going crazy trying to get at them. The otters were teasing him, going close to the edge, and back under as soon as he put his head over. Toby laughed and tried to bark like Barney. The dog got so wild though, I was afraid he'd knock her off the dock, so I carried her up the ramp and let her watch between the railings.

We threw stones in the water for a little while and then she got tired and wanted me to pick her up. It was raining harder anyway, and I thought school would get out soon. I didn't want to meet Andy or anyone, so I'd have to tell about Mom's being sick and me babysitting, so we went on home.

Bo was home when we got there, and he and Mom were having another humongous screaming fight. When we came in, Bo was yelling, "You're at it again—don't lie to me—I'm not that dumb—you gonna make another monkey kid?"

Mom got all mean eyes and shoved her teeth together and talked without her mouth moving. She said, "Shut up, Bo, don't let Tom hear you talking crazy."

Bo said, "Talking crazy—who's the crazy one around here? Tom's not dumb—he knows—and anyway, he's the one getting all the shit from what you already did."

I actually didn't know what they were talking about, but no way I'd ever give Bo the chance to think I *am* dumb. He only says it about a hundred times a day anyway.

I took Toby in the bedroom and changed her wet stuff. I got out the crayons and some old newspapers and helped her make a face on the paper.

Bo was yelling, "I better get every penny of my check, before you drop it at the bar!"

Mom's voice all of a sudden got real quiet. "Well, little one," she said, "tomorrow we're out of here. Orbiter to Man in the Moon: start packing."

"The hell you say," Bo said. I heard the front door slam.

In a minute, Mom came in the bedroom. She still looked shaky, and her teeth were still shoved together tight. She looked at Toby tearing up newspaper and throwing it in the air. Then she looked at me and said, "Ferry tomorrow, Tom. Put your stuff in your backpack. See if you can get Toby's clothes in, too, so there'll be room for more diapers in the diaper bag."

She stopped and rubbed her neck and head like they ached a lot. "We're outa here," she said, and went back to the living room.

JESS

This social worker. She speaks for multitudes—
*We only want to help—We need to know what
plans you have for October Rain—We may have
to file with the State if we can't arrange home visits—
It would be so much easier if you would cooperate
with Us . . .*

They're closing in. Friday, she says. At noon. Only
an informational meeting with the people from the State
office. They'll be out on the ferry Thursday night.

I have to think. Why can't I think anymore?

—If you eat HiFiBurrs you'll be able to think . . .

—If you let Jesus in you'll be saved . . .

—If you'll only cooperate, we will help . . .

—Let's listen to our audience reaction, Audrey . . .

The sink leaks. We have to get out of here—this doodly drunken town, clinging to the soggy edge of nothing. Bo is after me about everything like he's my guardian—only fifteen, a snot-nosed brat telling me what to do with my life, what right does he have to tell me anything?

See that eclipsed light coming through the back door? It's exactly the same light that is there all the time. All the time. It never alters. Smooth, flat light, hard as stone. Someday I'll take a hammer to it, fracture it so it sparks and dies.

What about this boat rolling under my head, this wall, this deck, whatever it is, rolling and pitching, a boat it must be—I can feel that little shiver, current against wave.

Boone, you have to help me, I can't do this anymore. I can't fix the sink and I can't fix my life and I can't get out. And the kids. You left them, too. And they'll take them away from me now, because I can't fix the fucking goddamned sink!

There are no arrows in that light. Smooth, hard as stone, it is. We're getting out of here, no matter what Bo says. I'm still in charge. I'm telling you this is true. This wall can hold the weight of that decision. This wall I'm leaning on, this deck, boat, whatever it is—can you feel that little shiver, the current against the wind?

PART TWO

BO

1

When we got on the ferry, I threw our stuff in the corner of the TV lounge. Tom wanted milk for Toby's bottle so I went through the cafeteria and picked up a carton of milk and a couple Cokes and some chips. There were still a few recliner chairs left up forward and I thought maybe we should move, but Tom had spread the sleeping bags out under the window in the last row of seats and Toby was already half asleep. He gave her her bottle and she was gone in a second.

We sat and drank the Cokes and watched a stupid movie about this girl who gets captured and raised by an Indian tribe. I mean, pretty romantic. Tom and I are half Indian and we both look all Indian, black hair and eyes—we could have played the extras, running around waving tomahawks and teaching the little girl how to sew animal skins with fish-bone needles. I mean no kidding, it was that kind of movie.

Tom got sleepy and got in with Toby, and I drifted around awhile checking out who was on board, if there was anyone I knew. It was so late, though—the ferry gets in to Tern Bay at weird hours, usually—the schedule is not too accommodating for our large metropolitan business district—so everyone was already crashed in the recliners or on the floor.

I glanced in the bar. Mom was sitting with the goon platoon at one of the tables by the window. Scar-face was holding both her hands on top of the table and leaning forward talking like he was pleading for his life. A couple times she smiled and shook her head. I had to put my hands in my pockets to keep from pounding on the window. That guy was such bad news—why couldn't she see it? I mean, the scars up his arms were probably worse than the ones on his face.

I went back where Tom and Toby were and tried to go to sleep, but this guy lying on the floor a row ahead of us was snoring. I mean, he was louder than the engine vibration coming through the floor, and not regular like you could sort of adjust your clock to it, but intervals of peace and quiet so you almost dozed off and then a huge rumble, snort, chuckle, wheeewwww with a whistle at the end. Sheeh!

I finally took my sleeping bag and moved to the forward lounge. It seemed like everyone in there snored, too, but at least nobody right in my ear. And the engine vibration was less.

I lay there seeing Scar-face reaching his hands across the table at my mom, staring at her like he was trying to hypnotize her. His face got all dim—I was casting a shadow across it. I was moving toward him, my fists too big for my pockets, when I realized the shadow wasn't mine—somebody was standing behind me. I whirled around and woke up fighting the sleeping bag away from my face.

I lay there trying to get my pulse rate slowed up, trying to think of something else. Like Sara. I needed Sara so much, needed her voice and her hands running up and down and her laughter . . .

It was pretty physical between us, but we held back, too, sometimes Sara did, sometimes me, but we really did hold back. I didn't want to impose on her. That is, there was certainly something I would like to impose on her every single time I saw her, but what I mean is, I wanted us to be lifelong, not just some high school romance, and there were funny things going on around Tern Bay that I worried were going to influence us, that could ruin our future.

For example, I know my mother was pregnant with me when she married my father. She would have married him anyway—they were like, a team? I mean, I think their children were a by-product, not a product. They would have had a life of their own without us.

I know kids who think their parents wouldn't have anything without them—I guess that could be true for some people—but not for my parents. There was something about them you couldn't ever intrude on, if you know what I mean. But they closed out a lot of options, right? Because of me?

Well, whatever . . . I just didn't want it to be like that for Sara and me—having to get married because of anything except that we wanted to be married to each other. Which we do.

But the other thing was, it seemed like all the kids in Tern Bay couldn't wait to leave there and go to more exciting places, but then they would do the exact same things as their parents—

boozing and taking drugs and getting each other pregnant with kids that would do the same things all over again, and almost no one got out of there, to actually stay. I didn't know what it was about the place. It was like some disease that never got cured.

The only time things were ever shaky with Sara was last year when this geek moved to Tern Bay from some place in southern California and started stalking around the halls like he was Mr. U.S. Weightlift Champion. A big, blond dude, looked like he should have been working the dock, not a freshman in high school. He gave Sara the high sign right off, and she kind of fell for it.

I'd see her talking to him between classes, leaning back on the locker with one foot braced behind her—had to make herself look like some poster dame, and he'd stand right in front of her with one hand leaning on the locker behind her head. I mean, way too close. I'd push them away because I had the next locker and they'd just slide along to the next one over.

I nailed her after school one afternoon, after that crap had gone on for a couple of weeks, and said, "I just want to know, just tell me yes or no, Sara, are you still going with me?"

She wouldn't say, either, just "Bo, we're friends, right? We're friends like, forever? So what do you mean?"

"You know what I mean," I said, "that guy, Jimmy—you know, I don't have to tell you. Just answer me, you're still going with me or you're not? Just say it, yes or no."

"Nothing's like, changed? I mean, my god, he's new here, at least you could be a little friendly."

"Friendly, right, hanging around his neck half the time. I should try that, I guess. Sara, just answer the question, yes or no."

Would you believe, a week later the guy got busted for sneaking into Billy Denny's house when Billy was working at the bar,

and stealing a hand-held VHF radio. Somebody noticed him coming out. He tried to tell the V.P.S.O. that he'd been sent to get it
by a friend and had just mistaken the house, but they couldn't
find the "friend," and Jimmy didn't know which house he was
supposed to go to. I mean, was it dumb or what?

Anyway, I was cool, I never said, "told you so," or let on I'd
accused her of throwing me over for that moron, and that was
the only time since I found her on the beach that we weren't together.

I lay there, thinking about Sara, her fingers tracing my mouth,
pressing my eyes shut, her fingers drifting here and there . . . I
turned over on my face so nobody would notice, even though it
was really dark in there.

WE GOT TO Sitka in the middle of the morning. I decided I'd
go into town—the ferry would be there for three hours, at least.
Mom had gotten her sleeping bag and was sound asleep a couple rows ahead of Tom and Toby. Tom was trying to keep Toby
happy with toys, but she had the attention span of a flea, and she
was trying to climb the backs of the chairs. When I told Mom I
was going to go to town, Tom heard and came over and asked if
he could go, too. She sat up and said to him, "If you take Toby
with you." I watched to see what he'd do.

There was this thing about Tom, I don't know what it was,
but it was like he was about a mile away from whatever was going on. Like he was just an observer. He hardly ever reacted to
anything, just nodded, said OK, shrugged. I didn't know what
it was. It was like he lived inside a bulletproof capsule or something. That's why him fighting with Andy was so strange, Andy
being his best friend—actually his only friend as far as I knew.

He said Andy was telling all these lies about Mom and everyone could hear him. But I mean, Tom put up with way worse than that all the time—Mom made him babysit and the other kids made fun of him right in front of him because of Toby. He was like, "What? What did you say? I can't heeear you." It would have made me so mad I'd have pounded some of those little rats to dust, but not old Tom. Just gave them that blank look, "What—what did you say?" and off he'd go, dragging Toby with him.

He tried to argue about taking Toby but Mom wouldn't listen, just buried her head in the sleeping bag. So he stuffed some diapers and pants in his pack and fastened it at the belt so Toby could ride on his back with her legs through the straps.

In Sitka, they use the school buses to take you to the Centennial Hall in town. I wanted to look around in the stores, but Toby grabbed everything and screamed when you took it away, so I told Tom he'd have to take her someplace else. Tom said I should come and take Toby halfway but I wasn't feeling too much like it. "Not here—Petersburg, OK?" I said. "I'll take her the whole time, promise." I figured he'd never remember.

IT GOT CLOSE to time to catch the bus, when here came Tom, Toby in his pack, and he was talking to this woman who was walking with them. He waved at me to stop, so I waited till they caught up with me. He said to the woman, "That's my brother," so she stopped and told me she'd found out we came from Tern Bay and she used to live there. I was kind of pissed because she said, "I think your brother could use a hand with the baby."

I just grunted, not looking at her, so she said, "Maybe you could take the backpack for a while."

I said, "It's his problem."

The lady stared at me a minute and then she said to Tom, "Well, nice talking to you," and walked away.

I guess it made Tom mad that I said that, because he caught up with me and dragged on my sleeve. "How come you said Toby's my problem?" he said. "I didn't ask to bring her, Mom said I had to."

I didn't say anything and that made him madder. He yanked at me again, and I reached down and untwisted his fingers from my sleeve.

I said, "Don't be such an airhead, Tom. Mom's making you keep Toby so she can booze it up. If you wouldn't do it, she'd have to quit or lose her kids. Now get off me. No way I'm taking her. You're the problem, see? Outa here, buddy." I pushed him off and walked away.

2

In the afternoon, Tom took Toby up to the forward lounge to watch the ferry go through Peril Strait. Mom was sitting in the cafeteria all by herself drinking coffee. There weren't too many people in there, only an old man eating a doughnut and a couple playing cards at one of the tables. I didn't want to get into another fight right then, so I sort of looked the other way and headed out the door, but she stood up and waved and called, "Bo, Bo, come here a minute."

I sat across from her and looked to see if she was really wasted, but she looked OK. I mean, OK for my mother. Her eyes were extremely green, like they looked sort of artificial. It's hard to describe—they were kind of wet-shiny, like she was always looking through tears, or like the way the ocean looks on one of those days when

it's black cloudy and a ray of sun makes a spotlight on the surface and you feel like you can see down through the green for
hundreds of feet. I know that's a lot to say about my mother's
eyes, but they were really extraordinary. People would stare at
her because her eyes startled them so much. No kidding, my
mother's eyes were astonishing.

So anyway, she looked OK, like she wasn't drunk or stoned,
but I could see she was thinking about something she wanted to
probably talk about, and I was ready to lose it completely. You
know how it is, when you're already mad at someone, and you've
been having one of those conversations with that person inside
your head with all the perfect comebacks, and all of a sudden they
want to talk about something unrelated. That sort of conversation
is totally programmed for the ring, one guy in each corner, right?

"Did you see them?" Mom said, for openers.

"Who?"

"Those social workers. Getting off the ferry in Tern Bay. The
people from the State office. You couldn't have missed them,
Bo, aliens sweeping down the ramp, glimmering, swivel-necked,
taking in the horrors of village life. One male, one female. The
man was short and nodding, the woman large, as large as Call
Me Gail, her hair streaming around her head like the tentacles of
a tube worm. You must have seen them."

"Mom, come on—that is totally one hundred percent para-
noid. Aliens with hair like tube worms? Come on!"

"I barely grabbed Tom back in time, he was so set on watching the ferry docking. I thought for sure they'd seen us, but they
hadn't. They were too busy chewing their first impressions."

All at once she went into one of her little talk numbers, the
me-and-you game with nobody but her included. Changing her
voice like a ventriloquist to answer her own questions.

"How can you keep children here in this godforsaken crook of the sea? How can you starve them, leave them alone, act crazy, drop acid, live at the bar? How can you do that?

"I'll tell you. It's easy.

"But we have to save the children, you have to cooperate, you don't want your children to grow up like you, do you?

"God forbid."

"Mom," I said, "Mom, listen. You're imagining that stuff. Nobody got off the boat. I didn't see anyone like that, and even if they did, they're still in Tern Bay, right?"

I waited for her to react, to see if I was getting through. She looked out the window, first, as though she thought maybe they walked on water. Finally she nodded.

"And we're on this fucking ferry, right?" I said.

Another nod.

"So what could be better—I mean, how could things get better than this?"

I don't know why, but I always got very, very sarcastic when I was trying not to get in a fight, and that maybe wasn't the way to go, exactly, but I couldn't help it, it was like the words just came out.

She didn't even react to the sarcasm, though, and I got to thinking I might not be there. Have you ever had that feeling? Like you're seeing and hearing, but you can't take part? Like you're a ghost that no one knows is there? Then I thought maybe Mom wasn't really there and I was, and I kept switching between me, Mom, me, Mom . . . Maybe it could be a gene thing, this craziness.

"You're wondering about the kids," she said to whoever.

"Why can't she look after her sons? Why does she make Tom take care of Toby all the time?

"It's simple. He does a better job. My sons know where they are in the world, they can find their way through the cement and glass and voices. They see the green arrows—You Are Here.

"Listen. When I was younger I could find my way up the mountain to the muskeg. I could look down at the Strait and tell you where every rock was hidden by the tide. I could cross the streams and the Sianuk River in the next valley, scramble over the boulders and trunks left by Undine Glacier in her last visit down the valley of the Sianuk, find my way home.

"If you go along Karen Creek, the path follows the deer trails until you come out at the muskeg. But over Harvey Pass, keep away from the ravine, because the sides of the creek are steep-to and you could fall a hundred feet without a single handhold.

"No one could ever mistake Karen Creek for Harvey Pass. But how about four corners with sidewalks, curbs, lampposts, one traffic light at each corner, all of them smelling of gasoline and metal?

"Metal doesn't smell.

"Put your nose down on the hood of your car.

"Don't argue with the lady. She's crazy. Who knows what she might do if thwarted?

"I can still find my way through Harvey Pass. But that's a different country. It smells of melted trees and something rising from the center of the earth still smoldering. Ashes, ashes, we all fall down."

She laughed and looked straight at me and her eyes were clear as water.

"Don't look at me like that," she said. "It's all right, Bo, I just have to air out the gray cells now and then. I'm really all right."

"Mom . . ." I said, and then I couldn't think of anything to say. "Really all right?" By whose standards? Who were you talking to just now, Mom? Yes, you're right, I *am* "wondering about the kids," one of them being me.

Sheeh! Now she had me doing it. "I'm kind of sleepy," I said. "Think I'll go crash awhile."

"Tom OK with Toby?" she asked, like she even cared.

"He could probably use a break," I said. "Well . . . later . . ."

Smart talk, wasn't it? No big fight, no big deal. Just, I couldn't breathe too well when I walked out of the cafeteria.

LATER ON, TOM came up and said he'd tried to get Mom to come out of the bar and take care of Toby awhile.

"What did she say?" I asked him, knowing perfectly well.

"She said, 'You do her tonight, OK, Tomtom, and I'll take her tomorrow, promise.' And she reached in her purse and grabbed money out—there were a lot of bills loose out of her wallet and the one she handed me was a fifty dollar bill. I never had a fifty dollar bill before. It seemed like Mom could have made a mistake, do you think? Like maybe she thought it was a five.

"She said, 'Get her some milk and she can sleep with you tonight, OK?' Then she said, 'Get yourself something, too,' and she kind of leaned against the wall and brushed her hand up my face."

"Yeah, she's out of it—waste of time talking to her," I said, thinking how she'd said, "I'm all right, really I am."

"Well," Tom said, "I all at once remembered what Grandma said about round-trip tickets. I was supposed to go to the purser's office with Mom after we got on but I had to stay with Toby so I forgot to remind her to get round-trip like Grandma told me to. So I asked Mom if she bought round-trip.

"She just stared at me and then she said, 'Round-trip?' And she laughed for a long time and then she said, 'There isn't such a thing as round-trip. You better learn that right now, Tomtom, we only go around once.'

"So of course I don't know if she bought round-trip or not. And also," he said, glaring at me, "I found out we get to Petersburg in the middle of the night, so you won't have to look after Toby like you said you were going to."

I laughed and he kicked me and ran off shouting, "Everybody's so dumb!"

Hey, sucker, I thought, maybe you are waking up. About time, Tombo.

By the time we got to Ketchikan it was night again because of heavy fog that hid the flashers in Wrangell Narrows. I watched out the window to see them unload. Tom came over and watched, too. A van got off with a trailer with four really cool Harley-Davidsons. I started trying to figure out how I could get one next year with my dividend check and a little of my fishing money, even though I was going to buy my own boat with it.

"What about your troller?" Tom asked.

"By the time I get out of school I'll have enough for the down payment and a Harley, too," I told him. "Mom's never getting her hands on that money—no way José."

Mom said, "Is that right, Mr. Rockefeller?" She was standing right behind us listening. "Get your stuff together, we're staying here," she said. "Five things—Tom, you take the diaper bag and one pack, Bo the other pack and sleeping bags, I'll take Toby and my pack—now move it."

I shouted, "Jesus Christ—Ketchikan," and a lot of people sat up in their sleeping bags. I was so mad I kicked my backpack all the way out in the hall and a man tripped over it and said, "Shit, watch what you're doing."

We carried everything up the ramp and hung around at the

top waiting for Mom. It was raining pretty hard and there wasn't really any place to get inside except where everybody packed into a little waiting room. I stood there tapping the railing like a drum and singing swear words under my breath.

It was pretty cold. The raindrops were thick, mostly snow, and the car lights twisted them into patterns. As soon as the last truck got off they started letting cars on. The ferry was supposed to be in Ketchikan three hours but we were so late they were going right on. Anyway, who would want to spend three hours in Ketchikan, Alaska, in the middle of the night?

Pretty soon Mom came up the ramp and I said, "I told you so," to Tom, because she was with Koz. Behind them came the short fellow in a blue parka and a gray Ward Cove sweatshirt that bulged out of the jacket because his belly hung down over his jeans. The frizzy blonde was with him and they were carrying duffel bags and walking very slowly, resting every few feet, leaning on the rail along the ramp.

"Too wasted to get up the ramp," I said.

When they came up to us Toby was crying and Mom said, "You take her, Tom, OK? Koz here'll get a taxi. This is Tom and Bo." She waved her hand and Koz sort of looked at us after he'd dumped his stuff down by ours. He felt around in his pockets and got a cigarette and then felt around some more and brought out a lighter and finally got it to light.

The other two came up then and threw their duffel bags down. Mom waved her hand at us again and said, "Bo, Tom, Toby," like we were the grocery list or something.

Don said, "Sorry we don't have room for everyone but we live in such a puny shack we can scarcely turn around. Tomorrow we can plan the trip . . . sun country . . ."

The woman, Lanny her name was, said, "Shut up, Lock-wood. Let's get the fuck outa here." She didn't ever look at us, just stared back at the ferry and blew smoke out of her nose.

Koz came back then with two taxis. He loaded our stuff in one of them and Tom climbed into the backseat with Toby. I got in and shoved them over and stared out at the stupid rain. Koz talked to Mom a second, then said, "Hillside Motel," to the driver. I looked back and Koz and Don and Lanny were putting their stuff in the other taxi.

The lady at the motel desk was the most gross, obese person I'd ever seen in my life, I mean sick. She definitely was not happy to see us. She made Mom give her one night deposit, one night paid. The motel room was the pits, man. It smelled like ciga-rettes and the carpet had a huge white blotch in the center of the floor. There were two double beds that looked like Army ma-neuvers had been held there.

The second we shut the door, I said, "No way we're going anywhere with those Mafia types. What're we doing in Ketchikan? You said we were going south. You just better give me my money."

"See your lawyer, honey," Mom said. Then she patted my arm and said, "It'll be OK. Honest, Bo. Wait'll you see those boats. I saw some pictures—you will go absolutely out of your mind when you see those boats. Wait'll we get down south—cruise, swim, lie on the beach . . ." She had her eyes half shut seeing that white sand.

All I could see was iced-up wheelhouse and green water over the bow. "Yes, dear," I said, as sarcastic as I could.

TOM

1

We were so tired we didn't wake up till almost nine o'clock in the morning, even Toby. We went next door to a cafe with a counter and two tables. We sat at one of the tables, and pretty soon Koz came in and sat at the counter and smoked and drank coffee. He asked us if we wanted to go look at the boats, his and Don's. Bo didn't know what to say because a lot he did want to and a lot no. But Mom said sure we'd go.

We got our stuff from the room and she put Toby in my pack and we all went to the boat harbor, Bo acting like he didn't know us. Koz's car was pretty old and small but I really like to ride in cars and we hardly ever get to. I put the window down and let my hand blow backward till Bo said close it, he was freezing.

Don's boat was tied up on the finger just north of the ramp, second slip. It was an old wooden seiner, painted blue and white, pretty big, way bigger than the *Sunny Belle* or the *Tykan,* flying bridge like on some castle, boom for a power block but the block was off, no skiff either. The deck was clean of gear, hatches for the fish hold and tanks screwed down, lines coiled and life rings hanging across the cabin bulkhead above the door with her name, *AnaCat,* in black on all of them. She looked pretty good, actually, like somebody kept her pretty shipshape.

Don came out on deck when Koz called, "Ahoy, *AnaCat.*" He let us go past him through the main cabin to the wheelhouse. Bo was pretending he didn't care, but then he saw the electronics and he about busted a gut he was so excited.

He kept on saying, "Oh wow, man, fantastic, awesome, what wouldn't you give, man," all under his breath but everyone could hear anyway. Don liked to show off what he had, you could tell. He switched on the batteries and all the instrument switches on the panel and everything started blinking and circling around. Global Positioning System, screen charts, sideband transmitter, Weatherfax—Bo just absolutely gave up he wanted to test that stuff so bad.

Don began showing him how to plot positions on the GPS and Mom and Koz and I went down the ladder to the fo'c'sle and looked around at the berths—eight bunks and two more fold-downs, and even a head below. We went back up and looked in the galley cupboards and Mom gave Toby a cracker from a box of saltines. There was way more food in those cupboards than we ever keep in our kitchen. One cupboard for only wine—special racks so the bottles wouldn't bang together. The refrigerator was empty though, I guess because he didn't keep it running if he wasn't on the boat.

Bo was turning dials, and maps kept shifting around on the screens. Don left him to play with them, and came over where we were trying the water in the sink. Mom asked him why it was called *AnaCat*.

"Guy I bought her from," he said. "He said his grandmother was some Russian royalty name of Ana Caterina. He mostly used the boat for crabbing. Then he got a seine permit but the second year out, the skiff shifted onto his leg and smashed up his hip and put him out of the fish biz for good."

I took Toby out on deck because she was getting fussy, and bounced her around on a fender that was hanging inside the rail. Don stuck his head out the door and said, "Hey, do you mind?" so we quit and just hung around till Mom said, "C'mon, Bo, we better go see the other boat." She said to Don, "He'll never leave all those switches—break his arm."

Don laughed, and he and Bo began switching off, Bo saying, "This is so cool, this is so excellent," all the time.

We walked along to the last finger beyond the ramp and almost to the end of it and there was the other seiner with her name, *Tenino,* on the bow.

"Pipe you aboard?" Koz said, and we all climbed across the rail, first Mom, and then I handed Toby over, and then me and Bo.

The wheelhouse of the *Tenino* was all polished wood like somebody must have rubbed it every day. *Tenino* was older and a little smaller than the *AnaCat,* the bridge open at the back, not all closed in like a castle, only one head that opened onto the deck. *AnaCat* had two heads, one on deck and one below.

Both of them had staterooms for the skipper with a door right into the wheelhouse, but *Tenino*'s stateroom had two bunks, plus a little table, and *AnaCat*'s had two big beds and thick chairs and a TV like it was somebody's living room. Most other ways, *Tenino* was pretty much like the *AnaCat,* but it only had LORAN instead of GPS and only VHF not single sideband, so I could see Bo thought it wasn't as great. But I really liked how it looked with all that nice wood inside.

The outside was wood, white hull and rail with two colors of blue stripes at the waterline, and blue trim on the rails and windows. I thought the *Tenino* was way more a nice-looking boat than the *AnaCat,* but of course GPS is very good, I guess. To hear Bo, you couldn't find your way to the bathroom without it.

Toby wanted to get down so Mom lifted her out. I got the leash out of my pack and fastened it to her overalls, and we walked along the dock to look at the other boats. At the end of the dock was a big tug all brand-new paint, red and black with shiny brass door handles and the name *M/V Albert Thompson* on a brass plate above the door. I thought I'd like to be a tugboat captain. You could go a lot of places and bigger ships would always be waiting on you to come and help them get through bad narrows or into the harbor.

Toby tripped over a coil of line on the dock and scrunched her face up because she thought she was going to fall in the water. I picked her up and talked funny like Donald Duck to make her laugh. When she got better I put her down and we walked back to the *Tenino.* Bo was standing there. He said, "Hey there, sucker," when he saw us. "Guess who gets to babysit today?"

I said, "You is who," and he laughed mean and said, "Not a chance. Mom went back to the motel. She said for you to buy Toby lunch. I'm going uptown."

I said, "How come always me, not you? How come it's always gotta be me?"

Bo looked at me funny and then said, "You're the only sucker, sucker. Nobody else wants her."

"Mom wants her."

"She's stuck with her, you mean."

"I don't get it . . ."

"That's the whole point—you don't get it. You're such a baby, Tom, a real baby, is all."

All of a sudden he gave me a push and turned around and started running up the ramp. He shouted back, "You're just a sucker, is all."

We walked uptown real slow because I couldn't get Toby into my pack by myself, and she didn't want to walk, but she didn't want to be carried much either. I saw Bo coming out of a store so I yelled at him to wait. When we got to him, I said I was going back to the motel to give Toby to Mom, and then did he want to go down and check out a few boats.

He shrugged and said he might get down there later, and he asked how would I get rid of Toby. I said I'd just leave her with Mom and come back.

He said, "Sure," and walked off.

When we got back to the motel I pounded on the door and nobody answered, but I kept banging on the door and finally somebody said, "Hunh? Wha'cha want?"

Finally the door opened a crack, and Mom was standing there wearing a flannel shirt. I pushed in with Toby and Toby grabbed Mom's bare leg and started whining. Koz pulled the blankets over his head and said, "Oh, shit," and Mom said, "Tom, I'm really tired, can't you look after her just till dinner?"

I looked at her and I said, "No, I can't," and I turned around and pushed through the door again and I walked away fast.

2

I went back down the hill across that creek or slough or whatever it's called, and hung around on the sidewalk awhile looking in store windows. I was feeling sort of bummed, sorry for leaving Toby but kind of glad, too. But my insides were squeezed up like they couldn't get any air. I don't know. I just felt weird, I guess.

It was raining really hard but I didn't exactly feel like going into any stores. After a while I thought I might just walk past the *AnaCat* and the *Tenino* again, sort of look them over. The harbor's a pretty long walk from downtown—it's closer to the ferry than to the stores. The sidewalk half the time goes right against the buildings and the buildings are out over the water. You can see water if you look down through the crack between the buildings and the walk. Pretty weird.

When I got to the boat harbor—Bar Harbor, it's called—I walked down the ramp and first went to the farthest finger to take a look at the *Tenino*. I passed the *AnaCat* which was just one finger beyond the ramp, but I thought I'd catch it on my way back. Two men were checking a gill net along the main dock and another guy had the guts of his Evinrude spread all over under a tarp he had propped up. Didn't look to me like it wasn't going anywhere.

I remembered the *Tenino* was almost last on that farthest finger. I started along it and there was Bo way down at the end checking it out, too. He had his fingers hooked in his back pockets and he was sort of turned sideways to the *Tenino* like he wasn't paying it any attention but he was really.

When I got up near him I said, "Cool, hunh?" He sort of jumped and then went on pretending he wasn't noticing much. I walked along the slip next to the *Tenino* and looked her over a little.

"He got a skiff for this thing?" I asked Bo.

"Koz, you mean? I dunno. He wouldn't pack the skiff around if they're not fishing. I guess they're going to buy for the cannery next year. Sheeeh, with a boat like this, why'd anyone want to buy? Pack some other dude's fish? You could make as much with a couple days seining as a troller gets all season."

"Maybe he hasn't got the rest of the stuff—the skiff and nets and stuff. Or maybe a permit. Probably they cost too much."

"Nahhh, the bank owns it all anyway. Bank wouldn't loan him on the boat without the rest of the stuff—how'd he earn the payments?"

"Well, maybe that's why he's packing—to make enough for the skiff."

"You're a skiffhead, Tom. You could pack with any old tub—you don't need a boat like this. Man, it is one wicked boat. Just excellent."

"Better'n the *AnaCat*?"

"Nahhh, not so great as that. The *AnaCat*'s got better stuff. Electronics. He's got that boat fitted like it was a tracker for the Navy."

"Wanna go aboard?"

"Sure, but we better not. Koz might not like it if he came down here and found us poking around. Anyway, where's Toby? You find Mom?"

"Yeah, at the motel. I left Toby and I just split outa there really fast."

Bo stared at me awhile and then he sort of turned his head and started scraping at the rail with his fingernail, like he was chipping paint loose, and he said, "They in the sack?"

"Koz was," I said. "He didn't want Mom to let me in, but I just kept pounding on the door so she did."

"What did she say?"

"Well, she said she was really tired, couldn't I look after Toby until dinner. I said no I can't, and I left. Only I feel sort of mean because I guess she could be pretty tired."

"Hungover's all." Bo looked at me like he was surprised I did it. "You going to get her back at dinner?" he asked.

"Hunh unh," I said, even though I'd been thinking I would. "Not me. I'm never going to take care of her except if Mom's at work. Not just so she can go booze it up like you said."

He sort of nodded and said, "Way to go," and then he said, "Wanna go check over the *AnaCat*?"

Bo never usually wants me with him even if he isn't doing

anything, so I was kind of happy he asked if I wanted to. So I said it'd be OK, I guess, and we walked pretty slow back to the first finger by the ramp. The two men were reeling their gill net onto the drum, one holding back while the other laid it on. The Evinrude didn't look any different, and I told Bo I thought it wasn't going out today. Bo laughed even.

We passed a big steel power skiff tied up by the inside of the main dock about three fingers down toward the *AnaCat*. The stern said *Ten Four* so we figured it was probably *Tenino*'s skiff. Like it was kind of a joke, see, Ten Nine and Ten Four? It was one bull of a skiff—Bo figured around twenty feet, maybe a hundred eighty horse power. Two hundred.

I really liked seine skiffs. They have to have a lot of power to keep the nets from the big boat stretched out against the current and all those salmon driving right into them. Is it ever great to watch a power skiff take off full bore, dragging the cork line back of it. Sometimes the net might get caught when it unwinds from the big boat, and the skiff could broach or flip and the guy get thrown in the water. It's pretty dangerous being the skiff man, but I'd sure want to drive one of those things, go charging at the rocks, net stretching out in back. Awesome! Probably I'll be a skiff man.

We walked along to the *AnaCat*. We climbed aboard after we sort of looked around to see if anybody was watching, and looked through the door and went up on the foredeck so we could see into the wheelhouse.

"GPS, sideband, Weatherfax, color radar, VHF," Bo was saying like he was starved and reading a menu.

"Everybody's got radar," I said. "That's not so great."

"Look at that radio, though. You usually gotta fish way off-shore to get one of those. I wonder why he'd get it?"

"What's GPS that's so great?"

"Satellites—bounces signals off satellites—tells you where you are anywhere in the world—always right on the dime. Man, this is such a cool boat. Would I give an arm for a boat like this!"

"Maybe Mom and Koz'll get married and then the *Tenino*'d be sort of like our boat."

Bo looked at me like I'd just crawled out of the cat's box.

"Married? You been dropped on your head, Tom?"

"Well, he must like her OK, saying like he'll take us to Mexico. You know, and being with her quite a bit?"

"In the sack, you're talking. See, that's all he's interested in."

I knew all about that kind of stuff, actually. What Bo was talking about. Andy Millins and I talked about it quite a bit—like about all the time . . . girls . . . well . . . you know. But that was different, really, not like your mom. Moms, it seemed like . . . I don't know, it just seemed like that would be different.

I didn't really want to say anything to Bo because he always thought I was so dumb and little, so I just said, "Well, yeah, I know about that stuff—you don't have to tell me."

"Well, you know what happened with Matt. You want that to happen with Mr. Shitface Kozloff?"

I tried to remember Matt. I didn't like him so much, I guess, but he was funny sometimes, especially when he'd been drinking a lot. He worked at the cannery driving the forklift. He had this old mud bike which he looked like a clown riding, because it was kind of small, and he was super tall and had a huge belly that stuck down over his pants so he couldn't fasten his pants up very high. When he bent over you could sort of see his butt.

One day he got so drunk he was wobbling the bike all over, and he rode it out on the boardwalk to the breakwater, and when he got to the top of the ramp he wobbled the front wheel so much that it all of a sudden turned and he shot down the ramp. It was a super minus tide so the ramp was about straight up and down, and he was going about ninety miles an hour when he got to the bottom. It was lucky the *Rae Ann* which is usually in that slip was out fishing or he'd have gone straight through the wheelhouse and been killed for sure. Since she was out he just flew in the air and hit the water like a torpedo. A couple guys who were down on the dock pulled him out when they stopped dying laughing, but that was the end of the mud bike. Was that ever funny!

Old Matt. Too bad he left, in a way, and never got to see Toby. In a way not, I guess. I didn't like him all that much. Suddenly I thought of Mom's story that night at home, how Matt had hit her and slammed her against the wall when he was drunk. I hoped I'd never see him again.

"Think Matt'll ever come back?" I asked Bo.

"You really are out of your mind, Tom. Why would he come back? To support his retardo kid? He's not stupid—just a fuckin' S.O.B."

"What do you mean 'retardo kid'?"

Bo stared at me a long time and then started to scrape paint with his fingernail like when we were talking on the *Tenino* and he asked if Mom and Koz were in the sack.

"Toby. Listen, Tom, she's super retarded. She can't even talk—she isn't even potty trained—she's three years old! Everyone knows it. She's very very retarded, is all."

"I knew that." I said it fast, knowing Bo would say, "Shuuure you did."

But he didn't. He said, "Then how come you talk like she's some magic act? Like she's smarter and cuter than anyone else's kid? I hear you say that, Tom. 'Look at her, Mom, isn't she cute?

She's thinking all those secrets she knows.' I hear you say junk like that all the time! Well, she's a brain case. She'll probably never read or write—maybe not even talk. If you know that, why do you talk that way?"

"Well, I knew it," I said, "but not for sure."

Now I was thinking about it. I was hearing him. It was like I had known it, but not the words, or something. I guess you can know something even if you don't know any words to tell about it. But then if you can't say the words, how does your brain tell itself about it?

Bo was looking at me funny like he wanted to say something else but then he didn't want to either. I thought about Toby never being able to talk, or go fishing, or read books, or draw pictures. Would you ever get any friends if you couldn't talk?

My brain started to get all funny like it couldn't think about thinking, but I had to. I had to. I don't even know, really, what I was thinking. If you think too hard about how you think, you get really messed up, like watching your own feet going downstairs and thinking how do you do that. Pretty soon you always trip.

Bo put his hand on my shoulder and I sort of leaned against him, only a little, but my brain was all funny, and I started to be not able to breathe a lot. I might have been crying, because Bo kept wiping his sleeve across my face and the button scratched, but I was pretty glad he was there. I knew I shouldn't have left Toby. She must be so lonely in there if she didn't have any secrets and she couldn't think with any words. I didn't know, though, did I?

I knew.

After a while, Bo said, "It was Mom drinking when she was pregnant with her. And she didn't drink hardly at all until Matt started hanging around. I'd kill that guy if he ever came back. God, he screwed our lives so bad—Mom alcoholic, Toby wrecked up."

"Toby's retarded because Mom drank?"

"Yeah, we had this film at school—it showed kids like Toby—looked exactly like her, you should have seen them—they got it from their mothers drinking when they were pregnant. And Mom never drank like that until Matt came around, and we're not retarded. I'd kill him if I even saw him one time!"

"But she didn't have to. She could just say, well I don't want any booze. Or anyway, she didn't have to get another baby, did she?"

"Yeah, but drinking makes you want to do it all the time. They were in the sack all the time, don't you remember? And if we wanted to go in our room they'd yell at us to get out or else sometimes they'd go off to the bunkhouse. Don't you even remember that?"

I did, sort of, but mostly because Bo was super mean that year, always punching me, and when he fixed soup or beans or Kraft dinner he'd just eat out of the pan and I could get what was left. But I only turned seven the week before Mom went to get Toby, so most likely I was too young to know about stuff. Six is all I really was, which is pretty little, actually.

We were sitting at the aft edge of the *AnaCat*'s cabin on the lid of a gear box that had a padlock on it—maybe survival suits in it, spare parts and stuff. I was sitting on top, flipping the handle of the box with my feet, and Bo was leaning his butt up against it and coiling a line. It was almost dark and the dock planks were all shiny from the lights and the rain. It reminded me of the boardwalk to the breakwater in Tern Bay, and I sure wished I was home and going to our hideout with Andy.

I started thinking maybe we could just go back on the ferry

the other way instead of go to Mexico or Disneyland. I said it to
Bo—"Maybe we can just get our tickets out of Mom's purse and
go back on the ferry. I don't even want to go to Mexico. I'd go
home, I guess, pretty fast."

Bo said, "You can bet there aren't any tickets. Mom would
have bought one-way only, because of maybe going with Koz on
his boat."

"Well, there must be a lot of money, then, and we could buy
tickets. She put money in a bunch of places."

"Yeah," he said, wrenching at the hatch cover. Then he
stood up straight. "I doubt it's anywhere now," he said. "Not
with how she's acting with those guys."

"Meaning like what?" I said.

"It's gone, I bet—she's getting supplied, is what, and believe
me, she's dropped a bundle already. If there's some left she'd be
sure it was hidden super safe."

"Maybe we could sneak on," I said. "We could be stow-
aways. And when they found us it'd be too late, we'd be already
close to Tern Bay so they'd just make us get off there."

"You're nuts, Tom. We're stuck in Ketchikan while Mom
gets fully strung out on whatever weird stuff it is those guys
trade. My god, what if she even gets pregnant again? Holy
shit—I can't stand it!" Bo kicked the gearbox so hard the whole
bulkhead behind it shook and the door rattled. "We could spend
our lives right here in good old Gateway City."

"We can run away," I said.

"Are you gonna take Toby or leave her with Mom?" he
asked, looking right at me.

I knew I couldn't leave her now that I knew about her, but
man, how could we ever run away with a fussy baby not even
potty trained?

"I don't know," I said. "Take her, I guess. I guess we'd have to, hunh? Probably we have to bring her with us."

Bo nodded real slow. I knew what was coming. "Shuuure we will," he said. "You bet, guy." He was quite a bit disgusted, I think.

WE WALKED UP to the street I'd been on that crosses the creeks and gulleys. At the top of the ramp was a stand like a hot-dog stand, all boarded up with a lot of torn posters on the boards over the window. There was a sign above the window in kind of Chinese-y writing, which said, *Chung Woo Mexican-American Cuisine*.

Bo punched me and said, "Look at that. Mexico!" He did a stupid Mexican hat dance and a guy and girl walking past laughed.

The girl said, "Sweet and sour pork tacos," and Bo laughed, too.

We stopped a couple blocks later and went into a cafe and got fish and chips in cardboard baskets. We ate it there because it was raining so hard. While we were eating, the *Taku* went nosing past, heading north toward the ferry dock.

"Sneak on?" I asked Bo. I still had thirty-seven dollars left from the fifty, so we could buy food, and anyway I knew Bo had brought some of his own, even though he'd never never think of mentioning a word about it.

"Nobody'd care once we got on," I said. "They'd just figure we were with our parents. And it'd be super easy to slide in when they're loading. All those people get off to look around and back on board while they're loading."

Bo was staring out watching the *Taku* and licking the grease off his fingers from the fish. He didn't say anything, so I just went on talking about how we could go to the motel and get our stuff and still have time to get there, because the ferry always stays at least three hours unless they're late, like when we came from Sitka.

Bo said, "Shut up, Tom. I already told you." He went on eating his fries, drawing lines in the ketchup with the ends of them, and then staring out the window and chewing real slow.

"Well, if we went on the ferry we could take Toby, it wouldn't be hard to do. We could buy her milk and stuff, and it'd be just like when we came down here."

Bo just kept chewing and staring out, so I quit talking and made a mountain of salt on a paper napkin to dip my fries in, after I dipped them in ketchup.

After a long time, when I was almost done eating, Bo said, "It's way more complicated than that. If we took Toby and ran away, or even if we didn't take her, Mom'd have to call the police or somebody, and first thing they'd start asking questions and finding out she's got problems."

He started drumming a major riff on the table with the salt and pepper. "Like that stupid snoop that kept coming around before we left. And next thing you know, they'd be talking about foster homes, or some dumb thing."

"You mean us? Take us away and make us live somewhere else? Like Andy's mom said? Mom said nobody could do that. Take her kids away."

"She's just talking"—*bammety clack, bammety clack*—"If they look at Toby, and start hearing that we ran away because Mom's drinking again and maybe wasted on drugs, we'd be dead ducks. You want to live with some old man and lady that make you wipe your feet all the time and be in before dark and never go out or watch TV?"

"Why'd they do that?"

"Who knows? That's how it'd be." He beat the table so hard with the salt and pepper I thought sure they'd smash. Then he shoved them back and grabbed the mustard and ketchup bottles. *Thud, thud, bonk, bonk . . .*

"Anyway, that's not the point. No way I'm going to get Mom turned in. Mom's got a bad rap with Dad dead and Matt cheating and getting her drinking, and now Toby. We're not cutting out on her. Not a chance."

"Well," I said, "we could take her, too. Her and Toby."

Bo didn't even answer he was so disgusted. He didn't even say, "Shuuure we can, Tommy babe." He didn't exactly have to say anything.

3

decided to check out the ferry and then maybe go back to the motel and watch TV. When I got as far as Bar Harbor I thought I might as well check out that skiff again, the *Ten Four*, since Bo didn't want to look at it that much. There wasn't anyone around so I climbed in and sat there thinking how cool it would be to run that skiff, haul the cork line toward the beach, the tow line back to the *Tenino*, hold the *Tenino* out of the net. Imagine getting caught by your own net like a salmon. All the time that huge roar—all that power—oh man, would I love to do that. Wicked!

I sat there awhile and looked at everything, played with the throttle and the gearshift, poked around the hoses. Underneath the exhaust hose there were a couple keys on a ring hanging from a wire. On the key ring was a piece of wood with a hole through it and some numbers scratched on it. I looked around sneaky and then took the ring off the wire and tried the keys in the ignition.

I wouldn't have started the engine, of course not, because of how much noise it makes, and anyway I don't know much about the gears so I could have bashed the dock, even though a couple times Grandma let me drive hers when I went to the island. But anyway the keys didn't fit in the ignition so I put them back on the hose wire and just pretended I was tearing through the water toward the rocks and the skipper was signaling north, go north, faster, faster!

I was getting pretty cold because it was blowing quite a lot, and of course raining, so I thought I'd go back and watch TV. Probably Mom would be there because of it being Toby's bedtime. Maybe Koz wouldn't want Toby around so he would've gone and we could get back to our trip to Disneyland.

There wasn't anybody in the room so I had to get the key at the desk and the lady didn't want to give it to me, but I told her Mom wanted me to get diapers for Toby so she did. I watched *Cosby* and then Bo came and banged on the door and I let him in. He had a couple bags of chips and a six-pack of Pepsi and we sat on the bed and watched *Miami Vice* and ate chips and I fell asleep.

When I woke up, I was lying on a half a bag of chips squashed into scratchy crumbs. There wasn't anyone there except Bo, asleep in the other bed. I got up and went to the bathroom and then got back in bed and waited for him to wake up. I didn't want to think about Toby, but I was so scared about what I'd done I couldn't stop thinking about her. I'd run off and left her. Mom might not have wanted to have her right then because of Koz, and Toby was retarded and didn't really know anything. She couldn't even say what she was thinking, not one little thing. And I left her.

But then I thought well, Mom would take care of her even if she didn't want to especially right then, because that's what moms do. They take care of you. But it didn't really make me feel any better because I knew I was supposed to be taking care of her, and she must have felt sad when I ran away and left her. I wondered if you could feel sad even if you didn't know the words for your brain to say you felt sad.

Anyway, where were they? They must have slept somewhere . . . maybe they went and stayed on the *Tenino*. They could be there now, actually, and then go and get something to eat when they woke up.

I decided to get up and go look for them. I got some jeans out of my pack because the ones I was wearing were still pretty wet when I went to sleep and the potato chip crumbs were stuck, sort of soggy-greasy on them. Then I thought maybe I better take the diaper bag in case Mom hadn't taken enough with her. I opened the bag and she'd taken quite a lot of them so I didn't know if I should take the bag or maybe just put a couple diapers in my pockets, and later I could bring Toby back with me. I took a couple out and under them was a Skoal can like Matt used to leave around. I didn't know why it would be in the diaper bag so I took it out and opened it. Inside was money rolled up in a rubber band.

I took the rubber band off and unrolled the money—hundred dollar bills—eight of them. Mom must have put the money for each of our checks in our own stuff.

I went through everything in my pack and there wasn't any. Then I started on Bo's pack and it was like he had a burglar alarm in his head even though I was being really quiet. He sat up and said, "Get outa that—what're you doing in my stuff?" and he swung at me but missed because he was only half out of the blankets.

I showed him the hundred dollar bills on the table and he went a little crazy. He threw everything out of my pack and his and Mom's onto the bed and unrolled the sleeping bags and turned them inside out. It was a big mess when he finished and no more money.

"She must have forgot she put some in the diaper bag," he said. "Tough. No way she gets this now." He folded up one bill at a time and put them in different pockets. Before he could get it all I grabbed the last two and put them in my own pockets. He swiped at me again but not like he really meant anything, so I guess he figured I should get some since I found it.

He went in the bathroom and slammed the door. I hung around till he came out and then told him I thought Mom and Koz might be at the *Tenino* and I was going down there. He said no way, they were for sure at Don and Lanny's house, and anyway he was going to eat, forget Mom, she could look after herself.

"And look after Toby, too?" I said and he said sure, her, too. So I went with him to eat, and he had pancakes and eggs and sausage, but I didn't feel too hungry at all, so I just had some fries and a glass of milk. I was very extremely worried. I felt like my badness filled up my whole insides. It kept making me feel hot in prickles, especially the backs of my knees and right under my ears. I was really scared for what I'd done to Toby.

After we ate, Bo went off to look around in stores, and I went down to the *AnaCat*. Nobody there. It was just the same as yesterday, nobody'd been around at all. I went along to the *Tenino* and nobody there either, so I went and sat in the *Ten Four* and put one key a little way in the ignition, all it could go, and pretended to drive. A couple men came by and one of them said, "Watch your wake there, Sonny," like I was coming in too fast or something, and he kind of laughed. They got on a troller, the *Donna Lee,* and took off.

That was some long long day, believe me. I went three times all the way back to the motel. Nobody there. I probably looked at every single thing in Hansen's Sporting Goods—fly rods, rifles, knives, flashlights, wool socks, Porta-Potties—just absolutely every single thing. Bor-ring!

This man in the store kept watching me, and asked a couple times if I was looking for something. I told him no, and kept looking at stuff, but then he said, "Listen, kid, either you buy something or you get. I don't like kids hanging around the store, see?" So I left, even though I didn't see why I should have to. Lots of people hang around stores looking at stuff they don't even want to buy.

Late afternoon, dark, I went and checked the boats again. Nobody. I stopped at the skiff and fiddled with the keys but I wasn't feeling like pretending anything anymore, only like finding Mom and Toby. I guess it's pretty hard to pretend stuff if you're feeling bad.

Then I went back to the motel. I still had the key from before so I didn't have to argue with the lady. I turned the TV on and watched on old, old, stupid movie about some crazy lady and her sister and everyone yelling at each other and running up and down stairs. I think I might have fallen asleep awhile because the movie changed to *Three Stooges* all at once and at the same time somebody knocked on the door. I figured Bo so I didn't exactly hurry, but it was Mom and Toby.

When I opened the door, Mom just stood there not moving at all. Toby was asleep with her head on Mom's shoulder. She looked like a little monkey clinging to Mom's coat, Mom hardly even holding her arm under her. After a long time, Mom said, "Hey, Tom, babe," and came in. She sort of slid her coat off, Toby still on it, and put them in bed and pulled the covers up over her coat and Toby both.

"Been Christmas shopping," she said when she straightened up. She was just standing there, not really exactly moving or looking at anything. "Party," she said. "Big Christmas party." She didn't look around or ask where Bo was or anything, just stood there and said those things, not looking at anything. Just staring but not looking. I don't know. Just standing there.

I didn't exactly know what to say to her so I just moved a little so I could see *Three Stooges* and after a while she went in the bathroom. She was in there a long time—the movie was over before she came out. Then she sat down on the edge of the bed across from Toby. She just sat there and stared at her hands. She started looking at her fingers, kind of turning them over in front of her eyes as if there was something on them or maybe they hurt or something. Then she said, "Christmas party tomorrow. Big party." Later on she said, "Shopping." She got in bed next to Toby but every few minutes she'd sit up and look at her hands.

I saw something was wrong with her, but I didn't know what. I got to thinking she didn't know I was there. I wished Bo would come. I wished he'd come because I was scared. And I didn't for sure want to go to any old Christmas party.

I watched Toby sleeping in Mom's coat. Her face looked the way it always did, little scrunched-up cheeks and wrinkles around her eyes that made her look old and wise. She wasn't any different. Bo had to be wrong. How could anyone believe she wasn't thinking a lot of things? It made me mad anyone would believe that.

I guess I went to sleep with the lights on because all of a sudden someone banged on the door and at the same exact second Mom sat up in bed and screamed. Then Toby screamed. I was so mixed up I didn't even know where I was. The door kept pounding and Mom was sitting there with her hands over her face and Toby was crying. I got up and went and said, "That you, Bo?" and opened the door for him. Then I picked Toby up and hushed her.

Bo looked at Mom sitting there staring at her hands and then he looked at me and said, "Told ya," and went in the bathroom. I didn't know what he'd told me. Everything, was all. Bo thought he knew everything. Anyway I was glad he came even if he does think he's so smart.

When he came out of the bathroom he looked at Mom again. She put her hands over her face like she was crying but no noise. Toby had gone to sleep while I was holding her so I put her in our bed and got in but Bo said, "No way—put her with Mom." So we both got in Mom's bed and Bo had the other all to himself. He is such a pig I can't even tell how bad.

BO

When the last movie ended, I couldn't think of anything else to do. The motel was it—I mean, even cement blocks are better than a park bench. My eyes were totally bummed—five movies can really kill you, especially most of them rated G because of Christmas vacation. It was raining hard, of course, and blowing, a hummer down the channel. It seemed like about ten miles back to the motel.

I didn't have a key so I pounded on the door, and pretty soon Tom opened it a crack with the chain on. "You?" he said, like he was thinking at least Santa Claus, and then shut the door again to get the chain off.

When I got in, he pointed at Mom who was sitting up in bed, staring at her hands like maybe they'd just grown there at the ends of her arms. I mean, she was gone?

"She just keeps doing that," Tom said, "Looking at her hands. She said something about a Christmas party, and that's all, ever since she got back."

"Yeah, sure, she's stoned," I said. "You don't recognize it by now? I mean, look at her." I wanted to shout at him, but what was the use. Tom was Tom. When he got there, at his own snail's pace, he was there. Till then, you might as well listen to the echo. Sheeeh.

It seemed like Mom heard me, maybe not the words I said, but a voice she knew, coming through the snowdrift, because she started on one of her little talk jobs, phony voices and all.

"She's ignoring problems, ignoring stress, ignoring happiness. Neglects her kids.

"Abuses them?

"Well, we don't think she beats them, we have no evidence of that, but you know, there are other kinds of abuse.

"Does she love them does she love them does it count if she loves them? I'll kill myself listening to their thoughts—noise pollution, rattle rattle, happiness, stress, play therapy . . .

"Slow down, woman, whose head trip is this anyway?

"Stop. I hear what you're saying: *I never know what you're talking about anymore—shadows flickering on the cave wall—birds flying, tortured tree branches, words armed with bayonets, dead swans—when you talk like that you're locking me out of your head.*

"Well, I want you to know this: I can't get in either. I must have dropped my keys back there somewhere—I wonder if you might have picked them up?"

She laughed, and then in one second she was crying, her hands, that seemed so foreign to her, twisting over themselves on top of the blanket.

Tom started to go over to her—I knew he needed to comfort her to comfort himself. So did I? But I didn't think it was a good idea. I mean, you hear all this stuff about not waking up sleep-walkers, and it was like she was sleep-talking, in a way. I don't know, I just didn't think we should intrude on her state of mind which was totally bizarre, I mean you should have heard her. It was like her voice was coming back from a space explorer. So I grabbed Tom by the arm and put my hand on his mouth to show him not to talk to her.

Tom looked up at me with eyes about as zonked as Mom's voice. I mean, they were holes in his skull? I think he would have fought me to get to her, only right then Toby gave a little shriek and jump and then started to cry, so Tom was distracted. I bet that kid would fly into a million pieces if he thought no one needed him. No kidding, Tom was born taking care of someone.

I got out of my wet clothes and crawled into the other bed. Tom tried to put Toby between us but I pushed them away. I thought Toby should sleep in the other bed—maybe it would keep Mom sort of fastened to the real world or something. Tom put her beside Mom and then climbed in next to her. In a minute, though, she started talking again, this time a low hum-ming sound, almost a song.

"I'm remembering more of you, Mark . . . are you ready? Are your eyes skittering across the truth of them looking for holes in the fabric, weaknesses you couldn't offer Annie? These are whole, Mark, pure. Pure death. Twenty-seven swans."

She hummed a little, and then sang in a hoarse voice, "*When the pie was opened, they were all twisted there, their own snowy crust deep in blood.*"

Tom was lying on his side facing me, his eyes wide and frightened. He sat up and looked at Mom, then slid his feet to the floor, pushed the blanket back, and got in beside me. He was shivering almost as hard as I was.

"Do you know the wingspan of a dying trumpeter swan stretched toward escape, not making it? Please take them to Annie, one by one, rocked in your arms, heads tucked safe under wings, your hand supporting their black stockings and platform shoes. They were headed to her, Mark, but they couldn't quite reach her, their long necks stretched out, wings beating down to drag those clumsy bodies over the snow. Not enough air beneath to lift them, that was all. No way to rise above the ratatat tat into the silent dome. Take them all.

"*Twenty-seven swans a-swimming in their own hearts' blood,*" she sang, "*no maids a-dancing.*"

She buried her face in her hands, but the song finished in my head. "*. . . and a partriiidge in a pear tree.*" Oh god. Tom's sobs shook our bed and I put my arm over him.

WHEN WE WOKE up in the morning Mom looked tired and sounded hoarse, but I was surprised at how fast she could come out of the wasteland—at least it must not be some drug she had to get on the hour. Lord, though, what it did to her brain while she was on the rush.

"We're going," I told her. "Not one more day in this dump. Shit, what a trip!"

"Listen, Bo," she said, "just listen to me a minute. I know you haven't had a great time, right? Tom either, hunh?" She reached over from where she was sitting on the bed by Toby and rubbed Tom's head. "But we're going south day after tomorrow. I promise."

"Well, you just listen to me," I said. "Those guys are no-good creeps. If you don't already know it you're blind stupid. Look at you last night. Mixing stuff, acid—god only knows what shit!"

I had to drum on something, anything—the TV, the chest of drawers, the chair back—shit, I was losing it, like totally? "They want your money, and that's it. They're just running the trade. I'm not dumb. I see it all the time in Tern Bay, guys wandering around the dock wondering where their ship's gone to. Camped under the boardwalk trying to get their heads straight, wondering what happened to them. Falling out the door of the Grizzly half dead when they've done too much mixing. I see it all the time."

Mom tried to interrupt, but I went right over her. "Those guys are going to have every cent of ours real quick if they don't already. Then what? Here we'll be, stranded in Sun City, you stoned out of your mind or dead O.D. That's what mixing does. Remember Joanie Eldon? Remember Arnie Dunn? They didn't just happen to drop dead of old age. Half the guys in my class are wasted all the time—I should know. We have to get out of here! My god, we're all so fucked up . . ."

Mom was half crying and walking around the room twisting her fingers all around. "Don't say that stuff," she said. "It isn't true."

She stood right in front of me, then, and grabbed my shoulders and made me look at her.

"So maybe I did mess around with the neon once or twice—couple of high flyers, maybe—but no more. Bo, believe me. No more." She tried to rock me back and forth by my shoulders. "And the guys are OK. Really, Bo. I don't want them to hear that junk. They're my friends."

"Junk's the word, right? It wouldn't be safe for them to hear it? They might decide we're a little smarter than they thought? You think they're gonna take three kids all that way?"

"Bo, listen. Listen . . ."

"No way any of us are getting on those boats. Hell, they don't even know anything about boats, I bet, just a way to pick up another haul. No wonder they have all the electronics. Fancy fuzz busters. They track the good old United States Coast Guard."

"Bo, listen, don't talk like that . . ."

"Not healthy? You bet!"

"Bo, listen. Please. It's not like that. No way. You've been watching too much TV. These guys are fishermen—real high-liners. They had a red hot season this year, is all. They made a lot of money. Why won't you believe it? You saw their boats."

"Sure. Look at them. Are they the type to be high-liner fishermen? Unh unh. You gotta work. You gotta be smart. Not street smart, real smart. You gotta work your ass off. Do they look like workers? They're bums. They're cheap, fucking bums. They don't know a boom from a butt."

"Wait, wait, Bo . . ."

"You work a hell of lot harder on the slime line than they ever worked pulling a net, I can tell you. You work for your money and then you hand it over to them. Know what they call that?"

"Shut up, Bo."

"When you run out of money, you know how to get it? How to make money for them?"

"No! Stop it!"

We stood there staring at each other. Then Mom said, "Jesus god, the chance of a lifetime and you want us to throw it away. You're crazy in the head."

She turned away, shaking her arms loose as though she'd gotten pins and needles from holding them so tight. "Listen, Bo," she said. "No more neon. No more booze, either, OK? I promise. I can quit—you don't believe it, but I can—I quit after Toby. You know I did."

She came over and grabbed my hands from my TV drum. "Take a chance, OK? You're such a chicken, Bo Rohlik. You never take a chance. Bet a few this time, OK? Just once? If I quit everything—we go to Mexico."

This was big time trouble we were in. I mean, no kidding. But I just didn't see a way to get her to give up. She was like, hooked into this fairy-tale stuff? About going to Mexico? On a purse seiner in the middle of winter? Give me a break! The one thing we might have going was the money Tom found. At least we could get ferry tickets. But if she didn't want to go back, I mean what, Tom and I could carry her up the ramp? Drag her kicking and screaming past the purser taking tickets? All I could do right that second was put her off—we'd think of something.

I shrugged. "Go fucking insane around here. Sheeeh! Let's go eat."

Mom laughed because she'd won. She said, "Come on—coffee, coffee, coffee—come on, Tom, bring Toby—she's starved." She picked up her coat which was still half under the blankets where Toby had slept with it.

"We went shopping yesterday—you guys'll go crazy when you see your presents. Today, we'll get food for the trip. Tomorrow, open stuff, and Christmas day, so long Alaska."

"Any idea what it's like out there in December?" I said. "Even the whales stay south. This is not a plan, OK? It sucks!"

"Wait—wait. At least wait till you see your present."

"It better be a survival suit and a helicopter is all I can say."

Mom was squatted down scuffling around in the diaper bag. She found the Skoal can and slid it into her purse kind of hidden behind her fingers. I looked at Tom a second and we waited for her to find out the can was empty.

She didn't open it, just put her purse over her shoulder and opened the door. "Come on," she said. "My god, if I don't get coffee soon I'll croak." Then she stopped and turned back and said, "And I do mean coffee. That's it from now on. Ok, guys? That's a promise!"

WHEN WE FINISHED eating, Mom started rummaging around in her purse on the seat beside her, not putting it up on the table, and I looked at Tom again. In a second, she sort of sucked in her breath oh, no, and I knew she'd opened the Skoal can. She sat there staring, I guess trying to remember if she'd taken the money. I was waiting for her to start yelling at us, but she just looked frightened, as though she'd seen the shadow pause beyond the door. Then she jumped up and said, "I'll be right back," ran out the door and across the muddy yard to the motel.

Toby started crying and trying to climb out of the high chair so Tom wiped her face with a paper napkin and tried to make her laugh playing peekaboo.

"She's having a fit looking for it," I said. "She thinks she took it when she was too wasted to know what she was doing. So that means it's all that's left, if she's that worried."

"We should maybe tell her," he said. "She's pretty scared, I guess. It makes me feel bad, her getting so worried."

"No way? First of all, it's our money, only half of what's ours since we both got checks for that much. Second," I held up fingers, counting all the reasons we were right to keep it, "we may have to feed ourselves, who knows how long, or get home, or god knows what. Insurance money, that's what. And third," I leaned across the table and half whispered in case anybody else could hear me, "if she gets it, you know where it'll go. They're stringing her, Tom, all this Mexico talk."

I drummed a long riff right under his nose. "Nobody sane would talk about a little vacation trip down the coast in December. Jesus Christ, that's the stupidest thing I ever heard. She knows it, too. She's just too blind now to let herself see it. We're in big trouble, kid. Real fucked up!"

What I was saying, actually, was "Tom, we gotta do something, what'll we do?" I mean, talk about desperate—I was actually asking my little brother what to do. No kidding, I think I really expected Tom to come up with something. After all, he was used to having to take care of everybody.

I was brushing up the salt Toby had poured on the table from the salt shaker when Mom came back. She was out of breath and she was in a big rush.

"I've got to do an errand," she said. "You guys keep Toby till I get back and then I'll take her all day, promise. You can go and play, go to a show, whatever you want. It'll just take a little while—half an hour."

She took a ten dollar bill out of her wallet and put it on the table. "You guys make up the rest, would you? I don't have any small bills—I'll break one and pay you back—there's the taxi . . ." She was gone before either of us could answer, and Toby hollering again.

WE WENT BACK to the motel and I switched on the TV— soaps, ugh. I didn't really watch, just sacked out on the bed and let Toby climb over me. "You know where she's gone?" I said. "To cash in the ferry tickets. Won't net her much, either. Two one-ways from here to Seattle is all, plus half fare for you."

"Now I get what Grandma meant, 'Be sure she buys round-trip tickets everywhere.' How come I always understand stuff too late? Why is that?"

I looked at him, his face so worried—god, it seemed to me he was actually getting wrinkles from worrying so much.

"I think we might be too late for the whole show, Tombo," I said. "It ain't just you, kid. I mean, what price to hear the fat lady sing?"

TOM

A woman came to clean the room so we hung around outside not to get in her way. The woman from the motel office came waddling along toward us. She was wearing a huge dress that didn't get littler anywhere from her neck to the bottom edge of it, and a little bitty gray sweater that was stretched over her arms but couldn't reach even a little way across her boobs.

She had on rolled-down socks made of that stocking stuff and blue fuzzy slippers and above the socks her legs, all gray with purple lines, were as big around as my waist, and got bigger and bigger until they disappeared under the edge of the huge dress. I didn't know how she could bend over—how would she get her underpants and socks on? I never saw anyone that fat before.

She came up to us and said, "Where's your mother? You kids been hanging around by yourselves an awful lot—how long you staying?"

Bo just shrugged and made one of those drop dead noises so I said, "Probably a couple of more days," and he stuck his elbow in the back of my neck which just happens to hurt a whole lot because he knows where to do it.

"I want to see your mother," the lady said. "Where is she?"

"She's just doing an errand," I said, dodging Bo's elbow. "She'll be right back."

"Shouldn't leave you kids by yourselves here," the lady said. Her eyes were real tiny behind the fat. I wondered if she got fatter if maybe she wouldn't be able to see because the fat rolls on her cheeks would get too tall to see over.

She turned around and started to walk away with her butt wobbling back and forth. It was flat, actually, like she'd leaned against a wall a long time and it had gotten pushed out to the sides.

"She owes me money. Tell her she better pay today or she can look for another place. I ain't keeping no homeless." She shuffled along the walk in her fuzzy blue slippers. "By noon," she said, sort of panting over her shoulder.

I was laughing pretty much at how she looked but Bo was totally pissed. The lady in our room set the vacuum cleaner out on the walk and went back in to put the towels in the bathroom. Just as she came out and started to push the cart to the next-door room, a blue station wagon pulled up in front of our room, Don driving. Lanny was next to him.

Koz opened the back door and got out and said, "Your mom around?"

Bo made his drop dead sound and I said "No," not wanting to say any more because of the elbow-in-the-neck stuff.

"Just 'no'? Just 'no, not here'? C'mon guys . . ." Koz was sort of teasing, like he wanted to be friends but we weren't being too nice to him.

So I said, "Well, she went on an errand but she'll be back in a little bit," and I moved around him pretty far off from Bo.

Toby was ducking her head and watching Koz from between my legs. He squatted down and put his hands over his face and played peekaboo and got her laughing. Then he stood up and went over and talked to Don. "I'll wait and you can go on," he said.

Don said they'd wait a little bit but Lanny looked mad and blew smoke right at him. He rolled his window up and we could see them arguing but we couldn't hear. Then they got out and went in our room. Lanny and Don sat on the sofa and Koz turned the TV on and sat down in the chair that had the burn hole in the seat.

Bo stayed outside but I went in with Toby. She was still hanging on my legs which made me walk funny and she was peeking through at Koz, seeing if he was going to play anymore, but he had a cigarette lit and was watching soaps. I pulled Toby off my legs and sat down at the end of the bed and helped her climb up. After a little she stopped feeling so shy and climbed down and started running around and climbing over everyone's legs. Lanny I could tell didn't like her and kept poking at her with her toe. Toby I guess thought it was a game and kept grabbing at her leg. Lanny gave her a big poke, actually she kicked her, and Toby sat down hard, very hard, and started to cry. I picked her up.

Lanny looked totally pissed and stood up and said, "Let's get out of this kindergarten," to Don. Then she said to me,

"Why don't you kids go on back home? Give Jess a break for god's sake—she needs three kids like a hole in the head."

Koz said, "Shhhh, Jesus, Lanny, not now." Then he said to me "Ignore her, she's just in a bad mood."

Lanny said, "Sure, bad mood. What about what you said last night, Kozloff? 'Why don't we just—'"

Koz said, "Shut up, Lanny," really mean with his teeth together like Mom when she's super mad, and he opened the door and sort of pushed Toby and me out onto the walk. "You guys want to help us get the boats stocked up?" he asked.

Bo heard him but didn't turn around.

"I guess," I said, but I didn't really feel like hanging around with that Lanny too much. I didn't know what else to say but in a second a taxi came and Mom got out.

"Sorry, sorry," she said when Koz came up to her. "Went to cash a check. Hope you haven't been here long."

She started to walk into the room and I pulled her back and told her in a whisper what the fat lady had said about pay by noon. She nodded but she was looking at Don and Lanny coming out the door and not really listening to what I was telling her.

"OK, OK, Tom," she said like she does when she's thinking about something else. She went past them, grabbed the diaper bag, came back out and picked Toby up.

Don said, "All set?" and got in the driver's seat. Koz and Mom and I got in back and Lanny in front.

Mom said, "C'mon, Bo," but he walked away in the other direction with a drop dead noise.

He said, "Not me."

Mom said, "Oh, leave him, he's such a grouch."

Don laughed. "Makes two of a kind around here."

Lanny punched his shoulder and laughed a little. "Send them home, Jess," she said. "He's old enough to handle it. Let your mom have them. What a drag!"

Mom shrugged sort of and squeezed my knee. "They're OK," she said. "I couldn't get along without Tom, here. He takes care of all of us, don't you, Tom?"

For some reason her saying that didn't really sound right. Like maybe she did think that but she was mostly saying it because of what Lanny said in front of me. I don't know. It just didn't sound right exactly. But probably she meant it. You know how mothers are.

We went to a big grocery store in one of those new shopping places with the parking lots on land that's been pushed out toward the harbor. There was a liquor store next door and Don said he'd take care of the staples and went in there.

The rest of us went in the grocery and we each got a cart. Mom put Toby in the seat of mine and the diaper bag underneath and said to me to go get diapers. "Fill up the cart," she said. "They might be harder to get in Mexico."

As soon as Mom walked away with her cart, Toby started to scream. I tried to get her to hush but she went on crying so I pushed the cart fast, then stop, fast, stop, until she decided it was a new game.

We went down the aisle to the diapers and I looked along till I found the kind we always get and I put three boxes stacked up, one underneath with the diaper bag. Then I pushed along looking for Mom. Toby wanted me to go fast again and started to fuss and try to stand up in the seat. To keep her quiet I started fast, slow, fast, slow and when I got to the end Lanny came around the corner and I ran the cart a little bit into her. Toby was still fussing and when I stopped she started louder. The top box of diapers fell off onto the floor and I picked it up and there was Lanny leaning forward, her face right above me.

"What can I pay you," she said, "to take this monstrosity and that ape of a brother and blow this town? How much, hunh? What would it take?"

I hated her so much, that very absolute second, I hated her guts so much I threw the diaper box right at her huge jiggly boobs and I turned around and ran toward the door.

Mom and Koz were coming along the end of the aisle. I shouted, "I'm going home!" and I pushed through a line of people at the checkout and ran out the door.

I heard Mom yell, "Tom, Tom, wait a minute," but I wasn't waiting for anyone. I never hated anybody so much in my whole entire life as that Lanny.

It was raining so hard there was a sort of riptide at the street corner. I just stomped through it about up to my knees and water flying in all directions. At the end of the block I looked back but I couldn't see anyone I knew following so I slowed down and walked a long way. I was very wet but warm because of running and also because of being so mad. Those people were messing up our trip and taking Mom away and acting like it was our fault. Like just being was our fault.

I started thinking how we would just run away and take Mom and Toby with us. Bo would get a gun, or maybe he couldn't get a gun because of not being old enough but he could get a knife, that was it, a knife, and pull it on them and grab Mom in one of those armlocks that hurt if you move even one inch. I'd grab Toby and we'd split so fast and then we'd hide, and when nobody was looking we'd get on the ferry. Or no, we'd go right in and buy tickets because Bo and I had all that money out of the Skoal can. That's what we'd do, we'd go right ahead and buy tickets straight to Tern Bay and in two days we'd be home.

Maybe while we were hiding, waiting for the ferry to come, I'd leave Toby with Bo and Mom and I'd go down and rip all the wires out of the electronics on their boats, and I'd take Bo's knife and cut the dock lines and make holes in things and the boats would get carried out to sea and sink from the holes. Maybe I'd do it when Lanny and Don and Koz were on the boats and they'd all get carried out and sink and drown. Or maybe I would tell the Coast Guard and they'd get saved at the very last minute when they felt really sorry how they'd treated Mom and us. They could get saved, I guess, because after their boats sank they'd never be able to come to Tern Bay because they wouldn't be able to pack next summer.

The *Chilkat* was leaving for the ferry dock to go to Metlakatla and I stood and watched it head south. Just a little ferry that hardly takes any cars, going back and forth only to Metlakatla. I decided to go look at the ferry times posted and see when the next one north would be. The sign said the *Malaspina* would arrive from Seattle at 7:30 P.M. and depart 11:00. If it was coming from Seattle then it would be going north and definitely, for sure, I, Tom Rohlik, would be on it. Even if Bo wouldn't go, or Mom or Toby, I for sure, would be on the *Malaspina*. And I hoped everybody else drowned. Everybody!

"Shouldn't she be in a home, or something?" Koz asks.

"She's in a home. Mine."

"Well, sure, I know, but I mean . . . since she's, you know, sort of not right, maybe you could get her in a home or something, so she'd get fixed up, like maybe trained some way, or something."

"Koz, forget it. She's mine. OK? She didn't ask to be here, right? I'll look after her. It's basically not your problem. Not basically, and also not number two or three or five million and eight, right? Not five or seven or one thousand forty . . ."

"Got it," he says, laughing and putting his hand

over my mouth. "It is basically not my problem. Only, what the hell do we do with her? We gonna drag her around Gateway City while we do the Christmas shopping and fix up the boat supplies?"

"You didn't get it, Koz. I am going to drag her around till they dig up Ketchikan and report what an advanced civilization it had. But she's basic—"

"—ly not my problem. Well, so let's go. Why don't you take that pack Tom carries her in? I could put her on my back with that pack . . . uh uh uh . . . I know . . . not my problem. You'll carry her. You want to carry her. She is your problem and you will carry her. So, let's go."

"I'm tired. I'd just as soon lie here till I mummify like a fallen tree. Till they dig this place up and say 'Oh, how quaint.' Till . . ."

"You're tired. Ahhh, Jessie, you'll be OK. You just gotta build your blood up a little, get your mind cleared out, see? Start over, clean slate, smooth sailing . . ."

"Right. Sun country," I tell him. "Yahoo."

Try to get a grip on things—you're a capable woman with an excellent education and there is no reason—I repeat, no reason at all, why you can't function with a few cinder blocks around you, a few cinder-block motel walls painted fuchsia.

Fucksya. Yes. He does.

Yucksya. Definitely yucksya.

I know, I know. What I don't know is how I got here.

THE FOLLOWED US everywhere today. Every time I looked back, there they were. At the drugstore they stood at the card counter reading Christmas cards. At the grocery they were hanging out in lettuce; at the liquor store they were glued to California reds.

I don't know what to do. I don't want to tell Koz I could get tapped by State officials. He'd be out of here yesterday, he's none too clean himself, you know.

A short, nodding man, and an enormous woman with electrocuted hair. Let's ask a question of our own. Here it comes, give us a drumroll for the inescapable, the ultimate, question.

Are they real?

Please. Clothe your words more gently; reduce their weapons capability.

All right. Does anyone but Jess Rohlik see them?

We have escaped them for the moment so that I can lie here on this droopy cat's pee couch, my stomach and head churning like a twin action washer. Koz has gone out to get tequila—he's got to make Oaxaca Headhunters, can't live without a Oaxaca Headhunter. Don and Lanny are in the kitchen cooking something that smells like boiled boot socks.

See Toby over there, diving into that pillow on the floor that belongs to the cat? Sound asleep, thumb dragging on her teeth. Do you put braces on the teeth of a child who has nothing else right? Look at her. Nothing. Pickled in utero. A perfect laboratory specimen. I'll get an A+ for science, won't I?

Jesus god, I just can't get anything right anymore. They'd be better off in a home, like Koz said. All of them. Can you see Bo in a home? We're laughing again, aren't we? At least we can laugh now and then.

"Get those kids out of my life," Lanny says. It sounds like she's grinding dishes in a blender.

"They aren't our problem, Lanny. I dunno what Koz thinks he's doing, but it ain't our problem."

"No? What's that pooper doing in the living room, then? More squid than kid. Jess should throw her off the ferry, if you ask me."

"So no one's asking you, right? Leave it alone, Lan. She isn't hurting anything. Koz wants to mess around with Jess, let him. He'll get fed up being daddy soon enough."

"When she runs outa green is when. She talks like she's orbiting Mars. Why the hell did he have to pick a looney?"

"She's pretty and she's loaded. What more can you ask?"

"Someone with a few brain cells? Someone without three ugly kids?"

"Let it cool, Lan—it'll cool, all by itself."

"Well, Mr. Cool-It, let me tell you something. Let me make myself perfectly fucking clear. None of those kids is going south with us. Do you read me?"

"They won't be with us, even if Koz winds up taking them. We don't even have to see them down there. We can go down and back and never see the backsides of one of them."

"Listen, Lockwood, I'll see those backsides right over the rail if they come near me."

She slams the crockery together and straps the armor to her words. Herds marching to battle. Battalions heard marching.

—REGRET TO INFORM you . . . result of enemy action . . .

—I don't know why he did it, why did he? Your friend, Billy Garcia.

—I wanted to save them both but I couldn't. Tell Dad and Mom I love them.

Mark, Mark—I do have one for you, after all. I've carried

her so long. Please. You have to take her. Even though I don't know her name, please take her. I can't carry her any longer, Mark.

She lives in a village, a hamlet in the elephant grass. She has no age, or maybe she does, maybe she's old now. I think she is old, but I can't remember right now. Her hair is long and black and her face is always hidden. She's been waiting a long time, but she doesn't know that, Mark.

The soldiers stumble on her village the way they stumble on punjee sticks and rotted bodies and coral snakes. They search and shoot the livestock and fire the hooches.

They are ready to leave now, but no—someone is left, someone hiding at the edge of the burned-out clearing, an old man squatting there, his knees making a shelf for the rifle. A soldier turns back, sees him and fires before the old man can raise the rifle from his knees. The platoon moves away along the path, watching their feet, watching the vines move and the grass move and the ground move. Watching over their shoulders, over their heads. Over their heads.

The last man turns and sees the child pull the rifle from the fetal body of the grandfather. She crouches and aims. She can scarcely support the heavy gun, but her aim is straight and her hand moves forward to the trigger. The soldier has to choose.

He has carried her so far now that she is old and her black hair has made a knot around his arm. He has carried her through the elephant grass to the river. He has carried her across the river and up the mountain to the muskeg where their faces are perfectly reflected in a pool. He has seen their faces splinter into tortured tree branches and birds flying overhead.

He can see the bottom of the pool now, like an answer. The

trees have broken. He can see them, the shapes burning, people flying and the trees all broken.

The soldier writes a letter. He writes the answer he has found to the armored words.

Mom was right. Tell Dad and Mom I love them. I love you, too.

Please take her, Mark. He can't carry her any longer, either.

2

What is this panic?

The money was there and now it isn't, like everything else in my life, like everyone else. Here—gone . . . flash of light, rattle of sound . . .

What's that! What am I thinking . . . one of those dreams . . . lights on a postcard . . . something right here at the corner of my mind . . .

All right, I can look after myself, no reason not. The ferry tickets are right here in my purse, and we won't need them since we're going with the guys. The kids have to have their chance—have to find out there's a world out there that doesn't include their hopeless, helpless mother.

Taxi driver looking at me funny. His hair sticks out in spikes from his red and white baseball cap. All the way in he smokes, hanging his arm out the window, leaning his hand with the cigarette on top of the steering wheel while he fiddles with the radio, a voice coming over it, hoarse phantom full of numbers and demands.

He'll have to wait for me. What will I pay him with if I can't cash in the tickets? I can, though. But what if no one's there—there's never anyone at the terminal except when a ferry's in. At the end of the dock, though—the blue hull, the stack with gold stars—it's in, something—*Taku, Matanuska,* whatever, it doesn't matter, it's there. Beyond it, across the channel, the little ferry that takes people to the airport poking in to its dock, floatplane drops down, skids on the surface of the water, throws up a tail of spray behind the pontoons. Everyone going somewhere, coming home again. I should go somewhere to come home. Where would I go to come home?

The taxi driver leans against the post next to the luggage cart, lights another cigarette. There's the steel ramp, the walkway, the purser waiting to take my ticket. Well, why not? I have a ticket, I can go, leave the taxi man waiting forever, standing there, watching me from under the bill of his cap, afraid I'll do it, leave him there, no fare, no fair. Go Jess. You're over your head, again. Out of control. Lying to your own sons, promising Bo, comforting Tom, not one goddamned thing you can do for them anymore when you can't even think.

They give me the money at the ticket window. No one looks at me funny for cashing in the tickets—the excuses sit on the back of my tongue, metallic and swollen.

We have money, we're safe in Ketchikan, the boys and Toby waiting at the motel, Koz coming by to go shopping for food to take on the boat, a Christmas party, the kids excited about their presents, excited about going on the boat, Bo will come out of his sulks because of getting to go on a boat with all that equipment. He'll learn how to use it, get skills he can use, almost a man, no, not yet, he still needs me, still needs me. Not a man yet, because he can't help me. No one can help me. Not now.

The taxi man opens the door and slams it shut, old door thunking on old car. Fuzzy dice swinging from the mirror, and salmon lures, hoochies, a lot of them, little squid eyes, plastic legs dancing when the taxi reverses, stops, turns across the loading lane between a Sea-Land tractor-trailer and a van hauling a Bayliner.

There's a picture of the taxi man, like a police-file mug shot, fastened to the visor. They should include a picture of the back of his head for recognition, those spikes of hair piercing the size band of his cap, gray fingerprints on the white part behind his ear where he pushes at the cap with the hand holding the cigarette.

They should include a picture of his hand holding the cigarette. How will I recognize him again, how will I ever know him if I see him on the street or in a bar or picking up his kids at school? How will I ever know anyone if I can't touch the backs of their hands?

THIS IS WHAT happened. What happened yesterday or this morning. They were following us, the elevated, honorable, sovereign Social Workers. I felt their stares on the back of my neck, so I turned around and looked straight into their fish eyes. They pretended not to know me, acted as though they were chatting casually with each other, commenting on the weather. But they were right there, hurrying along because Koz and I were walking pretty fast; it was cold, the rain blowing sideways along the hill. Koz was carrying Toby, trying to cover her in his jacket, but she wanted to see and kept struggling and poking her face out.

I walked a little faster and Koz finally said, "Hey, what's your hurry?" but I didn't tell him. They kept right up. I could hear their boots on the walk behind us, so after a while I ran. I had to. I couldn't stand them following me around with their thoughts.

This is what happened. Yesterday. I hid after I got around the corner. I slid between a broken-down cafe and a warehouse. The rain was coming down like rivets and the pavement back of the warehouse looked like a sheet of hammered metal, the bulb over the back door reflected it. I crouched behind a Dumpster and waited till I heard them all go by, Koz first, then the two following him *kuhlunk, kuhlunk* in their boots.

Right there, back of that Dumpster, was an old man sitting in the pool on the pavement, leaning against the warehouse, so filthy he might not have been able to sit up if you scraped off the dirt and bent his clothing. He smelled like stale booze and forty years of garbage collection. He was alive, breathing, every breath a history.

I sat there beside him, and now and then he opened one eye and rolled it in my direction. I fished around in my bag and took out a couple of those packets of crackers they give you with soup and I pushed them into his hand. He made a terrible face, pulled up his top lip to show two fangs, and screwed his eyes into knotholes. I think he was smiling.

I took the crackers back out of his hand and tore the packages open and pushed one cracker through the gap in his teeth. He let it hang there a couple seconds and then poked his tongue under it and it disappeared into his mouth. I don't think he swallowed it, maybe it just dissolved and ran down his throat, but in another minute he tilted to the side and flopped over on the pavement.

I put my arms around him and tried to prop him across my knees. He had no weight, but total gravity. We sat like that, a woman holding a man across her lap, waiting together, together dreaming the way out, until his head slipped from my knee into the pool. Our faces splintered into Ketchikan Public Works Department, letters reversed. No tree branches—no birds flying overhead. When the ripples stopped, the stones of the pavement rose toward us.

I am telling you what happened yesterday. Yesterday while Rick Kozloff led two social workers through the streets of Ketchikan, a man died. I am not making this up, it is not a head game or a bad trip. I sat beside a dying man who held three crackers in his lap. We did not need the social workers—it did not relate to stress or happiness, this death, it had to do with food.

I left him there. What else could I do? This is not a woman who can call the police. Anyonymous tip? That was what I meant to do. Handkerchief over the telephone receiver.

When I got to Koz and Don and Lanny's house, Koz was there with Toby. He was angry at my running away till I told him about the social workers. Then he laughed and said, "Poooor thing, are they after you now?" He hollered at Don and Lanny, "Hey, we gotta fix this little girl, she's being followed by aliens with glittering eyes."

Things got put into my hands and Koz put his arms around me and let me slide down to the carpet with him, waves lapping at the edges, licking up the time and washing over the man, the dead man, washing his clothes and his skin, filling his mouth, hiding his two teeth, carrying him out to sea. Gently gently taking him. It was only food after all, not happiness.

Listen. I ask you to forget this man. As I have. As my grandmother, rocking on my shoulder, has forgotten him. We will wake from our dreams remembering nothing.

3

My hands were shrinking. Hands that shrink can't touch anyone. There are people all around me, talking to me, laughing, not noticing that I'm disappearing. I'm talking and laughing myself, drinking my drink from this white foam cup that feels like dead flesh. This Jess is watching that Jess laugh and talk and hold her cup without hands.

I have to keep moving. Everywhere I am, I break the space. There is a spatial catastrophe I cause by existing. I should be only a mind. I must move—I've used up this space long enough.

ALL OF THE people here are very familiar. Very familiar. I know every one of them. There is the man with the beard and the small nose, the one with the scars below his eye, who blows out every time he takes a swallow from his beer can, makes his lips quiver like a horse.

Next to him, the bony woman in the leotard top with the long frizzy hair and the chipped tooth, the woman who holds her cigarette with her fingers over the top and flicks the ash behind her without looking.

There is the short, half-bald man with the big belly over his jeans and a gold chain around his neck where the black hair comes over the V of his flannel shirt. A plaid flannel shirt. He is that man, the one that wears the plaid flannel shirt and the gold chain.

I know them all, all, because they are the same ones that are here wherever I am. I always talk with them and laugh with them and step aside when one of them or another gets hot and wants to punch someone. Oh yes, I know them well.

I love them. I love them because I know them so well, and I love them because they don't care at all that I'm not with them. They are lovely, lovely people who love me even though I've shrunk so far away, gotten so small now, they probably can't even see me. But it doesn't matter to them. They love me anyway, especially because they can't see me, because they can't see love, so love and I are just the same.

"I am love." The words sound familiar. But of course they are, because everything in this whirling space is familiar. Everything is love.

TOM

It was another very long day. Super long. I didn't want to go back to the motel because of the fat lady and Mom probably wouldn't have paid even though I told her what the lady said. I walked along the street toward town, didn't see Bo or Mom and Toby, went back to the grocery store, nobody. No way I was going down to the boats. They were probably there, stowing the food and diapers and staples. No way I'd go there.

When the ferry came I would just go down, buy my ticket, walk right on, goodbye Ketchikan, goodbye jerky booby lady, goodbye creepy guys. I didn't exactly want to leave Toby but no way would I go find them. I knew what they'd do. They'd force me to stay, go on their dumb boats, drown myself instead of them. Not a chance!

It got pretty late afternoon and I thought I might go eat something and then it would be around seven-thirty and the *Malaspina* would be there. I walked along above the harbor and tried to see if there were any lights or people around where the *AnaCat* and *Tenino* were. I could see the *AnaCat* from up above—it was dark, nobody around. The *Tenino* was out too far to see but I couldn't see anyone on the dock out towards it. Probably they'd finished putting stuff aboard and went to get something to eat. Who cared, anyway? Not me, for sure.

Up the hill above the boat harbor a couple blocks there were a lot of lights poking along the hillside and making circles on the clouds. I stood on the sidewalk and watched the circles moving around at the ends of long thin sticks of light and thought I'd go check it out, see what was making them.

In one block I could hear a lot of tweedledee music jumbled up. One more block and there was a huge store all lit up with Christmas lights and three searchlights pointing crisscross above it from the back of a truck. In the parking lot was sort of a carnival, like at the fair in the summer. There was a merry-go-round and a Ferris wheel and a couple stands for throwing rings and shooting ducks and a couple food stands. The jumbly music was from the merry-go-round and Ferris wheel. The store was giant cement, no windows, and the sign all the whole length of it said, *Seaview Sav-U*. What a dumb name. I guess it was an everything store like a Kmart or Fred Meyer and it must have just opened because there was still one of those frames along one end for climbing on to paint or put up the roof.

I thought I might look over the Ferris wheel. There was a line with a few people, mostly kids, and wood steps you stood on to get into the seats. Little lights blinked on and off all around the edges of the wheel. An old man in a Santa Claus suit was running it, pushing the long handle to make it go, slow down, stop. He was a real skinny Santa with a wrinkled face and no beard. The Santa suit was kind of worn out; the red velvety stuff was rubbed off at the sides of the coat and he had a paper bag in one pocket which I guess had his whiskey in it, like Simon Kaminsky keeps his in a bag in his pocket.

He stopped the Ferris wheel and let three kids off and a man and woman and a little girl get on. Then he pushed the handle forward and moved the seats along two more, then two guys got off and two kids got on. Then he pushed the handle all the way forward and the thing turned fast and everyone screamed and laughed and the music played very loud.

After a couple minutes he pushed the handle back and everything slowed down and then stopped. While people got out of the lowest seat and more got on, I all of a sudden heard my mom laughing and then Toby crying and crying. I looked around and then up where the sound was coming from and there in the next to highest seat was Koz holding Toby, and Mom sitting next to him. Mom was laughing, and shrieking and grabbing at Koz's arm and he was rocking the seat back and forth and holding Toby out over the bar so she was hanging way up there above the machine that ran the Ferris wheel. I could see her twisting and struggling and hear her screaming. The Santa Claus moved the seats one forward so I was looking straight up at Toby's legs kicking to get back on the seat.

My knees and neck got all hot pins and needles and I jumped onto the steps and bumped into the Santa and knocked against his whiskey bottle in the paper bag. He said, "Fuckin' brat," and gave me a huge push. I fell backward off the steps onto the cement. I saw his arm above me push the handle all the way forward and the Ferris wheel came whirling down. The music was everywhere and the blinking lights, and those moving circles in the sky were coming right down on top of me. I knew Toby was screaming and whirling but I couldn't save her and I was scared out of my head.

I got up running. I ran and ran, stumbling all the time in gutters and puddles and planks but I finally got down to that skiff. I climbed over the side and lay down on the floor of it where nobody could see me between the seat and engine box, and I put my head on the hoses. I was out of breath for sure, but not too out of breath to cry.

I guess I must have been kind of crazy from crying and being so scared. Everything got weird. You know how water trickling and slapping along the side of a boat sounds like people talking? Voices, it sounds like, talking just a little too far away to get the words, but definitely people talking. I kept raising my head thinking the voices were getting closer and closer. The water under the dock against the pilings sounded like footsteps on the planks. I'd raise my head and listen and then try to get flatter down in the skiff. I have never been that scared in my whole entire life.

I kept seeing that Ferris wheel coming down with the lights blinking and that Santa when he pushed me off the steps. His eyes were all red and one of them looked sort of smeared and covered up with something like jelly so he probably couldn't see out of it.

I wished I hadn't seen that eye. How could I anyway, when he was pushing me and I was trying to see Toby and Mom? But I did see it and I couldn't stop thinking about it when I was lying in the bottom of the skiff listening to the voices and footsteps. I think I must have been out of my head. Totally right out of my head.

I guess I lay there for hours. I don't actually know, but any-way it seemed like hours. Some of the time I played with the keys hanging under the hose. I took them off the wire and jangled them, felt of their edges and ran my fingers over the numbers carved in the wood chip, but all the time lying on the bottom not even wanting to pretend I was driving or fishing or anything.

I got so cold my hands were shaking and I was shivering so hard it make the skiff rock. I decided I better go back to the mo-tel because I was so freezing, so I sat up and looked everywhere to be sure that Santa wasn't creeping around.

The dock was shiny wet and it seemed like there were lights blinking on-off in the shine. I got out but looking around all the time and even walking backward partway because it seemed like there were footsteps behind me. The trolling poles on some of the boats were clanking because the wind had started coming up and the fenders creaked against the dock and I just wished I was dead. I just about was dead of being scared. But I think being dead was what I was scared of. I don't know. I was crazy for sure.

From the top of the ramp I could see the funnel of the *Malaspina*. The lights lit up the gold stars, the Big Dipper and North Star from the Alaska flag, and also the rain blowing in twisty worms around it. I stood there staring at it, shivering so hard my feet hardly stayed on the walk. I could walk down there in two minutes, buy my ticket, get aboard, be home in Tern Bay the day after tomorrow. Or I could go back to the motel and see if Bo was there, or Mom and Toby.

But there was the fat lady. If Mom hadn't paid by now maybe the fat lady would call the police. If I went back maybe they would put me in jail if I didn't pay. I could pay with the two hundred I had from the Skoal can. But then I couldn't buy a ferry ticket.

I'd better take the ferry. There wouldn't be another ferry north for probably three days. But what if I went back to Tern Bay all by myself? If I left Mom and Toby and Bo in Ketchikan and went and lived there all alone? Probably that snoop lady would call the police and they'd send me away to that foster home like Bo said where you can't watch TV and always have to wipe your feet. But it seemed like I shouldn't really do that anyway. Go away and leave Mom when she was having some troubles. And Toby was retarded. I couldn't go away and leave Toby if she was retarded. Or maybe that didn't matter. Leaving her or not.

I was actually crying not knowing what to do and anyway cold, and any second that Santa with the creepy eye would show up. In fact I could hear footsteps pretty loud and slow right behind me and someone breathing like they were very tired. I slid behind the Chung Woo Mexican-American Cuisine stand and leaned against it in the shadows where no one could see me. The footsteps and breathing got louder. Somebody was whispering, "Tom, Tom," and this humongous black monster, all swelled up on bone legs, came around the corner of Chung Woo and reached out its arms and grabbed me.

The monster whispered, "Shhh, don't, it's just me."

"Just me" turned out to be just Bo. He had three backpacks on his back, and he slid them off to the ground and leaned against Chung Woo to get his breath. I was shaking so hard, Chung Woo was rattling, and the sign on it was banging. I grabbed Bo's arms when he dropped the packs. I still wasn't sure it wasn't that Santa, or someone worse, and I just couldn't let go of him. He didn't even seem like he cared. I never was so glad to see anyone in my whole entire life.

At the back of Chung Woo was a small step, not very wide, and we sat there. I could feel Bo's leg shaking against mine. He'd been half running and carrying all the backpacks, mine and his and Mom's. He was puffing pretty hard and a couple times he tried to say something, but he wasn't talking yet until he got his breath. We sat there squeezed together on the step, and I quit shaking so hard because of Bo being warm next to me. Also I was not so scared. Hardly at all, actually.

We sat there long enough for Bo to be able to talk, and he asked me if I knew where Mom was. I told him no, I'd left her in the grocery when Lanny was after me about why didn't we leave Mom alone. I tried to say how much I hated Lanny but my voice got all runny in my nose and eyes, so I just shut up and wiped my face on my sleeve, which sure was no use, since I was soaking wet all over from lying in the skiff in the pouring rain.

Bo said, "That bitch. We gotta get Mom outa here. Besides, the cops'll be looking for us because I grabbed our stuff from old blubber guts in the motel. She locked up our room with a padlock and put our stuff in the office. She was just waiting to call the cops when I walked in, but I grabbed the packs and took off. Only two sleeping bags, though. The other wasn't fastened to the pack, and no way was I stopping to tie it on. She grabbed the phone and started yelling and I took off. I kept up the hill till I got above the harbor. There was a cop car on the street below, with its lights going, so I was ready to jump if it turned up."

He stopped, still to catch his breath, I guess. He must have really run hard. "I figured you guys would be down here at the boats. Where is everyone, anyway?"

"I don't know," I said. "I was maybe going to the ferry or either back to the motel. I saw Mom and Koz and Toby on that Ferris wheel up where the new store is, and I was going to stay with them, or anyway get Toby, but this Santa guy pushed me off the steps. And anyway, something's wrong, I guess."

My voice was getting all yucky in my throat and nose again. Bo put his hand over on my shoulder, like almost he had an arm around me. Like almost he was hugging me. So my voice got a little better. "Mom was trying to keep Koz from dropping Toby out of the seat. Koz was holding Toby out over the machine that makes the wheel go, and she was screaming and kicking, and Mom was pulling on Koz's arm. But she was laughing, too." I stopped because I was shivering again but I had to say it, even though I was crying again. "Bo, I hate all of them, Mom, too."

He didn't say anything and I felt really bad that I said it. It wasn't true I guess, because you wouldn't ever really hate your own mother, even if you were very, extremely mad at her. Of course you wouldn't hate her. Like she says, you just take what you get and love it. But she had to look after Toby because Toby was just little, and now she was retarded, too. Well, not now, she came that way, so she'd always been retarded. But now she needed Mom because of being a baby and retarded. But she always had. Needed her, I mean. Geez, I was getting so mixed up, and I just couldn't, couldn't stop crying. Why not I don't know, because I wasn't even scared anymore with Bo there, or very cold either.

Bo said, "Yeah, I know. I feel like that, too, sometimes. She isn't bad, though. It's like she's more sad. Like, she's so sad inside, ever since Dad died, she tries to make herself feel better. She maybe thought Matt would make her forget Dad. And booze. And whatever they've got her into now. It seems like she's forgotten everything now."

I was trying to stop crying, rubbing my face on my knees and hands, while I was trying to hear what Bo was saying. He took his arm off me and put his hands together between his knees. It was so dark behind Chung Woo I could barely see his hands right there in front of us, twisting all together.

After a little, Bo started talking again. "She knows it won't ever be like with Dad again. All that stuff makes her not think about him."

He shut up then for a while, so I thought he was thinking something else, but then all of a sudden he said, "When Dad and I were fishing she'd call up on the VHF and ask if he'd got a lot of 'shakers.' He'd say, 'Just one,' and he'd punch me. Then he'd say, 'It's a real puny one, think I ought to bring it home for supper?' And she'd laugh and say, 'Better'n nothing, I guess. Better bring it.' Then she'd say, 'Love you guys.'

"Can you believe? Right there, out loud on the radio, and everyone could hear. 'Love you,' she'd say.

"Dad'd say, 'Better believe it, woman.' He'd punch me and say, 'Your mom's an OK lady, guy, she's a keeper, all right.' He used to say that about us, too—'Lucky we only got keepers, Mom,' he'd say. 'Look at 'em—no shakers in this haul.'

"He really loved us, and Mom, too. She just can't make it anymore, is all. She can't make it without him. She's gonna go down if we don't do something. Dad would have wanted us to do something. Trouble is, what? I don't know what."

It seemed like Bo's voice got kind of funny, too, when he was saying that about Dad would've wanted us to do something, and he put his hands over his face for a second. I felt a little better because of him saying that about Dad, and that Mom was sad, not bad.

"Is Toby a 'shaker'?" I asked. "Would Dad think Toby was a shaker?"

Bo didn't answer for a while. Then he said, "No, Dad wouldn't have thought any kid was a shaker. Not even Toby."

"So anyway then, we gotta take care of Toby, even if we can't think how to fix things for Mom?"

"Yeah," Bo said. "Toby, too. Toby and Mom. We gotta do it."

I all at once heard the *Malaspina*'s horn, long and deep, like the sound was coming up from underwater. Two long blasts. I didn't have to get up and walk around to the front of Chung Woo to know she was leaving, those worms of rain twisting out in the lights behind the gold stars. It was the saddest sound I could think of, right then, knowing she was leaving and we couldn't go on her. Maybe never. Maybe we could never leave here or get Mom out of her troubles. I took a deep breath so I wouldn't start crying again. I was getting cold again, too, sitting on Chung Woo. I put my hands in my pockets.

Bo said, "There goes the ferry. We'll have to wait for the next one. But we can find Mom before then. Maybe we could stake out the motel. They'll have to go back there sometime. All Mom's and Toby's stuff is in the packs except what she has in the diaper bag. What the hell are you doing?"

He pulled sideways away from me on the step, and tried to look down in the dark between us. I was turning something over and over in my jacket pocket so my hand kept jabbing his leg. I pulled my hand out, holding the keys from the skiff.

"Oh gosh, the skiff keys. I forgot to put them back on the wire. I gotta go back down there." I stood up, kind of stiff, not wanting at all to go back down to that creaky dock.

"What keys?" Bo said. "Skiff? The *Ten Four*? You got the keys to it?"

"Hunh unh. They don't fit, I tried. They're just hanging there under the hose, I don't know what for. They got numbers on this piece of wood."

I held them out dangling from the wood and Bo took them, but he couldn't see anything in the dark.

"What numbers?" he said.

"Ten, slash, nine, slash, zero," I said, from looking at them so much when I was down in the skiff. I said it again, this time thinking about it. "Ten—nine—Oh! *Tenino*. Bo, geez, they must be the *Tenino*'s keys. Oh my god, I took the *Tenino*'s keys! I gotta get down there before they find out."

Bo stood up and grabbed my arm. All of a sudden he was whispering, even though we'd been talking right out loud, nobody around there that time of night in the pitch dark.

"That's it," he whispered. "Grab your pack and move it, buddy."

He threw Mom's pack over one shoulder and lifted his. I picked mine up and got one arm through a strap, and then backed against Chung Woo to push the pack up so I could get the other arm through. Bo was halfway down the ramp under the lights before I got my pack up.

By the time I got to the foot of the ramp, Bo was miles ahead, almost to the last finger. I saw him turn his head when he passed the slip next to the *AnaCat*, but he didn't slow down. The wind was ripping down the channel, pitching the boats and clanking the rigging on the poles. By the time I got to the *Tenino*, the pool on top of my pack was full and running over down my face by my ear, and I was pretty cold and super tired of that dock. The lights reflected in *Tenino*'s windows and I could just see Bo through them, moving around like he was a reflection, too. I lifted my pack over the rail and climbed aboard.

Inside, the light reflected off all that polished wood, and I could see pretty well, the binnacle and wheel and instrument panel. Bo was feeling around in his pack. He came out with a flashlight which he turned along the instrument panel. He was muttering the labels out loud—"VHF, radar, depth . . ." Then he looked around kind of sneaky, bent forward and pressed the starter button. There was a growl from way deep in the boat and he let up the button before the engine actually started.

"Running," he said. He flashed the light along some gauges. "Full tanks," he said. "Yahoo!" He took the keys and stuck them in his pocket, flashed the light around, turned it off and sat down on the floor, leaning his back against the locker under the chart table. "Now to find Mom," he said.

"We gonna take this boat?" I asked him, not for a second believing it.

"We're gone," he said. "Just have to find Mom and Toby. Soon as we get home they can have their dumb boat back, but we're outa here, buddy."

"You know how to run it?"

"Sure. All the same, once you get going—just bigger, is all. No prob, kid." He switched the flashlight on again and flashed it around. "Somewhere is their name and address. That's where everyone is, wherever Koz and Don live." He stood up and started shuffling through the chart bins above the table.

I saw it, though. Right off. From where I was sitting on the floor, I could see a paper in a frame on the bulkhead next to the door. Some license or something. I grabbed the flashlight and shone it on the glass and there was the name, Richard A. Kozloff, and underneath his address, 149 Reynolds Street, Ketchikan, AK. Bo read it out loud while I shone the light, and we said it together to remember it, "149 Reynolds Street."

"If Mom's there, how will we make her come with us?" I asked him. "No way she'll want to quit partying and come with me and you and Toby."

Thinking of stealing that boat, like it was about a billion-dollar boat we would be stealing, was so scary, I didn't see how we would be able to go to the owner's house and act like nothing was happening.

"We gotta see, first," Bo said. "Maybe I could go in and tell her you were sick, or something. Or we could just sort of go to the party and grab her when nobody was exactly looking."

I was thinking how I'd been planning that, when I was running away from the store. Bo pulling out a knife, me sinking the boats. No way, that wasn't a plan. Not at all.

We walked back up the ramp, the rain not so hard, but the wind still gusting so it suddenly pushed us sideways against the rail.

"Where's Reynolds Street?" I asked.

"Look in the phone book, I guess," Bo said. "Oughta have a city map. That store down the street probably has one. But we gotta watch for cops, remember. Because of Fats at the motel."

We walked past Chung Woo, out to the street and down the block, kind of keeping to shadows and doorways. The store was closed, but the phone booth actually had a phone book. Reynolds Street wasn't very far, either—straight up the hill above the harbor, one block over. It was a short street, not joining anything at the next block. A dead end.

We looked for cops before crossing, and then ran the first block to get away from the main street. Then straight up. Man, it was. A mountain, actually. And when we got to Reynolds Street, it turned out to be half street, half stairs, which went straight on up. I was out of breath trying to keep up, Bo half a block ahead, his bone legs not even noticing how steep it was, I guess.

No trouble knowing which house. You know those cartoons where the walls go in and out when there's loud music, or a big fight going on? Halfway up those stairs is where it was. We could hear it a block away, mostly drum and electric guitar. Closer up, we could see the house, even though it was very, very dark out, with rain, and not any streetlights up the stairs. It was an old house, I think, pretty big. Anyway, a lot bigger than our house in Tern Bay. A walk went over to it from the street stairs, and then there were more steps up from there. I could see light coming out of the curtains on the windows, but not much, like they only had one little light on inside.

Bo was standing on the walk just beyond the street stairs when I caught up, not going any closer to the house. He didn't say anything, just sort of moved his hand for me to follow, and started up the front steps. Then he changed his mind, came down and went around the house toward the back, pushing through the bushes at the side, and once tripping on something that clinked, like empty cans or something. I followed, trying not to trip. The bushes grabbed my jacket and once poked my eye. Bo was tall enough so his head was higher than the bushes, but I went right through.

Around back was a porch clear across the back of the house, no railing, just a couple steps to the ground. There was a door with glass in the top. We could see through to the kitchen and along a hall to a room with a light on. I could only see the ceiling of that room. Shadows moved across it like people must be moving around in there.

We stood there listening to the music booming out and clashing. I just could not imagine what we were going to do. No way was I going in that house. I could tell Bo didn't want to, either. He was standing really still, keeping back in the dark between the house and the huge tree behind it.

All at once the light through the window in the door was cut off, because someone was standing there. Then the door opened and someone came out. The music blasted out like a drum explosion, and then got a little softer when the person closed the door. We didn't move or even breathe. There was so little light, we couldn't see the person, exactly, just a black shape. And whoever it was was wearing all dark clothes, too, so there wasn't any way to see them, black pants and a black shirt, the person's face a little lighter above, not enough to actually see.

The drum explosion changed to a slow song, sad, with the tune winding around behind, like it was looking for something lost. And the person started to dance. The person danced very slowly, just a black shadow dancing, holding its hands out toward someone who wasn't there. We were the only ones there.

The minute Bo moved, I knew it was my mother dancing. In one step he was on the porch. He faced her, his arms raised above his head, and moved with her like he was her mirror. They danced, not touching, until the music slowed down to end. Then Bo slid his hands over her head and down to her shoulders, and she reached up and touched his face. He bent a little, lifted her, and came down the steps carrying her. Her face was against his neck—I don't think she saw me or anything at all.

"Get Toby," he whispered, and then he was gone.

I went on standing there. I couldn't get my mind changed over to Toby. I kept seeing Bo and my mother dancing. In the pitch dark, dancing there like they had always known the same song. I wanted it to be me, so much, I couldn't stop seeing them. Me dancing like that, slow and sad, knowing every move before we made it. Me dancing with my mother.

Then I went up the steps and opened the door before I could think no, don't do it. Because I had to get Toby. Of course I did have to. I wanted to dance with my mother. I wanted to run away. But I walked in, and shut the door behind me, and went to look for Toby.

Smoke and the smell of booze made me cough. The light from the living room came through thick smoke. People were leaning against the sides of the door at the other end of the hall. Above their heads I could see the top of a Christmas tree, with little blinking lights and an angel bent crooked to one side. The music was so loud I couldn't really hear voices, just noise, sometimes laughing, like screaming. There weren't any lights on, except somewhere in the living room, and the Christmas tree.

I didn't want to see anyone, for sure, so I stood at one side of the kitchen door to look down the hall. There were three closed doors, one on the left, two right. I thought probably bedrooms and bathroom. Probably Toby would be sleeping in one of the bedrooms.

Two people were standing in the middle of the doorway to the living room, at the far end of the hall, with their backs to me, blocking the door. I stepped forward and opened the first door on the right. It was pitch dark, so I felt along the wall for a light switch. Then I heard a lot of rustling around. Some man said, "What the fuck!" and a woman said, "Christ, who's there?" so I shut the door very, very quietly.

Just as I did that, a man came out of the door farther along on the other side, switched off the light, and went down the hall to the living room, where he had to squeeze between the people standing in the doorway. Before the light went off, I could see a sink and mirror, so I knew it was the bathroom, and it must be empty. I could stay in there while I figured out what to do.

I closed the bathroom door as quietly as I could, turned the light on, found the door lock and turned it. It was a big bathroom, as big as our kitchen, with a huge tub with bent legs, not going all the way to the floor at the sides like ours. I thought I heard a funny noise from over by the bathtub, so I walked over and looked in.

Toby was there, asleep on a folded-up blanket. She was sleeping on her back with her thumb in her mouth. The noise I'd heard was from her sucking her thumb. She was wearing a Christmas dress, red velvet with white fuzzy sleeves, and red tights, like someone had dressed her up to be a baby Santa. I could tell she'd cried herself to sleep. Her eyelids were all stuck against her cheeks. Her face was smeared with snot. Her skin was puffed up instead of wrinkled, and there were red and white streaks like fingers, across one cheek. Somebody had slapped her. I hoped it was Lanny who'd slapped her. I wanted it to be Lanny.

Suddenly somebody knocked and rattled the door. I made my voice as deep as I could and said, "Yunnnh," like one of Bo's noises. I heard someone walk off, then, a man's footsteps, and go to the kitchen. I waited, and after a while I heard him walk back. He rattled the door again, said something under his breath, and went the other way toward the living room.

I scooped Toby up in the blanket and grabbed the diaper bag. The blanket wasn't ours, but if we were stealing a boat, I didn't think a blanket mattered much. She smacked away on her thumb and I held my breath, hoping she wouldn't start crying, but she only went "uhhh, uhhh," that funny sucking breathing, when you've cried so hard you're still trying to get your breath back.

I switched the light off, unlocked the door, and tiptoed, half running, down the hall, across the kitchen, through the door, and down the steps, not even closing the door behind me. The music blasted all over while I tore through the bushes, trying to keep Toby's face from getting scratched. Just as I got to the walk below, lights came on in back. Someone had turned the outside lights on. Probably they wondered who'd left the door open in all that wind and rain.

I went back down the hill as fast as I could, but it was kind of hard to keep Toby from sliding down in the blanket, and carry the diaper bag, too, which we sure did need. I got down to the main street above the harbor, no one around—I guess it was one or two o'clock, or later even—just one car way down the street. I crossed, trying to get a better hold on Toby, and the car down the street all of a sudden turned on flashing blue lights and came at us full bore. I ran, then, hard as I could, toward the harbor, but the cop car swung into the parking lot above the ramp. I ran, bending down, and got behind Chung Woo.

I knew when they opened the car doors, because I could hear that scratchy voice, like in a tin can, coming over their radio. I heard one door slam, and then another, so I guessed they both got out, but I could see the light flashing above Chung Woo, so I knew the car was still sitting there at the top of the ramp.

I couldn't hear anyone coming over toward us, so I looked around the end. No one in sight, so I inched to the corner—still nobody. There was a green van parked near the top of the ramp. I ran across the lot, went behind it, and looked down at the dock. One cop was halfway along the finger straight ahead of the ramp. The other was walking along the main dock to the left. The *Tenino* was the last finger to the right. If I was going down at all, I had to take a chance they'd see me on the ramp, so I went for it.

I just ran. Way down at the end then, Bo came around the corner and waved me on like I was in the 440, which I felt like I sure was. When I got to him, the blanket was dragging on the ground, and Toby was starting to cry from bumping against my shoulder. Bo grabbed the diaper bag and threw the dragging end of the blanket up over Toby's head, and we ran faster than we'd either of us run in our whole entire lives.

We reached *Tenino*'s slip too out of breath to say anything. Her engine was thudding away, waiting. Bo jumped the rail, bent over and grabbed Toby, said, "Cut her loose," and disappeared through the door.

I turned to get the lines. Bo had unfastened all but the bow line and one spring line. He'd left those with a single turn on the cleats, so we were loose almost before he'd put Toby down and taken the wheel. I threw myself over the rail as he put her in reverse. The huge screw ground up the water behind us. We backed out of the slip, roaring and grinding, and caught the current while the bow swung clear. Then Bo put her forward and we moved slowly along the breakwater, past the red and green markers at the entrance. In the channel Bo swung her south, shoved the throttle up, and we were flying. Oh man!

I dragged the fenders up over the rail, and looked at the water hissing past, all white foam against black—hoooeeee! We were really cruising! In the cabin I said, "South?" but Bo couldn't hear me over Toby's screaming, and the engine, and the banging and thumping that were going on out there on the deck. I didn't care, anyway. I was shaking too hard and much too tired to care where we were going. Only so long as it was somewhere *else!*

PART THREE

BO

After we got out of Tongass Narrows, away from the lights of Ketchikan, it was so dark I couldn't see the tops of my boots. Tom was messing around trying to get Toby settled down, and now and then I'd hear that thumping on the wall of the head where I'd shut Mom in. She'd been so wild—I was scared she'd jump if I didn't keep both arms tight around her, and I didn't know what to do with her, figuring Tom would come tearing down at any second with Toby, and we'd have to patch out of there.

I kept unlocking my fingers from the wheel and pushing on the veins that were throbbing in my neck—man, that was some run, Mom struggling every inch. I kept telling her, "It's me, it's Bo—Mom, it's OK, it's OK, you're all right," but I don't think she ever like, registered? Nothing getting through except seeds and weeds. Sheeh!

Tom got Toby to sleep on the bunk in the stateroom off the wheelhouse, and came back in. I was running off the radar and now and then getting a LORAN position and roughing it onto the chart, but I slowed way down after we got past town and out into Nichols Passage. I figured they'd head straight north looking for us. There was a good chance they wouldn't even notice till morning that we were gone, brain-dead bastards like them. I thought we could head around Cape Chacon on Prince of Wales Island if we had even a little luck on weather out in Dixon Entrance. Once we got around the Cape we could stay inside the outer islands most of the way back.

"What's wrong with your face?" Tom said, squinting at me in the light from the screens. "Looks all scratched up. You get in those bushes by the house?"

"Hunh unh. Met a wildcat."

"Wildcat? What do you mean?"

"Mom," I said. "Yeah, those are real scratches, dear Tom, and they don't feel like love to me, either."

I was waiting for Tom to say, "Mothers always love their kids no matter what," or some dumb thing like he does, but he just stood there, rubbing his hands up and down the sides of his pants and staring out the window. Finally, he turned around and walked out of the wheelhouse. I thought he was starting to face up. I felt cruel and glad.

Love was what Sara felt like. I wouldn't have gotten in this mess if my mom was like Sara, not that I'd want Sara for a mother, believe me. That was not my picture of Sara, not at all.

■   ■   ■

TOM HAD DISAPPEARED—I didn't know what he was doing, but I was getting flaked out—the clock said 3:17 A.M., and
it hadn't exactly been a restful day and night. We were out in
Clarence Strait and the radar wasn't showing anything near us,
so I put the chart light on and hunted up an anchorage across on
Prince of Wales. I figured with the radar and the sounder and
that huge bank of floodlights the seiner carried, we could make
it in all right.

Tom came back in, then. "I heard all this thumping on
deck," he said, "like something was loose out there, so I went to
see what it was, but it stopped and I couldn't find it."

"The wildcat," I said. "Locked in the head."

"*Mom*, you mean? You locked Mom in the head?"

I kind of shivered. I was hanging on the wheel so tight still,
my fingers felt rusted to it. "She would have run or jumped in—
tried to more than once. I didn't know anything to do with her
except lock her in."

"I can't stand this," Tom said. "Mom, and everything. What
do people do when they can't stand it anymore? Nothing, is all.
What can you do? Nothing."

I shrugged. "We're doing it, aren't we? At least, we're doing
something. I sure wouldn't be here if it was nothing we were doing, Tombo."

Sometimes Tom seemed so damned helpless. But then, other
times, he really came through. Like getting Toby? No kidding, I
don't think I could have made myself go in that house. Really. If
I'd had to go in there and make up some cover story to get Mom
out, or hunt for Toby, I doubt we'd ever have gotten away at all.

"What if Mom's sick?" Tom said. "Maybe even she could be
dead? But she isn't, is she, Bo? People can die of too much booze,
though, can't they? And if they take pills or stuff, worse, even."

"She's not dead, Tom, she's just sleeping it off in there. I'll get her out once we're anchored. I'll put her in there in the captain's room with Toby and that way we can keep an eye on her, whoever's at the wheel. You take the wheel a sec—here, I'll set her on auto, but watch—and keep an eye on that radar screen."

I went back and opened the door onto the deck. I had to push hard to get it open, and then it was nearly ripped out of my hands by the wind. We were leaving a huge wake, and waves like snow-capped mountains were piling up behind us with the northerly. The wind was so cold I had to put my hands over my ears.

I pulled myself over to the door of the head, hanging on to the winch and the hydraulic gears so I wouldn't blow over the rail. I pressed my ear against the door. Nothing.

"Are you there?" I said. "Mom? Mom, are you there?"

She must be asleep. But Tom's question had sort of scared me. I should get her out of the head. It must be cold in there, and she probably wasn't feeling too great. I dragged the door open. She was slumped down, her head on her arms, pillowed on the closed toilet seat. I pulled her out and she muttered and sort of thrashed around, but didn't wake up. It was hard to get her up, her dead weight and the wind beating at us, but I finally got over to the cabin door, braced her against the bulkhead while I got the door open, then carried her in and put her on the bunk next to Toby. Tom had found a sleeping bag to put Toby in, so I unzipped it and got Mom into it, then zipped it up and left them there, neither of them even noticing the change.

Tom was propped on the wheel, his head on his arms, sound asleep. Some first mate—good thing we weren't an oil tanker. I shook him awake enough to steer him down the ladder to one of the bunks in the fo'c'sle.

The radio was on, switched to Channel 16. The Coast Guard

report came in all of a sudden: "Hello, all stations . . . switch to Channel Twenty-two for Notice to Mariners . . ." Which I did. The usual . . . some buoy missing, a log boom destroyed . . . "hazard to navigation . . . Mariners should exercise caution in transiting the area." Nothing about a boat named *Tenino*, stolen from the Ketchikan boat harbor. Good. The longer they didn't report, the closer we'd be to Tern Bay.

I got us anchored in a narrow passage between two small islands, like a bowl, land all around us. It took me a while to figure out the hydraulics for the anchor windlass—every boat seems to have a different deal on hydraulics. I wished we had the *Sunny Belle*—at least I would have felt familiar. The *Tenino* seemed enormous, even though the wheelhouse seemed cramped, and the equipment and switches weren't where I was used to finding them. The truth was, I was too scared to let myself think about how scared I was, if you know what I mean.

After a while it got light enough to see a little, everything gray-black, black-gray, like the color switch was broken. The gulls started screaming over something in the water behind us. The tide was changing and swinging us around. Just about high slack. There wasn't any waterline on the rocks. December high. Hah, hah, joke.

I shook Tom and drummed a riff on his skull.

"I gotta sleep," I told him. "I'm dead. I can't do it any longer."

"Where are we?" he asked, jerking his head away and trying to get his eyes open.

"Moira Sound," I said. "Behind some islands. We can hide out till we find out what's happening. But you have to listen to the radio. I think they'll start hollering for us soon. Or they might call the Coast Guard, but I doubt that. It's almost light, but I can't do it anymore. If we can hide out here until tomorrow, I'll be OK. They'll think we headed north, anyway."

I yawned and pushed him over so he had to stand up. "Mom's sleeping it off. I hope, anyway. Food we got. Galley's stocked like this was a cruise ship. When you get time later, start throwing the booze over. Enough booze on board to float the damn boat. It goes, buddy."

For one instant before sleep struck, I wished I was home with Sara, not floating around on a stolen boat, with Mom wiped out. And then, for some reason I remembered—it was Christmas Day. Well. Merrrrry Christmas. Mom—Tom—Toby . . . ? Merry Christmas for sure!

TOM

At one o'clock, it came over the radio.

"Calling *Tenino,* calling *Tenino.* WYP4577. Over." Koz's voice. I was ice-cold prickles, scared to move. It sounded so loud and clear, like they must be rounding the tip of the island next to us. Toby was whining, and climbing over the seat by the chart table. I said, "Shhhh," and pulled her down, which only made her fuss louder. In a couple seconds he came in again.

"Calling the fishing vessel *Tenino.* Urgent contact. Come in, *Tenino.* Over."

I climbed down the ladder and shook Bo. "Koz is calling from the *AnaCat.* What'll we do?"

He groaned, rubbed his face, said, "Nothing. Not a damn thing. Just listen. If he gives his position, write it down. Or if he says go to a working channel, do it, but don't answer."

No way I'd answer. Imagine telling them where we were. Was Bo nuts? He'd already gone back to sleep.

I got back up just as Koz signed off—"No contact—over and out." His voice sounded as clear as if he was standing there—I guessed they must be headed toward us.

Toby. What to *do* with her? All she could do was climb and grab and whine. I tried to think what she could play with, but all I could think was, it isn't fair. Not fair Toby is retarded, not fair I always have to take care of her. That rule about fair is so dumb!

I put her life jacket on, just in case. It was pretty hard to make her happy because there wasn't much she could do and not break anything or get hurt. She'd crunched up a lot of crackers all over, and I'd given her Cheerios and milk, and opened a can of applesauce, but she didn't want it, so I ate most of it. Mom hadn't woken up, and Bo hadn't even turned over. I put some more milk in her bottle, and put her on my jacket under the binnacle, and she went to sleep after a little while.

Around half an hour they started calling again, this time Don, I guess, anyway another man, but I only could recognize Koz's voice.

"Calling *Tenino*. Urgent. Come in, *Tenino*. Over." He repeated that a couple times, then said, "Calling *Tenino*. Go to Channel Six Eight for urgent message. Over."

I switched to Channel 68, and in a minute he said, "*Tenino*, we have your present location. We are proceeding in your direction. Do you read? Over."

I was holding my breath, scared he could hear me even though I wasn't on the transmitter. After a couple minutes he came on again.

"Calling *Tenino*, calling *Tenino*. Proceed to Ketchikan, all speed, *Tenino*. We will overtake you on present course by seventeen hundred. Suggest immediate return. Do you read? Over."

In two more minutes he repeated the same message, and after another minute said, "No contact—over and out."

I found a piece of paper, an old envelope, and wrote, "1:35, Ch 68" on it. Then I wrote, "overtake at 1700," in case we better get out of here before then. I thought about that, and wrote, "They know our position. They want us to go back."

WHEN BO WOKE up, I told him what the guys had said on the radio—"We know your position—overtake—seventeen hundred," all that stuff.

Bo said, "Bullshit—no way they know where we are. We'll head out tomorrow morning. I don't want to travel at night if we can help it. But if we travel from first light to when it gets real light, and then late until dark, it'll be hard for anyone to identify the boat. We'll get in maybe four to five hours a day. If the weather stays OK, which I wouldn't bet on, we'll make it easy before New Year's. I'm starved. Good thing they stocked up."

He opened the refrigerator and took out a package of meat of some kind, and got out a frying pan. I had to swallow, looking at it. It turned out I was super hungry, too. I opened a cupboard and found a box of mashed potatoes, and got out a pan to make it in, but Bo grabbed it.

"Go listen," he said. "I'll cook."

I headed back toward the wheelhouse. Then I heard a funny noise. It sounded like Mom was crying and talking with a sore throat. I looked at Bo but he just shrugged and pointed, and I went.

All the rest of that day and some at night they called us. Sometimes they switched to a working channel. Their voices would get angry—they'd order us to make contact, tell us they were closing in. The rest of the times they just repeated the name on Channel 16. "*Tenino*, calling *Tenino*."

Every time, though, it made me scared. I wanted to switch off but Bo said no, we had to know if something changed. Pretty soon, he said, we'd be out of range of their transmitter, and if we didn't listen we wouldn't know when we'd gotten far enough away.

"How come they don't call the Coast Guard and tell them 'stolen boat'?" I asked him.

"They aren't too hot on getting the Coast Guard's attention, I'd say. Drugs, see. They're smuggling. Perfect place, you know—long long coast, way too much to police. I'm gonna figure out what they're up to. Then, if they start making us trouble we'll have something on them. Soon as I get time I'm gonna search this boat. They're sure to have left something—you can bet on that. They're not too swift, you ask me. Real small-time. Beat by a couple kids."

"Not yet," I said. "They could really know where we are, like they said."

"Bull. They haven't got a clue. Couldn't find their own butts in the dark. We'll be in Tern Bay while they're still hunting for the exit to Bar Harbor."

As soon as he said that Koz's voice came in, no call numbers, just "We're right behind you, *Tenino*." Then he said, real soft, "*Tenino, Tenino, Tenino*. Watch out."

All of a sudden, another voice boomed out, "This is United States Coast Guard Group Ketchikan. Channel Sixteen is for calling and distress only. Vessel calling *Tenino* please give your call sign."

There was silence. The vessel calling *Tenino* sure wasn't identifying itself right then. Not even though they'd already given their name about a zillion times. I guess Bo was right. They didn't want the Coast Guard hanging around.

"See?" Bo said.

I did, but it was creepier, in a way, when they just called our name, real soft, *"Tenino, Tenino."* I was sure sick of being scared, but everything kept going right on.

After Bo and I ate, and Toby went to sleep with her bottle, Bo messed around with the LORAN and radar and sonar. He said he wanted to get better at plotting and reading the screens. He put our position from the LORAN on the chart, and told me he'd decided to go around Cape Chacon, south of Prince of Wales Island, and up Cordova Bay. He showed me on the chart, and made the route with a pencil.

"They'll think we went north. Everybody goes up Wrangell Narrows, especially in this weather. We'll squeeze up Rocky Pass and cross to Chatham Strait while they're still messing around above Petersburg. Up Chatham and around the corner to Icy Strait, and run home, buddy!"

"Home run, you mean," I said, and he punched me like he got the joke OK. He was super excited, I could tell that, mostly because he wasn't treating me like something that crawled out of a hole.

"You think Mom's OK? I mean, is she going to get OK? She sure acts funny," I said, "like if we're not even here."

"Just say we're not," Bo said. "To her." He fiddled the dials, not looking at them.

"Meaning?" I said.

"She doesn't give a shit what happens anymore. Anyway, not to us. Not chicken shit for any of us."

"So why'd we kidnap her? We have to save her. You said." I felt sort of mad, like it was all a trick on me.

"Kidnap! That's all right—joke, boy! We *kid*napped our mother." He wasn't really laughing, though. "I don't know why, and that's the truth."

"Well, because of her being our mom, is why. Of her loving us even if we mess up. Like she says."

"Like you keep telling me, you mean. Shuure she does. Look at her, holed up in there, loving us every living second. You think she's lying in there loving you? No way. If that's love, forget it."

"But the booze and stuff made her too sick, is all. She just needs to get better. And she's had some troubles, you know. You said, Bo. Dad, and Matt going away. And Toby."

All of a sudden it seemed like we'd already said all the same stuff back in Ketchikan. Only Bo was saying Mom had got a lot of troubles so we couldn't leave her, and I was saying she didn't have to drink so much which probably made Toby retarded. Now backward. Bo was mad at Mom and I was sorry about her. A lot Bo sounded like he wanted to wash his hands of her. A little bit I guess I did, too.

IN THE NIGHT I woke up and in one second I was hot and prickly all over, thinking what we'd done. Way worse than when I ran off and left Toby. We stole a boat. I tried to make myself think of something we could steal worse than a boat, and I couldn't. I couldn't think of one thing, only maybe a bigger boat. A car, no. Nothing compared to a boat like *Tenino*. A huge trailer rig, maybe, for the same money. And the real owner needing it to earn a living, too, like Don. Maybe a truck would be like a boat. But you couldn't hide with a truck very well. Not at all, actually.

It kept getting worse, and my legs kept jerking and kicking trying to get rid of the hot prickles, until Bo sort of woke up in the other bunk and said, "Jesus, what's wrong, can't you lie still a second?" and I said "No, I'm too mad that we stole this boat and got in so much trouble now," and Bo said, "Aw, shit, it's nothing—go to sleep." Which he did.

I tried to hold my legs still. I made a list of things I'd stolen. Mostly I got in trouble for them, too, and if I didn't I was scared just as much, anyway. When I was four I stole a bag of M&M's from Trader Market. My mom made me take it back and tell Marty Olson, who owns Trader Market, that I did it, and say I was sorry, and pay him for the M&M's. How come practically the first thing I can remember is something I did bad? Probably it's the same for everybody.

That wasn't the earliest thing I remember, though, because I remember my dad carrying me on his shoulders on the dock, and letting me steer the *Defiant,* only probably just pretending I was doing it. And that must have been first, because the *Defiant* sank when I was three. I thought I couldn't remember my dad at all, but I do because I remember that. Him holding me, me steering.

Anyway, my stealing list. Andy and I stole a couple things from kids' lockers after school, once, Andy a pair of gloves and I got a Seahawks cap. But they weren't any good because we couldn't've worn them since everybody knew who they belonged to.

I stole some money, $1.50, from my mom's purse once, and spent it, and she found out and made me stay in for a week and clean every day when I got home from school.

I started wondering if you could even get in trouble for kidnapping your own mother. Maybe just if she wanted you to get in trouble, if she got away and called the police and said "Arrest my kids—they kidnapped me, and my baby, too." Mom wouldn't do that, though, no way. Except she seemed very mad about being with us. Or very something, I couldn't tell what, since she wouldn't talk to us or look at us. Maybe she was just waiting to call the police and get us put in kids' jail. Or sent to that home where you have to wipe your feet and stay inside. She said nobody could take her kids, but maybe now she'd want them to.

Bo poked me with his foot from the other bunk, then, for rolling my legs back and forth, so I tried to lie still again and think about something else. I tried to think about Andy and me building a new hideout, but that didn't seem like it would be very great anymore. So I tried to think about being on a spaceship heading toward another galaxy. I listened to the water voices slapping the hull. I tried to pretend they were aliens talking about our spaceship. We'd just landed. The voices were super excited, but I couldn't quite get the words. I listened and tried to catch what they were saying. I listened and listened until Bo was shaking me to get up, it was time to head out.

BO

'd started dreaming about those shadows, again. I was walking along a street I'd never seen before, huge buildings like canyon walls on both sides, and a strange light that made the window glass milky, like glacial outflow. My shadow on the walk in front of me was long, the legs bony, my shirt loose at the waist, hair a little below the ears, baseball cap making a mound on top. Then the shadow began to grow around the edges. The head enlarged and something radiated from it, billowed out like a mane of hair. The shoulders rose like a huge hump. Someone was so close behind me he had consumed my shadow. A hand reached around, the shadow of a hand . . .

"Bo, wake up, Mom's talking," Tom said, and I grabbed him by the throat.

"Stop it," he said. "Bo, cut it out."

I couldn't get my eyes open, the shadow hand, the strange milky light . . . Tom's voice the only familiar thing . . . I loved him for saving me. And hated him when I remembered where I was.

"What," I said.

"Mom's talking."

"So? Maybe she's coming out of it."

I looked at him and his eyes were full of tears. She wasn't coming out of it. I knew, looking at Tom's face, that whatever words our mother had spoken were not of this planet. For one second I wanted to put my arms around him, hang on to him because he was so real and solid.

"But she talks so weird," he said. "Like she doesn't even know I'm there."

I thought of our conversation in the cafeteria. "I'm all right, really I am." After she'd been babbling about finding her way over Harvey Pass. What was it she said then? "Ashes, ashes, we all fall down." Sheeh!

I sat up and pushed Tom away so I could get my boots from under the bunk. "All right, all right, I'm coming," I told him.

He wiped his eyes on his sleeve before he went back up the ladder, and I thought maybe he was pretty pushed for a little kid. I mean, how many ten-year-old kids have to rescue their crazy mother? I thought I'd try to get off his back a little more, but it bugged me that he acted so young. I mean, why couldn't he at least act his age. That made me sort of laugh, though, because actually, he probably was.

■   ■   ■

WE RAISED THE anchor and headed back out into Clarence Strait. It was light enough to see where we were going, that gray light over everything that doesn't reflect back, clouds sitting over the islands so low the shore was just a dark line against gray sky, here and there a tree spiked through like a nail holding down the land. Fog covered Dixon Entrance—we'd have to feel our way around Cape Chacon, but at least the wind and seas were calmer. I checked the chart and calculated a compass course to get us down to the Cape.

All the time, Mom was in there on the bunk, talking. Tom stood in the doorway, his hands rubbing up and down the sides of his jeans the way he did when he didn't know what to do, when something made him like, nervous? I tried to concentrate on the course, watch the fog eating up the shoreline, look over the switch panel and equipment so I'd know it better. I couldn't shut her out.

"The whales are singing. Between the island and the shore they're rising . . . pipe wrench of God . . . singing . . . language I learned long ago. The only one . . . the only one . . ."

The radio, then—blast them, they kept right on us.

"*Tenino Tenino.*"

"Vessel calling *Tenino* identify yourself."

Well, at least the Coast Guard was hounding them.

"Ten I know. I dent if I. Now I understand this language, the one the voices whisper . . ."

Tom came over and stood very close to me. He fiddled with the spokes on the wheel, then began rubbing the sides of his pants again.

"What's wrong with her?" he said. "I wish she didn't talk like that. It doesn't make any sense."

"Well, it does in a way—she hears *Tenino* and turns it into 'Ten I know.' And "identify"—she thinks it's 'I dent if I.' I mean, it makes sense in a way, if you're zapped and screwed up and really wasted. I mean, she doesn't know where she is, really. So she's just trying to make sense of the noises."

"I am zapped screwed up wasted—secret language words for broken. Ten I know, I dent if I am screwed up for good."

She laughed, as though she'd made a joke, and sat up. She said, "Now I am better. I am fine, now. Look at those waves crowding onto shore. Over there sitting on those rocks is my grandmother. Do you see her? She is staring at something. She is watching my dad mow Brady's hay field across the road."

Tom looked up at me with his eyes filling up his whole face. He put his hands over his ears for a second, then turned away and grabbed the binnacle with a death grip.

I thought about shutting the door into the captain's room so we wouldn't have to listen to her, but in a way it was like, fascinating? I mean, you got hooked on it, you could see a sort of thread of logic to it, but it was so freaky at the same time. When she said, "My grandmother's sitting on those rocks over there," we both turned and looked. I mean, in a way she was really convincing. So I didn't shut the door, and I could see Tom wanted to and didn't either, so we had to hear it all.

"She knows him, the field hand from the next farm, notices how he pushes his straw hat back to loosen the sweat band, pulls it forward to stop the glare, wipes the back of his neck with the tired bandana.

"She can see him clearly in the noon sun, a flock of crows rising like a coda each time the tractor passes.

"She has remembered those rocks to sit on, each breath more rock, rocks made real by remembering. She will sit there until the field is mowed and my dad drives the tractor across the road and up the track to the barn.

"He vanishes behind the barn and she starts to forget.

"She wonders who that was mowing. She thinks she saw someone drive a tractor behind the barn and she wonders whose barn that is right over there with the huge haymow and the loose boards at one end.

"Someone should fix those boards but she can't remember who to ask and anyway it is not her barn.

"She has no barn, how could there be a barn out here in the sea where these rocks beneath her are disappearing?"

She started to cry, and then she shouted, "Goddammit you aren't even *listening*."

That brought Tom up, I'll tell you. He just about lost it right that second.

"I am, I *am* listening, Mom," he started shouting.

He went in and held her face between his hands and made her look at him, even though I doubt she saw anything except a swirl.

"We're listening to you. We're all here, Mom—me and Bo and Toby, we're here, we're right here, don't you see us? Just look at us!"

"Leave her alone," I told him. "For god's sake, just let her talk. She'll come out of it after a while. Just let her alone."

All at once I remembered my dad holding me, hugging me up tight to him, crouching so his eyes were level with mine—how old was I—not more than five, I'm sure, and he was wiping my face and saying, "It's OK, son, she loves us very much. She loves us. She knows we're here, it's just that sometimes she thinks she can't reach us. So she goes inside her head to find us, that's all. She'll be back. Don't worry, she always comes back."

Remembering him holding me peeled my skin right off. I felt like I'd been sandpapered—the air hurt my face and my lungs and the palms of my hands on the wheel. He was the one who hadn't come back, who hadn't loved us enough to come back.

How could I think like that? My dad loved all of us so much it should have saved his life.

I must have been a little crazy myself right then. I mean, is there any logic to that kind of thinking? I tried to get a grip on myself—Tom was the one who had lost it, not me.

I felt so sad for him, then. Because he couldn't remember our dad's voice, or how his arms felt holding him. And Tom turned into the person who held people, held Toby, held our mother's face when she talked like a crazy woman. Nobody ever held him. Where did he learn it?

"Hey, Tom?" I said. "Listen. Dad told me once, he said, 'She knows we're here, but sometimes she thinks she can't reach us, so she goes inside her head to find us. She'll be back.' He said it every time after that. 'Don't worry, she always comes back.'"

Tom nodded without turning around. "Yeah," he said, "well, maybe."

She went on talking, though, and even hearing my dad's voice in my head, I found it hard to be convinced. After all, in those days she wasn't into booze and drugs.

BY EVENING, IT seemed like we were carrying on a sort of three-way conversation, except that Mom, as usual, was talking to one person only. Not us.

"There isn't a lighted buoy this side of the Strait, why the hell is it so dark in this entrance, everyone uses this bay," I said to Tom.

And Mom reported, "It is night and I can see Bo dark against the window. He has no depth. He is worried about the depth when there is none to worry about. Bo, don't worry. I will save you, because you have no depth.

"Bo is looking at the chart. The chart shows where Boone is. Bo is looking for his father who is dead at the bottom of the sea."

All at once she got out of the bunk and stood in the doorway. "Where are we going on this boat?" she said.

"Home," I said.

"It feels so fierce," she said, "this dying, this going going after death. Voices keep coming from the bottom of the sea, hissing through the water. 'Ten I know, ten I know.' No one I know. 'I dent if I, I dent if I.' Why do they keep calling through the water?"

"It's on the radio, Mom." Tom said. "It's the *AnaCat* calling. Don't you remember? The *AnaCat* and the *Tenino?*"

"I will save you," she said. "Don't be afraid. I will save you. My voice croaks, but that is the way of the dead."

I SPREAD THE charts out on the chart table and turned the light on over them. "We gotta cut through," I said to Tom, and traced a course on the chart with my finger. "Through here, through Rocky Pass. Otherwise we gotta go outside Coronation Island to Chatham Strait. No way with that weather report. We already got big seas, even in here. Look at how we're icing. We'll have to hole up, maybe, ride it out. I don't want to get caught."

"Outside," Mom said. "I can do it. I know Outside. It is where I live, it is home, I will take us there."

"Where?" I said.

"Outside."

"No, I don't want to try it. And you don't know from nothing how to steer a course."

"Yes I do know. I know how to steer a course. Dead reckoning."

She shuddered and turned back toward the bunk.

"Now he knows," she said. "He knows I live Outside. That I am the dead reckoning."

Tom hugged her. He came and stood by me and looked up at me. "Mom's better," he said. "Isn't she?" He rubbed his hands up his pants.

She lay down next to Toby and went right on with her monologue, filling in, as usual, the other voices she heard.

"I am better. Better die than kill. Words I recognize. I know what they are saying. Listen.

"Dear Jess, I killed a little girl. Mom was right . . . better die than kill.

"Dear Jess, I don't know why he did it, why did he? I wish it was me . . ."

"What's she talking about now? Who killed a little girl?" Tom said.

"I'm not certain, but I think it was her brother that got killed in Vietnam. I have this weird feeling that something happened, like he maybe cracked up because he killed somebody, and so he walked into enemy fire, or stepped on a mine or something. I didn't know it was a kid he killed, though. But that's what it sounds like, if you can believe anything Mom says."

"You mean like, he killed himself on purpose? Nobody'd do that, would they? I mean, if you were in a war, all you'd want to do would be get away from bullets and stuff, wouldn't you?"

"I don't know—I just have this feeling—Grandma won't talk about it, and of course not Mom, but I kind of picked up some ideas of it from EJ once, listening to her talk to Grandma. It's like he must've cracked up over there. A lot of those guys did, or when they got back they like, couldn't get over it? Like they didn't know what to do if they weren't under fire or something?"

"But Mom makes him sound like he was someone who wouldn't have killed anyone no matter what. I mean, all the stuff she tells us about them playing out on the island, and him taking care of animals, and all that. I mean, he'd never have killed a little kid, Bo, I know that for sure."

"Maybe he didn't have any choice. I mean, sometimes there could be situations where you didn't have any choice if people are killing each other. I could see that, how he might have had to do it, and then he felt so bad he just went wacko and killed himself."

"Hunh unh," Tom said. "I don't think so. I don't think he would do it, not in a million years."

"So OK, he didn't do it. So shut up about it if you know everything, why don't you? You asked, not me."

THE RADIO BLASTED us again. "We're right on your stern, *Tenino*."

"Think they're close to us?" Tom asked.

"No way," I said. "Probably never left the harbor."

". . . never left the harbor never left the harbor . . ." Mom said. "*Patrols which never left the harbor attacked three vessels in Tonkin Gulf* . . . Tom Tom, the miller's son, stole my life and away he run . . ."

"Then we couldn't hear them all that clear, if they were still back there, could we? Clear through Prince of Wales?" Tom said.

"Yeah, maybe not. Yeah, could be not. So maybe they did get going, but no way they'd know we went south around Cape Chacon. They wouldn't ever think we'd do that in this weather."

"So how come we hear them so clear?"

"Jesus, Tom, can't you shut up for even one second? I gotta figure out this course."

"Jesus is Lord, praise the Lord for his everlasting salvation . . . Praise the Lord and pass the ammunition . . ."

"This is *AnaCat, Tenino. Tenino,* over."

"Ten I know, ten I know . . . who is that? Tom and Bo ignore the voices the way I do. I am a good mother. I have taught my children to ignore the voices. My mother is a good mother, too. She is writing down the story so we will remember ourselves. We remember mountains where there is only white sky sealed to water and we remember islands on unbroken sea, and we remember ourselves standing on islands on unbroken sea, and we remember ourselves standing on islands staring up at mountains. We who are imagined by the moon salute you.

"You be the salmon, Jess, I'll be the swan. . . . This was an entirely unprovoked attack; our ships were on routine patrol. We invent everything."

There was actually silence for a little while. I thought maybe she'd gone to sleep, but all at once she said, "You're lying to me. You say you're listening but you don't even know what silence is."

She rose up on her elbow and stared straight at us. "You know who you are . . . you don't have to keep looking over your shoulder to see who I'm talking to."

Tom started sobbing and I shut the door.

The boat is rising on gray mountains, skiing down the sides, crossing blind water, green where a dagger of sun stabs through. Tom is sitting on the floor under the binnacle. The binnacle. See how I remember words? And I remember my sons who are saving me and I remember my daughter that I broke. All the good ones are broken but I am not broken. When we are broken we are good.

Bo and Tom are dressed in black rain gear. They are covered with water. It is dripping in pools and they hang their gear by the door and the water runs one way then the other like a reversing river, the river flowing with the tide, we are all going with the tide on this boat.

"Hey, Tom, we gotta hole up in here—that ice is way

too bad. Look at the stack—must be six inches. Every wave is breaking on us."

Breaking on us breaking on us. Every thing is broken. Every body broken now.

Bo is putting his gear on again. Bo is shouting and shouting and Tom is putting his gear on again and the river runs everywhere under our feet.

"We're dragging! Fucking anchor's too light with all this ice—too much surge. We gotta drop that other hook. They got another anchor in the lazerette. We can set it with the winch for the net."

"OK, I'll come," Tom says.

"Unh, unh. You start her up and steer off that rock there—see it? Toward that tree sticking out of the cliff there. When I shout, put her in neutral, and then back her down to port after I drop it. Go slow till you feel her pull—she won't swing like on the first anchor—just sort of jump."

Bo is slamming out to the deck and Tom is scared starting up the engine. The boat is bucking and twisting with the river of water all spread out now on the floor drying up high and dry.

Bo is waving his arm and Tom is dragging on the wheel. Bo is screaming through the door. "Back," he screams, "Give it everything you got! Get some way on, Tom."

The engine is roaring and struggling and the boat leaps in the air and I fall to the floor. Tom stops the engine and it is very quiet. I lie still on the floor and listen to the silence rising all around me.

"Mom. Mom, are you all right? Did you hurt yourself, are you OK, Mom?"

"I am all right, Tom. I am here. Can't you see, Tom? I am Here."

"We OK, Bo?"

"Yeah. Lucky to get in, though. This is gonna be one humongous blow."

"We can ride it out?"

"Yeah, we'll be OK. We're protected in here, but I don't like the anchors they got on this thing—seem way too light, 'specially when we're iced up—stuff weighs tons. At least they aren't hunting for us now, I'll tell you. Seventeen hundred they'll be head over bucket."

THE BOAT GNASHES at its leash. I have to concentrate on wind like pain. Toby is crying and crying and Tom tries to hold her but the boat rolls them to the floor and Toby screams and throws herself backward.

"Mom, Toby's scared," Tom says. "I'm scared, too. The storm's terrible."

"Don't be afraid," I tell him. "I know what to do in a storm."

He smiles a little at me and struggles to take Toby up again in his arms. The wind thunders and Toby arches over from the force of it.

"BO, IS IT OK?" Tom asks.

"Yeah. Bet it's blowing ninety knots outside, though. Last report said sixty gusting eighty. Seas to fifty feet. We just made it. I wonder where the *AnaCat* is. Shit, is it blowing! Hope we don't lose anything on top. She sure is sawing on those anchors."

"Think this'll last a lot more?"

"Probably blow itself out in a few more hours. I hope. Man, listen to it."

"Toby's pretty sick, I guess. She threw up a couple times and had a fit screaming. Mom has her in the bunk."

"So Mom talked to you?"

"Yeah, she said 'give her here,' like she knew she should look after her."

"Man, listen to that."

BO IS TURNING the switches on all the instruments and checking. Nothing is broken.

"Where are we?" I ask him. I am glad because my voice is not broken anymore.

"Same damn place as yesterday. El Capitan Passage. We gotta go tonight if we're gonna stay ahead."

"Stay in the head. I was there. I know I was there, something smooth, water whispering, 'are you there are you there,' four walls touching. I stayed in the head."

Bo looks at me and laughs his no laugh. His broken laugh. "You remember that? You must be better."

"I am better. I remember. I stay ahead."

Bo shakes his head. He mutters in the secret language too quiet for me to hear. He talks and watches the green light circle.

WE HAVE GONE to sea again climbing the sides of gray mountains into the gray sky motion lovely, rising inside me, lifting the boat. I am not sick. My body is gone so I am not sick I am well and rising on the water.

There is a line of dark land now, low across the water we reach the mountain peak, but gone in the valleys, snow foam curling above the boat before it rocks to the top again. Bo is steering the boat toward dark land. He has to pull the throttle back because green water is breaking over the bow.

The boys keep whispering about Rocky Pass. I can hear them, because I can hear all voices.

Rocky Pass. The *Defiant* inching through that moonscape, razor grass and kelp everywhere, shifty, shallow bottom, depth alarm screaming and screaming while Boone dragged the wheel around, hairpin turn between reefs like frozen lava, sea lions hoarse with barking.

We hit slack tide too late. It turned so fast. Sudden grind, keel jolting on rock, hurled us to the deck, Boone pulling on the wheel from his knees, frantic, throwing the engine to stern, too late.

Water whined past, abandoned us to the rocks it had covered. The boat listed, would it stop, would it go down under the spiral tide into the mud, never rise? Rocks everywhere, pockmarked like the moon . . . rocks would break the boat, hole the boat . . . rocks caught it, held it up.

Boone rowed out and dropped another anchor. When the water remembered and came back, the boat lifted and we pulled out to the anchor. We were floating in the blackest night with the grunting hoarse sea lions and we were saved.

—*Jesus saves, too.*

—*jobs in town, there's money, Boone, it's safe, you'd come home at night.*

—*you want me to put up with all the shit I'll get from some Indian-hater chewing my ass?*

—*the boys need shoes, the dentist . . .*

—*why didn't you marry some goddamned rich logger?*

—*don't go for halibut, we'll get by some way.*

—*sure, like hell we will, you running off to town, making it with some logger.*

—go then, goddammit, see if I care.

Jesus saves, but two anchors can save you, too. I know. Because of Boone and Rocky Pass. We won't break because I know. I dent if I know. But don't break. Something is here. Something I almost know . . . something I *do* know . . .

—Lenny's making trouble, Gus, there's talk in town—a strike, ugliness—he's no good, you ought to get rid of him.

—I can't pay him enough, that's all—five kids and nobody to look after them—his wife left him.

—you're kidding yourself, Gus—he's the kind that hates everyone.

—he doesn't hate people, Bekah. He's poor.

No. No, I was wrong. It is nothing I know.

YOU LIE . . . YOU say you hear me but you keep looking around . . . Haven't I shaved my words, tipped the points enough to pierce your noisy heart and leave it silent?

Are you listening now? Are you watching that fog bank eat up the sea? Try to see through it—strain your eyes. See that dim outline over there, trees on the shore, gone now in a winding sheet? Were they trees at all, or only another idea? Should we steer for them, or away? How do people know these things when there are only shadows on the water, birds crying somewhere, waves expiring, their breath rising over the phantom trees. How can I save my children when I can't even save myself?

—According to the most recent body count we are winning in that area.

—three, four, five . . .

—don't look, Jess, come back, don't look—take my hand, we're going home now, don't look.

—eleven, twelve . . .

—*somebody crazy, that's all, some sad, sad person—come on, we're going back.*

—seventeen, eighteen, nineteen . . .

—*stop counting, come on, it doesn't matter how many, it's all of them, all of them gone.*

—twenty-six, twenty-seven.

—*A RAMPAGE, BEKAH. Lenny Carter on a rampage, getting back at me. I wish Jess hadn't seen it. All those swans dead. Oh god, Bekah, I wish I hadn't seen it either.*

I HEAR HIS feet on deck, he's coming in, wet steamy salt smell, motion, salt smell around me, boat surging with Boone inside me, planks cool, my fingers in Boone, in his seams and his curves like the planks . . .

Run my hands along these wooden boards to find the notch for my fingers, notch I always find with my fingers when I turn on my side after Boone slides away from me.

My fingers are looking along the smooth planks—I hear his feet on deck. Boone is coming to me, I am turning toward him, wanting the wet salt of him, my fingers looking and looking not finding not finding . . .

"Hi, Mom."

The scream is breaking through . . . Arms hold me so tight my breath is gone, I can weep without breathing. All the salt that is Boone and the sea passes through me.

Listen . . . listen to me . . . *I am not the sieve for your grief!*

We had to hole up in El Capitan Passage for two more days because the weather was so bad and we were icing up. The boat would pull up from its roll too slow, Bo said, so we could get trapped under a wave and ice up more.

Bo decided to search the boat. "There's gotta be something," he said. "I don't think they could run the trade without leaving some evidence."

"What do you mean, 'run the trade'?" I asked him. "Like drugs and stuff?"

"They got it perfect, see, they pick up, I'm betting they're getting it offshore from those foreign factory trawlers. Then, see, they've got the perfect distribution system—those geeks never set a net in their lives—they just run out and put up the *Cash Buyer* sign, only they're cash sellers, see. But where do they hide it? Coast Guard'll rip out your planking if they think there's a chance you're smuggling."

Bo was just talking to himself, not really me, and all the time poking at things, tapping along the planking, lifting up the floor in the fo'c'sle, reaching around in the bilge. I looked in a couple cupboards and the refrigerator. It seemed to me like the refrigerator would be good, fill up some milk cartons or something like that, jam jars, cottage cheese containers. Bo said no, though, it was too obvious.

We kept looking, and Toby thought it was a game. She'd lift up the edge of a cushion and shake her head and laugh and then pick up another one. So I traded back and forth with her between the cushions, and every time I lifted one up I'd say, "Peeeek," and she'd laugh and then all of a sudden she said, "Peeeek." I couldn't believe it, so I did it again and she did it again. I started yelling, "Bo, listen, you got to come here and listen to Toby."

Pretty soon he came back in the galley and I said, "Listen," and I peeked under the cushion and then she peeked under the other one and said, "Peeeek."

Bo said, "Hunh."

I said, "See, maybe they're wrong, maybe she will talk when she gets ready."

Bo said, "Not a chance. She's just making noises." But he started watching her, I could tell, and once when she grabbed his leg when the boat rolled, he reached his hand down and scrubbed his fingers in her hair.

We didn't find anything, and Bo quit finally. "I know it's here," he said. "I'm gonna tear this boat apart when I get the chance. Those guys oughta be in the slammer for a hundred years for the way they goof people up and wreck them."

"Think they know where we are?" I kept asking Bo that and I know it made him mad but I was actually pretty scared.

"Hunh unh, not yet. I told you, Tom. Why don't you just shut up about it?"

Well, I think he was sort of worried, though, because even though it made him mad my asking, he just kept on talking about it, trying to figure out how come we could hear them.

"Maybe they got everyone they know to start calling on their radios. Like, they could have called one of their gang over in Craig, say, or right ahead in Port Protection, and said, 'Call *Tenino* and tell them we're gonna get 'em.' See? Then we could hear them anywhere. So maybe it isn't *AnaCat* but *Molly Joe* or *Sea Otter* or whoever, calling. They wouldn't actually have to know where we are at all. They probably put out calls all over— Petersburg, Wrangell, places like that."

"But maybe *Molly Joe* and *Sea Otter* are out here, too. Looking for us, I mean. What if they put out of Craig? They'd be right behind us, hunh?"

Mom all of a sudden said, "What they?"

Bo caught on to what she meant. "The *AnaCat*," he said.

Mom nodded and said, "The what and a cat?"

Bo just started turning switches and stuff so I said, "The *AnaCat*—they're chasing us, trying to catch up with us."

Mom bent over to Toby and said, "Baby, baby, baby don't cry. I will sing to you about the cat."

Toby listened to the song about a cat. "The Baby and a Cat." "The Lady and a Cat." Toby laughed and meowed. She knew that cat's meow. I thought, well she can't be all that retarded, can she? But I knew. Really, I did.

The next day turned out clear like somebody turned the switch back on, everything so clear you could see the snow blowing off the tops of the mountains fifty miles west on Baranof. There was a lot of surf still piling up against the shore because of the storm—it takes a while for the ocean to get calm after a big blow, but the water was so blue it was like the nicest summer day. Bo, of course, didn't like it, not at all, so what else was new?

"Too clear," he said, "we'll have to wait till late to go—spot this boat at twenty miles in weather like this."

"Well I like it better than fifty-foot seas and iced up windows," I said. "At least I don't feel so scared, like throwing up all the time."

"Sure—except we can't go till dark, and we'll have to run all night, so you better crash now, because you won't do it later."

"We going through Rocky Pass?" I asked him. "Rocky Pass—it's really bad—Sam knows someone sank his boat on a reef in there."

"So? We got radar, and it's a lot shorter than going around. Especially with the weather likely to blow up again any minute. And they'll never follow us in there, you can bet on that. But we've got to get across Sumner Strait to Rocky Pass. They might turn out along the Strait instead of going up Wrangell Narrows, if they've figured out we didn't go the way they thought we would."

LATER, BUT IT didn't seem like much later, he shook me and said, "We gotta go."

"Sorta rough still, isn't it?"

"We can handle this. The wind's let up a lot, and we can always duck into Hole in the Wall, or Port Protection, if Sumner's too rough."

He started up the engine and then went out on deck and waved at me to go forward over the anchor, but right away the aft anchor chain pulled tight, not letting us go. Bo let a lot of chain out so we drifted back over the aft anchor. He went back and winched the aft anchor off the bottom.

He waved to me again, forward, forward, and when we got straight over the chain, he started the windlass. When the anchor came up it was covered with mud and a purple starfish sucking the air, and then slipping down, all those yellow suction cups winking.

Mom started singing "Starfish and a Cat," and Toby laughed and meowed some more.

"Seems like Mom noticed that starfish, didn't she, Bo?" I said.

"Yeah, she might be like, coming out of it pretty soon, all that singing to Toby, and stuff."

I hoped that meant she wouldn't talk to herself anymore. She'd talk to us, not some person that wasn't there. I felt so sad that she believed nobody listened to her. Wouldn't that be sort of like Toby—locked inside your own head, nobody you could talk to? It made me think what it would be like to be inside a closet or a box or something, and you couldn't get out. Or like that film I saw before Mom made me turn it off, and they were burying somebody alive, closing down the lid of the coffin, dragging it toward a grave—eeeehh—I still couldn't stand to remember that one. Mom and Toby buried alive in their own heads? Eeeehh!

IT WASN'T REALLY dark yet, more like mid-afternoon, when we turned north out of Shakan Bay and headed across Sumner Strait, but Bo figured nobody'd be out at that time of day after the blow. It was really rough, huge seas breaking on us so we could only see out in between waves crashing on us. Mom put Toby in the bunk, but she threw up and I had to get a lot of paper towels for Mom to clean her up. But at least Mom had her, not me.

We got about halfway across when I all of a sudden saw another boat east of us. The sun was way below the horizon by then, after three o'clock already, but a sort of pointer of sun came out that made that boat light up even though the water was dark. It was blue and white; I could see it perfectly.

We'd sink down in the troughs, then lift up, see the boat, the wave would break green water over the bow and windshield, then we'd sink, lift, boat in sight, crashing water, sink again . . . but every time we went up I could see that boat perfectly, and it was blue and white, and it was a seiner—you could tell by the way the bow was so high and the way the side rails curved down.

I didn't have to say anything to Bo, only waved my hand at it, and he said, "Oh, shit, it's them." Then he didn't say anything more right away, just looked at the LORAN to get the speed, and poked in the numbers for Rocky Pass so he'd know how far we had to go. I started to ask him how far, could we make it before they got to us, but he said, "Shut up, Tom," so I decided I better wait.

The sun got off them so they were dark against the water and that made them seem not so close. I thought maybe the sun might have been in their eyes when we could see them all lit up and maybe they wouldn't have been able to see us. I said that to Bo, and he said, "Look at the radar screen, stupid," so I did, and of course there they were like a yellow bullet on a video game. So of course we were on their screen the same way. But they maybe couldn't tell who we were.

After about a million hours, Bo said, "Take the wheel, Tom, I want to look at the charts." So I took the wheel and tried to hold her like Bo had her, around 335 or 330 degrees with the compass correction, since we were actually heading pretty straight north toward Rocky Pass, but it was really hard to hold her with those waves every couple minutes jamming us. When we came up I tried to see the boat. It was getting too dark to see except on the radar screen, but it was sure getting closer on that.

Ahead of us I could see an island, and in front of it a long line of surf. We were getting pretty close to it, it seemed to me, and I knew it was shoally, you could see a long line of surf breaking, but Bo wasn't saying anything, so I just dropped the course off to more like 315, 320 degrees.

Bo came over from the chart. When we came up, he saw how close we were to that island and he said, "Yeah, that'll do, maybe—that's Strait Island."

He took the wheel. He turned way off west so we rolled in every trough and I thought sure we were going down. One minute I was looking at him on the ceiling above me and the next one I was on the ceiling looking down at him. Bo was just fighting to hang on to the wheel.

He kept that course so long I thought we must be going into some place on Kuiu Island, the big one west of Sumner Strait, but then all at once he turned us almost back the way we'd been coming. He had to throw his whole weight on the wheel and sit on it while the boat came around through the waves. It was like it must have been on that Ferris wheel in Ketchikan, rising and then dropping so fast it left your stomach on the roof of your mouth. But once we got turned, we were really moving, surfing on a following sea that picked us up and threw us ahead. We were totally flying.

When I got my feet back under me, I took a look at the radar screen and I couldn't see the boat anymore, only Strait Island.

"Where'd they go?" I asked Bo.

"Keep watching," he said, and in a second or two I saw a little blip, then bigger, bigger, and there it was, going south along the other side of the reef. We were moving way faster than they were now, because we had a following sea and they were bucking it.

"Was it them?" I asked Bo.

"Who knows?" he said. "I sure as hell wasn't going to wait and find out."

When the island got between us and we couldn't see the yellow blip anymore, Bo turned north, which slowed us down since we were quartering the waves again. But already I could see the black line of land ahead.

I was very extremely glad to see that light on Point Barrie passing us on the east. We were close enough to get into Rocky Pass before they caught up to us, if that's what they were trying to do.

"*Tenino*, we're right behind you. Get ready, *Tenino*."

"Fuck you, come and get us!" Bo shouted it so loud I thought they could probably hear him even though he wasn't on the radio.

"This is United States Coast Guard, Juneau Communications Center. Vessel calling *Tenino*, on Channel Sixteen, this channel is a calling and distress frequency only. FCC regulations require vessels using Channel Sixteen to identify with call sign. Request you give your call sign and position."

"Can't you make the kid shut up, Tom?" Bo said. "Jesus, how can I concentrate on the chart with all that racket?"

"Well, you told me to take the wheel," I told him. "How am I supposed to look after Toby and steer the boat at the same time?"

Bo ignored me, as usual. "Be hard to find the entrance I think—it's pretty low around there, not much landmark," he said. "Listen to this, what it says in the *Coast Pilot* about Rocky Pass. 'Devil's Elbow is the most dangerous part of the pass. The channel here makes a full right-angle turn.' And get this: 'The Summit is very shallow and should be attempted only with local knowledge.'"

"Do we have local knowledge?"

"We got great electronics like I keep telling you, right? So just shut up, would you? We'll go through on a rising tide. That way if we get jammed we'll lift off. And we'll have enough water under us. In a falling tide, we'd be in big, big trouble if we went aground—she might go over and crush the prop or the rudder, or hole the hull."

"We gonna get through, do you think? Can you steer?" I just couldn't stop shaking. "I can't see anything—geez, I don't like this too much," I told him.

"No?" Bo said, not very nice. "I really just love it—this is so fun I wish I could spend my whole life right here in the dark on the rocks!"

"I don't think they'll try to follow us into Rocky Pass, do you?"

Bo said, "Hnnnnh." Never ask Bo anything, that was the only thing I knew.

BO

We had to anchor for two or three hours for enough water to get in the channel, before we started through the Pass. The high would be around midnight, pitch dark, naturally, but with the radar I figured we could get through and anchor at the other end, which was only about ten miles.

Tom took the wheel and I went out and released the windlass brake, listening to the chain rattle out—the whole damn place was way too shallow for my likes—we were down around ten feet out there at the entrance, and we drew at least six. Not a great prospect. Like, I didn't really want to do it? No kidding, I was extremely concerned, you might say.

■   ■   ■

WE DECIDED TO kill time by cooking ourselves a real dinner. We got the stove cranked up and threw three T-bones on the grill. They'd stocked the galley, all right. I made a salad and Tom fixed instant mashed potatoes which were definitely his best thing. Toby woke up and Tom piled up cushions so she could sit up at the table in the galley.

We debated trying to get Mom to come out and sit at the table with us, but Tom got this scared look on his face and said, "I don't think she's ready yet," meaning, "I don't think I can handle her talking like we don't exist."

I took a plate in for her, even cut her meat up like we did for Toby, so she wouldn't have to exert herself. She rolled over and poked the meat around with her finger, looking at it like it was some biology specimen she had to examine.

"You gotta eat something," I told her. "It'll make you feel better. You haven't had anything to eat for a long time now."

She looked up at me as if that puzzled her. As if the whole idea of eating was something she'd never heard of. Maybe she wasn't coming out of it. She didn't seem much better yet.

"Eat, Mom," I said. I jammed the fork into a piece of meat and held it up to her mouth. She opened her mouth, took the meat, chewed, nodding like now she got the idea. I sat down on the bunk next to her and stabbed another piece, then scooped up a little potato, and she kept nodding and chewing. I was feeding my mother the way you feed a baby. I wiped her mouth with the paper napkin and fed her a bite of meat. I couldn't stand to sit there and feed my mother like a baby and I kept doing it and doing it?

Tom came in wondering why I hadn't come back to eat, and seemed pleased that Mom was eating. "That'll make her better, won't it?" he said.

"I can't stand this," I said. "Why can't she at least feed her-self?"

"I'll do it," he said. "I'm almost done, anyway. You better eat."

I looked at him. Tom the Caretaker. What was wrong with him? I stabbed another piece of meat and held it up to her mouth. Shit, what was wrong with me?

Later, when Toby had exhausted both us and herself, Tom gave her a bottle, took her in and put her in the sleeping bag next to Mom. I went in with them just to be sure Mom was still breathing.

I don't know whether it was our being in there, or it was just time for another talk session, but as soon as Toby was tucked in, Mom sat up and started in.

"These things haven't happened yet, because it isn't evening." She stared over our heads as if she was watching a movie on a screen.

"When it is evening, I will walk down the hill toward the harbor, someone with me, Toni and Diane are with me. It's dark and the lights of the town are all laid out like a postcard, red and green running lights on boats coming in, light on Kialik Point sweeping past, Diane telling how she put one over on Mr. An-derson in biology today, Toni laughing . . . like a postcard, the lights, and we're turning on Harbor Street, walking toward the boat ramp and the lights . . .

". . . something tears the postcard, lights are tearing it, per-forations of light and sound across the postcard, tearing it. Toni and Diane are screaming and everyone is screaming and running and I'm running because I'm late. I'm the late Jess Rohlik."

She laughed.

Tom had a death grip on my arm. "She's talking about her dad getting killed. Bo, she did see it—she saw the whole thing . . ."

I tried to shrug him loose—I was pretty freaked out, myself. I could feel him shaking against me. I should get him out of there, I knew, he was too young for this kind of stuff, for hearing the kinds of things that make people crack up. But I couldn't leave. I mean, I had to know.

And besides, it didn't seem right to leave her alone. It seemed like she'd carried this stuff around inside her all her life and now it was coming out and it was like, we should take it off her some way? I mean, if you're transmitting and no one's receiving, you're out there all alone, right?

So we stayed, and probably we shouldn't have. Afterwards I thought, we shouldn't have.

"The whale inside me is rising," she said. ". . . pipe wrench of God . . . look at that lovely silver dawn . . . look at it turn rage red . . . dawning outrage . . . *why don't you leave me alone!*"

Tom shuddered and buried his head against my arm. "We better go," he said. "I don't think she wants us to hear it, Bo."

"She isn't talking to us. She doesn't even know we're here."

I put my arm around him and tried to talk calmly. "Look, if you want to leave, it's OK. She's talking about things that happened a long, long time ago."

I gave him a little push. "Go on. I'll stay—in case she might need for somebody to be here. You go on."

I could feel his head shake, and he took a deep breath and stood straight again.

"Bekah, so sorry—goddamn goddamn—so sorry—Lenny Carter come screamin' in there to the dock, level everything in sight with that gun a' his—no one could do nothing—Gus and Arnie and the others—all a' them dead—Lenny, too, sure

*enough, turned that gun his way after. Goddamn, Bekah . . .
Bekah, I give anything . . ."*

"Who is that?" Tom said. "It's like somebody else is talking,
not Mom."

"Shhhh—listen."

*"It was Jess's fault! She was late to meet him, wasn't she?
She's always late, Sam. He'd be alive if Jess hadn't been late!"*

Tom was on top of her before I could grab him. "Stop it," he
screamed, "Stop it." He held his hand over her mouth. "It wasn't
your fault, it wasn't it wasn't it wasn't—"

I grabbed him by the shoulders and flung him off her. Mom's
eyes were shining like green ice. She wrapped her arms around
herself and smiled. The smile was the worst of it. I knew we'd
never reach her.

I pushed Tom out the door and down the ladder. He was
sobbing and shaking all over. He crawled into his sleeping bag
without taking his boots off. I unzipped it and pulled his boots
and jeans off and then covered him up again. I got into my own
bunk across from him and lay there listening to him cry into his
pillow.

So she'd been walking down the hill toward the dock when
it happened. Sam must have brought her out to the island with
the news—*"Bekah, so sorry—Lenny Carter come screamin' in
there to the dock . . ."* and Grandma cried out, "He'd be alive if
Jess hadn't been late!" God, what a thing to carry.

"Tom," I said, "you want to come over here?"

I unzipped my sleeping bag partway down in case he did. He
didn't move for a while, and I could hear him snuffling his face
in the pillow, trying to stop crying. Then he backed out of his
bunk and came over and slid himself down next to me. I put my
arm around him and he turned on his side away from me. I

could feel his tears on my hand and I wiped his face with a corner of the sleeping bag, and then my own.

Having him there reminded me how I'd wanted him in bed with me after our dad died. Grandma came over and took us out to the island in the skiff. She put Tom in Mom's old room, and me in Uncle Tom's, thinking we'd like to have rooms all to ourselves. But we were used to sleeping in the same room, and I needed him.

At eight, I guess I didn't really believe in death—couldn't imagine that my dad was never coming back. I think my sadness was more fright at seeing grown-ups crying and acting like children. But every night after Grandma tucked us in and went back to sit by the stove, I'd sneak into Tom's room and get him and put him in bed with me. Later, I'd wake up and hear Grandma coming down the hall, padding along in her slippers, standing in the door like a ghost in her flannel nightgown.

"I see Tom came and got in with you," she'd say. "Would you like me to carry him back to his own bed?"

"No, he can stay," I'd say, "he's sound asleep."

We kept up that pretense as long as Tom and I were there, night after night for several months, till Mom finally needed us again. I realized, later, that Grandma had kept up her side of it to save face for me.

I lay there thinking about Grandma, how she'd understood me, how gentle she had always been with all of us, and yet, she'd accused my mother of the most terrible thing anyone could be accused of. How could she have done that? No wonder Mom had gone crazy, thinking it was her fault her dad had died.

I pictured Grandma coming into the harbor in her old wooden skiff, standing there behind the tiller in her black oilskins, ignoring the rain beating into her face. One time, right before Toby was born, and Mom was off with Matt, Grandma had come over and fixed dinner for Tom and me. She told us stories while we ate, about how she and Grandpa came to homestead the island, and about waiting too long to go to town when Mom was born.

Then tears started running down her face. She said, "It's too bad, isn't it, that children come packaged in hope. Because it isn't their hope, is it? Do you think it's their hope we carry like whips?" She shook her head, wiped her face, and told us about the time she got left high and dry by the tide while she was picking salmonberries.

I knew now that her hope had been the price she paid for her cruel words.

I wished I could have stopped Tom from screaming at Mom like that. But maybe anyone could just lose it if things got bad enough, even Tom? Or maybe everyone in our family was programmed that way. Like, we were genetic time bombs waiting for the trigger? Sheeh!

Tom rolled onto his back and said, "I hate Grandma. She's mean."

"I don't think she could have really meant it," I said. "Like, she was probably so upset when Sam told her about Grandpa, she just said whatever came in her head."

"She meant it, though. You could tell, the way Mom remembered it exactly. The way she said it, you could tell."

"Well, maybe Mom didn't understand her right. Mom saw it happen, remember, so she must have been out of her head, in a way. I mean, who wouldn't be, seeing their dad killed."

"You're treating me like a little kid, Bo."

I lay there thinking about the way words get carried around, getting heavier and cutting deeper all the time, maybe not even the words that were said, just the words that were heard. Maybe I'd done that to people I cared about. Like Sara. Maybe I'd said things she thought were different from what I'd really said, or maybe she remembered words that weren't even important to me. Maybe she was carrying them around like a brain bomb that would blow us up someday.

All at once, talking seemed to me the most dangerous thing in the world. And then, about one whole day late, I heard what Tom had said.

"Tom? I don't think you're a little kid anymore, OK? I mean, no kidding. You are not a little kid anymore."

"Yeah," he said. After a little while, he sighed heavily, and a minute later his breathing slowed and his feet twitched against mine as he let go and slept.

I MUST HAVE slept, too, but I woke when I felt the boat beginning to swing as the current eased, a little like it must feel to float in space. As though you were suddenly weightless. My dad used to tell me it was the ocean holding its breath. I got up, put my boots on, and shook Tom awake. I hated to do it—he was so sound asleep, but I needed him. He was not a little kid anymore, not for this trip, at least. "Wake up, Captain—time to hit the road," I said.

When I got up to the cabin I was surprised to find Mom sitting at the table. She was rocking Toby and singing "Scarborough Fair" like a lullaby, Toby leaning over her shoulder and sucking her thumb. Both of them seemed sort of peaceful, as though they were comfortable finding each other again. I gave Mom's shoulder a little hug and she looked up at me and smiled, almost like her old smile before she flipped out. I thought maybe it could be worth it after all, worth all the grief she'd given us. And the terror.

Depth, eighteen feet. I let Tom start the engine and warm her up, get the hydraulics going, while I tried to memorize the chart, and took a LORAN position. The LORAN was screwed up, though, because we were surrounded by land, and the reading showed us way west of our actual location, right up on top of Kuiu Island, in fact. No help there—we'd have to run on the radar, and just feel our way with the searchlight if we had to.

We pulled the anchor and I put her in gear, keeping the throttle forward only enough to have a little way on, but the flood current was carrying us, so we moved fast. I watched the screen, rocks everywhere and no radar markers underwater, despite what the *Coast Pilot* had promised. Tom kept his eyes glued to the depth sounder, reading aloud, his voice more and more scared as the depth fell.

"Bo, it keeps flashing eight point five, then four point five," he said. "We couldn't be in that shallow of water, could we? I mean, we're over six feet, the boat is, isn't it?"

"Maybe it's reading the weeds," I said, "kelp, stuff floating off the bottom."

"Now it's steady at seven point three—is that enough for us?"

"If we're only six, it is," I said, not knowing the *Tenino*'s draft. Six feet was only a guess.

"It's shifting again, six point one, six, six point eight, six . . . Bo, we better wait a little."

I'd started thinking the same thing. The *Coast Pilot* said the channel was dredged to five feet—that would be at low tide— and we should be at more than half tide now, but the depths sure didn't show it.

"OK, you're right . . . we'll drop the hook again and wait for more water. Man, is it dark."

I switched the floodlights on and the shoreline on both sides leaped at us, black and much much too close, as though we really were on the top of Kuiu Island.

"Put her in reverse so she's got enough way on to stern to hold against the current," I said. "Here—about like that—there's a reef all along the side there, so keep over—right there is good—sight on that jaggy-sharp point on shore, see it? Give her a little more to stern when I let the anchor go."

I dragged my rain jacket on and went out on deck. The wind had come up and roared through the passage, something on the rigging played like a guitar string, and the water poured past us at about seven jillion knots. We still had a lot of forward way on, too much to drop the anchor.

I pounded on the window and shouted, "Back—give her a little more to stern."

Tom nodded and I heard the screw churning as he urged the throttle up. The drive to stern gradually overcame the current and the water seemed to calm as the two directions equalized. I was about to release the brake on the windlass when I heard Tom scream, "No, Toby, get off me, let go . . . let go . . ."

The boat swung and I felt her grind over something, then a jolt threw me against the wheelhouse, and we were dead in the water.

I leaned against the wheelhouse and stared into the darkness, listening to the engine drum uselessly and the wind roar over my head. I didn't think "rock," or "aground," or "holed." I didn't think anything sensible at all. When a thought finally got through, it was "home." "Thank god, we're home now." Why?

Maybe just the sense of being no longer afloat, no longer hammering into the seas and wind. We'd arrived.

Then I clicked in. "Christ, Tom—turn the floods on—that switch at the bottom . . . God, look at that water screaming past! It's jamming us on harder. Give her more to stern—no, wait, we don't know if we're holed. Get down there and check the bilges—see if water's pouring in anywhere. I'll see if I can keep her off if she lifts."

"I DIDN'T SEE anything," Tom shouted as he came back in, "but I couldn't hear even if it was pouring through because it's so loud outside."

"But you didn't see any running into the bilge?"

"Hunh unh, not even in the hold either."

"Wouldn't be holed back there—we hit bow on. I'm going up on the bridge and try to see how we lie. Hold her in reverse till I get back. Hold her right where she is—don't let her swing or go forward if she lifts. Right here. Got it?"

"So why don't we call the Coast Guard? Like, they could send somebody?"

"In here? Most they'd get in here is one of those little dory jobs. I'm going up."

I looked at Tom's face. It was striped in black and white from the floodlights, his eyes driven deep in his face. He looked like someone behind bars, tortured and terrified. Exactly how I felt, too. "Tom?"

"Yeah?"

"If anything happens while I'm out there . . . you know . . . bad . . . like if the boat heels all the way over and something happens to me—you know—call the Coast Guard. They could at least get a helicopter in here."

"What's Mom doing out on deck?"

"Who knows. I'm going—keep some way to stern, Tom—hold her off if she lifts."

I slammed the door and went up the ladder. The canvas on the bridge had turned into a giant bass drum in the wind, and the floodlights made interlocking circles of kelp streaming past from cratered, treeless rocks. I moved from side to side, trying to see the rock under us, but we must have hit near its peak—nothing ahead of the bow. If we'd hit near the top of it, we might lift off at any moment, the way the tide was pouring in. I felt a little calmer—time and tide—dead certain, right?

Then, through all that drumming wind, I heard a call, far away as a loon's cry.

"Mom's   over   with   To . . . beee . . . Bo . . . o . . . come baaack . . ."

PART FOUR

TOM

If you've ever stood on the deck of a boat and looked out at empty water where somebody should be floating, you know about nightmares. Black shining tide rips, nobody there. It seemed like forever happened in a minute.

I must have yelled—I don't remember, though. But suddenly the Zodiac inflatable came slamming down from the bridge onto the water where the floodlight was turned. Then Bo dropped off the ladder to the deck, handed me a line, grabbed a life ring off the bulkhead, and rolled off the aft deck into the Zodiac. He jammed the oars into their locks, grabbed the line out of my hand, and shouted, "Get up there and try to aim the lights," and then he was gone—out in that water all by himself. Bo wasn't always so great, maybe, but really he was. Really he was very very great.

I got the rope ladder out of the lazarette and cleated it by the rail where Bo had gone in. Then I went up and flashed the flood around, but I couldn't see anything with it—no Zodiac, nobody floating in the water. Mom and Toby and Bo were gone and for all I knew they were all dead.

The light showed the current screaming past the hull so fast it looked like we were doing ninety knots to stern, but we were totally dead in the water. The bow was tilted up on the reef and the stern was way down close to the water. I thought that maybe the tide couldn't lift the bow off before the water came up over the stern. Maybe the boat would fill and sink before Bo got back. *If* Bo got back.

Another forever I stood there, and then there was the Zodiac back in the light. Bo was rowing against the current like he'd never rowed in his life. I ran back and there he was trying to lift Mom up where I'd put the ladder over.

She looked dead, not moving or trying to climb aboard. I pulled and lifted on her while Bo pushed her up till we got her over the edge, and then I let her slide down flat on the deck. Bo reached down in the Zodiac and stood up again and he was holding Toby.

He handed her up to me and I couldn't stand how she felt, like nothing at all, like a drowned seagull washed up on the beach. I yelled, "Are they dead, are they dead?" and Bo didn't answer, just pulled himself up the ladder and hung on the rail awhile, and then climbed over and cleated the line from the Zodiac.

All at once the boat jarred and then it started moving and swung all the way around. I could tell from the way we were moving that we were going to get carried toward Devil's Elbow, which is just nothing but rocks and a hard turn. Nothing but rocks. I didn't know what to do—try to turn the boat, try to stop us, try to make Toby and Mom be alive. I don't think my brain was working anymore; it wasn't making any words to say what to do, just shivering all by itself.

Bo went tearing into the wheelhouse and threw the engine into reverse. He was watching the radar, which was totally dotty with rocks.

"Get their clothes off," he shouted at me. In a minute I heard the rattle of the anchor chain. Bo came back to the wheelhouse, revved the engine to stern, the boat swung, and he shut her down.

He was past me before I could move, tearing Mom's soaking stuff off and rolling her in the sleeping bag, rubbing it up and down her from outside like she was a log he was rubbing the bark off of.

So I did the same thing with Toby, and she kind of squiggled around in my hands when I started rubbing her and made a sound like a little kitten mewing, so I knew she was at least alive, and I guessed Mom, too, or Bo wouldn't be rubbing the sleeping bag on her like that.

"They're so cold I don't know if we can do anything," Bo said. "I'm going to heat water—make water bottles to put inside the sleeping bags—you keep rubbing till I get back. You're supposed to warm them slowly—not their arms and legs first."

He went out, and I kept rubbing Toby, but she was making noises, so after a minute I put her down and started on Mom like Bo was doing. Bo was back in just a second and took over so I went back to Toby, then back to Mom while he fixed water bottles. He emptied a couple big juice bottles and a jam jar and put warm water in them and stuck them in the sleeping bags, and then he got in the sleeping bag with Mom and told me, get in with Toby.

I can tell you that was one long night. I don't think I slept one second—every time I shut my eyes I saw that black water, rips and eddies whirling around after Bo disappeared in the Zodiac—it was like something was down there waiting, smacking its lips, waiting. Mom couldn't have wanted to be in that water. She must have gotten mixed up some way, thought we were at the dock when we went aground, something like that. No one would ever, ever go into that wild water. She thought we'd gotten home, that we were tied up at the dock.

I kept Toby pressed tight against me and rubbed my hands up and down her, and she sometimes made her little squeaking noise, but she didn't try to push away from me, so I guess it felt good to be getting warm next to me. Every hour or so Bo got up and heated water and refilled the jars. I never could hear Mom moving around or saying anything, so I didn't know if she was even alive. Once I asked Bo if she was doing OK, and he just grunted. Sometimes I didn't know if it even mattered that Toby didn't talk because actually Bo didn't either.

IN THE MORNING, or I guess morning, still dark of course, Bo got up and made some tea and propped Mom up and made her drink a little, just a sip at a time. After a while she opened her eyes and looked at us like she wondered where she was, kind of looking all around the cabin like she'd never seen it before. After a couple minutes she took the cup in her own hands and started drinking more, and when it was empty she said, "Thanks, Bo," only her voice was croaky and it was hard to hear her, but I felt like she would be all right.

Bo looked over at me and all at once he said, "Aw, dry up, Tom," in this funny voice, like he was really mad at me, and he jumped up and ran out carrying Mom's cup. It turned out I was crying and I didn't even notice it. I didn't know you could be crying and not even know it, that seems so weird. I felt pretty dumb. Bo sure would never cry just because Mom turned out to be alive. Would that be weird!

WHEN IT GOT light enough to see, I thought it was a good thing we couldn't see much the night before. The tide was way, way out, and we were like on the moon, or somewhere with rocks everywhere, black rocks covered in kelp everywhere we looked. We were actually looking up at the reef next to us, the one we'd hit. It was a good thing we stuck on that rock as long as we did. What would I have done if we'd come loose while Bo was out there with Mom and Toby? Nothing, is what. Nothing I could have done at all. I think that rock saved our lives.

JESS

1

This pool has no bottom . . .

NEVER . . . THE BOTTOM of this pool is Never . . . a man is missing in the pool . . .

. . . I CAN REACH him if I keep swimming . . . he shouldn't be here shouldn't go out in the water he must not do this swimming and swimming and not swimming and sinking and sinking

—WHOOSH, NOTHING LEFT

■   ■   ■

. . . TIN TUB—TIN tub . . . whispers . . . *are you there, are you there?* I know the answer but . . .

TIME TRICKLING DOWN my legs—giving birth to Time. Small. Too small . . .

. . . TIN TUB—TIN tub *Mom are you there*

. . . TOO SMALL, WHAT I gave birth to . . .

—NO SHAKERS HERE, only keepers

. . . TOO SMALL IT is only . . .

—YOUR WHOLE LIFE . . . do you know how long that is?

. . . SO SMALL IT is only my . . . Self

IS THIS SOME shitty trip, or what? Why are we on this boat? Bo is here—I can see him in the wheelhouse, wrestling with the wheel—look at how his sweater hangs like a smock—his bones never touch it below the arms. One foot braced against the binnacle, muttering under his breath—he's saving us. I can see that. The rescue hangs as heavy as his sweater.

Why is he doing this? Jesus god. Madness runs in this family, doesn't it?

Are you laughing? My kids are rescuing me from something and I can't even remember what it is.

"Bo, what's going on? Why are we on this boat?"

"Don't you remember those creeps in Ketchikan?"

I don't remember. Wait a minute. Splinters. "Did one of them have a fat belly and half a head of hair and a green cap?"

I do remember. I want to hold it away from my head and get clean of it—it's slime, the memories pouring back in. Don't let me think about it—crack was the best of it—what else did they throw in? Blue acid, brain-burners . . . I've never crashed like this before.

I have to touch him. I really have to touch somebody, get my arms around someone and hang on. Everything's flooding back—fragments everywhere . . . a carnival, the world turning like a Ferris wheel—my whole head is just sinking under all the horror I'm remembering.

I get out of the bag and grab some sweatpants that are thrown on the foot of the bunk, and a gray sweater that's lying there. Right off I can smell the diesel, fishy, sweaty smell that Boone used to smell like when he got home from his fishing trips, and it makes me go all wet and clammy, that smell. The flood in my head is drowning Boone all over again. I'm just empty space, pretending Boone is coming, Boone is out fishing, not dead, not sunk with the boat to the bottom of the sea. I'm just the empty space waiting.

God, I must be wasted still, to think that kind of stuff. That's crazy thinking, isn't it? Please. Don't say it.

I stand behind Bo at the wheel and put my arms around him. "Yeah, I do remember a little—I wish I didn't. Bo, it was terrible, wasn't it? I was totally wasted. Bo, hey, I'm so sorry."

He doesn't say anything, naturally, but then he turns a little and slings one arm behind him, and hugs me against his back, like everything's going to be all right.

I keep asking him what happened. I have to know, but I don't want to hear it. Like waiting to hear your sentence. Jess Rohlik, sentenced to life.

He's just starting to tell me a little of it, when a voice comes over the VHF.

"*Tenino, Tenino,* we're right behind you. You'll never make it. You haven't got a chance, *Tenino.*"

Something about that voice—what is it? It doesn't seem to come from anybody, but at the same time, it sounds familiar, and I know I've heard it before.

"Bo, who is that calling? That's a weird kind of call, isn't it? Seems like I've heard that name, but why would someone call and say, 'You haven't got a chance'? Who's *Tenino?*"

"You don't remember? Check out this boat, Mom."

"This boat? This boat's *Tenino?*"

"Rick Kozloff's boat. Don't you remember? *Tenino* and *Ana-Cat.* They talk like they're right on our stern, but I don't believe it. I think they've got a relay going so we'll think they're right behind us."

"You stole it? Jesus god, Bo, we could get twenty years, something like that. This boat's worth at least a couple hundred grand. That's no misdemeanor, kid!"

Would you believe? My kids have stolen this boat! I get the

shakes again just thinking about it, or maybe because I already have them pretty bad from the shock treatment. Electric ice water. How did I get into that water? Wait. Yes, I know. I know. Jesus god.

Finally, they tell me some of it, both talking at once, arguing about how they did it, how they took Toby and me from that house where I'd gone into orbit. I know they're leaving out half of it because they don't want me to feel bad anymore for getting so stoned, for abandoning my own kids. Mostly they want to tell me about getting off the reef in Rocky Pass, and hauling us out of the water. Listening to that I have to sit and put my head between my knees.

Tom gets white as a ghost talking about it. They were so scared, those kids, and no one to help. But Tom got up there on the bridge in all that wind and rain, kept the spotlight trained while Bo was out there in the dark rowing for our lives. Can you even think of kids doing that? It makes me think of Boone calling home on the radio, "Got any keepers there, lady?"

I can't keep from crying when I think of that. Shock, I guess. And maybe knowing I left them. That I meant to leave them forever. Can they know that?

Can they not?

MY FEET ARE as shaky as my head, and Toby starts fussing and trying to get out of the sleeping bag. I have to go back and get in with her and rub her back to try to keep some circulation going. Her little body's so sparrow-thin it's a wonder there's any place for blood at all. I leave the door open, though, so I can watch the boys.

Toby dozes off again. She feels pretty warm, except now and

then she shudders all over, as though she's remembering that water. The boat's rolling and pitching like a carnival ride.

Carnival. Jesus god. Koz, holding Toby out over the seat on the Ferris wheel. I can see it. Psycho. That man is psychotic.

I SHOULDN'T HAVE had Toby. But I did. Remember how EJ tried to throw us out of the bar—she knew I was going to wreck up that baby. If it'd been anyone else I'd probably have listened, but she was in my mom's pocket, I knew that, she was just telling me what my mom thought. So I didn't listen to a word of it, just barged in there, forget you, and now look.

EJ didn't earn her old "statue of limits"! She should have made me stay out of there. She was dead a year later. Serves her right for not kicking me out, doesn't it? God, EJ, how could you die? How could you let me down like that?

There was so much life left in her. My mother should have given her Instructions for Staying Alive. What did you say?

To you, too.

Well, I'm here, aren't I? Hear hear, I'm here.

After EJ went to the hospital in Juneau, Mom and I visited her as often as we could. Her wild hair was gone—they gave her a blond sausage-roll wig to replace it. She'd yank it on when she saw us coming, pull it down at an angle over one eye and leer at us, jiggle a bare hip out of the sheets.

Toward the end, she slept most of the time, all that painkiller, but now and then she'd rouse. The last time we went, all at once she said, "Charlie never came back."

"Smart man, that one," Mom said. "He knew you had a gun trained on him."

EJ looked at her squinty, and then grinned her old grin.

"He was just good for one thing, that little shark shit, but I . . . Bekah, you really thought I'd shoot him?"

She actually winked, but I saw tears in her eyes. "Bekah, you asshole," she said. She dozed off then, and her kids were the ones with her that night when it ended.

Poor EJ. All that time, and we never understood about Charlie.

Poor Jess, too. You're feeling pretty sorry for me, too, aren't you? Her poor damned kid, and her poor stupid cracked-up brain—blaming everyone on earth but Numero Uno.

Is this woman gonna spend her life a fool, or what?

Reality check: Bo and Tom Rohlik have stolen a boat, kidnapped their mother and sister, and are escaping from a gang of drug dealers through the North Pacific in a winter storm.

2

We're anchored at Hood Bay alongside an old cannery ruins. Rain has melted it away, the boards all slimy, crisscross collapsed. A lot of people must have gotten their hopes collapsed, too. Everywhere you see remains on the shore—cannery buildings, old homesteads—as though the forests and the rain are the local Bureau of Reclamation. There isn't much here, is there, except the forests and the rain? A wraparound world: velvet upholstery, gray gauze drapes, wave-pleated rugs. Exterior Design Award.

Think of all the failed dreams, the people who came and saw wealth here, or escape, or peace. And they were right. It's all here. But there's never enough, is there? Such a strange word. Enough. A word for something which never exists.

Most of these people went back to town, or back south, gave up and did something else. I should have done that, after Boone died. Taken the kids and gone south, figured out a way to make a better living for them. But you know, we've done all right, the pick-up jobs I get and the Permanent Fund checks. Not this year, though. I really blew it with those checks. We'll tough it out this year. Tough we are, though, right?

I'M SURE NO use, yet—so shaky, and this terrible dizziness. But it's getting better. I can take care of Toby, change her diaper and give her a bottle. Tom said we were out of milk, but then he hunted around and found a huge carton of powdered milk, so we have plenty, only please let us get home soon. Kerosene in every vein in my body. I can't hold my legs still, and I can't stand having the door to this room closed—claustrophobia, or something. But Toby's recovering. She's pretty much back to her normal self. Normal, abnormal, you might say. Toby's going to outlive me. I think that every single day of my life.

Who's going to look after her then?

Tom can.

Perfect.

No, I'll tell you who. The government.

The taxpayers?

The oil money—the Permanent Fund! That'll do the job.

Write to the Governor. Jess, what a genius!

SO NOW WHAT? Weathered in on the wrong side of Chichagof—can't get home, and those bastards closing in. No, they're not, either. Think they'd be out in this? No way.

When I press Toby hard against me and brush her eyelids with my finger, she squirms and pushes back a little. She has crow's feet around her eyes—only three years old and aging skin. Look at that darling face, all screwed up tight as though she's concentrating, her hair stuck down in little curls on her scalp, worry wrinkling her forehead.

After Tom fed her, he brought her in and I put her in the sleeping bag with her bottle. She cuddled right down and went to sleep. Tom fiddled around touching stuff on the shelf and poking around at stuff on the floor till I wanted to scream, what with kerosene in my arms and legs, and dizziness.

Finally he said, "Bo says Toby's, like, retarded? That she might not learn how to talk? I always thought she was just thinking stuff, secrets. That she'd tell what she'd been thinking about when she got ready."

"No. Wrong, Tom." I said it fast and mean. I can't stand to hurt him—his eyes get all flat and black and you can't see into them. "She's not going to tell us secrets."

He stopped looking at me and got real quiet, not poking at things anymore. I hated saying it.

"She's where we put our secrets," I told him, and he looked back at me with those blank eyes. "She's the place we can put our secrets, and she won't ever tell them to anyone else."

His eyes got clear, then, and he laughed. "She's a keeper, then, isn't she, Mom? Toby's a secret keeper!"

How could I ever have thought of leaving them?

Do you know how hard it is to hurt your kids? All right, all right, I hear you. You know. I've hurt them a lot more in other ways, though, haven't I? What words did they hear when I went into the water? "I don't love you enough to stay with you"? Armed words. Bayonets. Jesus god. That's what those social workers kept telling me. "You don't love them enough." Wrong. They're wrong! You know what? Those social workers aren't even real!

NOT A TRACE of light from outside. Toby keeps making little sucking noises next to me, and once I heard Bo muttering down in the fo'c'sle. That kid even mutters in his sleep. Why has he gotten us into this mess? Maybe it isn't actually his fault. Aha. Getting sharper, there, Jess. You could be right for once.

What a strange kid. Why would he do it? He could just as easily have gone off alone, gotten on the ferry and gone home, or taken Tom if he'd felt that responsible. I don't get it. Why would he feel he had to look after me, after I went off and left them?

Maybe Bo's crazy. It runs in the family like I told you. People in town call my mother "Crazy Bekah," the way she lives out there on the island all alone, never taking anything from anyone. Anything she can't do for herself doesn't get done. No way can you tell her anything. Move off island? Stop felling trees with an axe? Stop setting crab traps because she might get dragged over? Forget you, baby.

That's where Bo got it, though—from my mom. Bo's just like her, crazy independent. That old-man face—it breaks my heart—eyes shielded, skin stretched like canvas. You know who had eyes like that? My dad. I could never read his eyes, either. But my dad at least had flesh on his bones, not like this skeleton I raised.

I haven't raised Bo, though, not really, not since Boone died. I've just let him grow. Go. Let him go. He owes me nothing. All right, all right—I hear you laughing.

■   ■   ■

BO IS TELLING Tom we'd better head in—Freshwater Bay, he says. I hope we make it that far. We're putting the rails under on every roll. Lord, how did we get into this? This is the worst mess I've ever gotten my kids into—I never had to wonder if they'd survive before. If anyone gets wind of this, they'll take them away from me for sure. Then I would not survive. If we get home they'll take my kids away, and if we don't, we'll die. To-gether, though. At least we'll be together. And Boone, too, some-where he must be. Under all this water blowing over us. Blowing in the wind. All the flowers and all the soldiers, and all of us blowing in the wind.

Sing, Jess. Make us all happy.

EVERYONE ELSE IS asleep. Through the door I can see those little indicator lights on the panel in the wheelhouse. Twice there've been calls over Channel 16, but there isn't much radio traffic this time of year—smart people stay home. All at once something else comes over the radio. Whispering.

"*Tenino, Tenino, Tenino* . . . die. Die, *Tenino,* die."

It's just whispering, but it's right here on the boat with us. I must be tripping again, I'm so freaked by that voice. The whis-pering is all around me. It keeps going, soft, like something brushing against the hull, like waves hushing across, little rip-pling sounds, "*Tenino,* die . . . *Tenino,* die."

And all at once, I know we will. We've struggled and fought back, and the boat's still floating, but now we're going to die. All of us. That voice, floating from the wheelhouse, that voice is Jesus Praise-the-Lord Himself, telling us the end has come. I can't move or cry out to warn my children. My body is stone. Paralysis of the Dead.

Wait, wait—I know something—I know it . . . We don't have to die because we always can. Don't you see? As long as we can get out, we're safe. It's the emergency door. We don't have to pull the handle, but it's there. So we're safe! You, too—everyone's safe.

Now, lying here in the whispering dark, I'm seeing something from the other life, the one that happened first. Before Boone. Before I started to disappear.

My dad disappeared, too, disappeared in the dark, and I never saw him again. Till now. Now I see him, lying there, fallen back in the skiff, blood everywhere, someone grabbing my arms and turning me around, tiptoe dancing away from the darkness shrinking toward me.

I've never told my kids about my dad. About the tearing light and sound. About the blood. I couldn't, you see. It was in the other life. When I stop crying this ocean, I will tell them. About Lenny Carter who took a gun and killed twenty-seven trumpeter swans, three men, and himself. I'll tell my sons about guns and madness. About my dad who died one night when I was late.

BO

Mom came in and said, "Hey, guys, let's go. Tern Bay or bust. Pull the hook, put that thing in gear, pedal to the metal." She was dancing around, bumping into the wall when the boat rolled, hopping up and down.

"Pins and needles," she said. "Kerosene in my veins. I need to do something, get off and run on the beach, I don't know . . . We'll be out here for another week at this rate."

I laughed, turned on the switches and started the engine, warming it up while I rolled up the charts.

"Hey, what did you think I was gonna do, lady, sit here all day waiting for them?" I said.

I switched the radio over to the weather channel and we stood there listening to the next low moving out of the Gulf of Alaska heading into Southeast, "snow likely, reducing visibility to near zero." I looked at Mom.

"Go, anyway, Bo," she said. "Plenty of places to duck in if it gets too bad."

"Yeah, sure. Icy Strait—my favorite place in snow."

"So? Are we gonna sit here like ducks in a row waiting for Koz and those other junkies to show up?"

It seemed like Mom had gone crazy in the other direction, now that she was feeling better. Like she'd gotten a rush just from being alive? Well, I mean, who wouldn't, only it was kind of confusing when I thought about it. First, she throws herself off the boat, then she's jazzed because she didn't drown.

I kept seeing them out there in that howling dark, kelp wrapping them like mummies, the press of the current holding them in place. The kelp actually helped—it buoyed up their bodies, and held them against the rocks. I could haul in on it like rope, hoping the roots would keep their hold.

The shock of that cold must have sort of paralyzed them both. Toby was tucked into Mom's arm, but that arm wasn't holding anymore, it was floating up, drifting back—I grabbed Toby with one hand just as she slid off Mom's shoulder, dropped her into the Zodiac, trying at the same time not to lose my grip on Mom.

I had to lean far over to lift Mom up—the kelp was tangled around her legs, so I had to lay her across the inflated side of the Zodiac while I unwound her. Not once did either of them move—I didn't dare stop long enough to see if they were breathing—that they were still floating seemed incredible.

When Mom was all the way in finally, I felt for a pulse in her neck, and thought I got something, but I had to row—we were getting carried farther and farther up the Pass—the floodlights seemed miles away already. I should just have pulled to shore and tried to revive them. Reviving them was all that mattered. But the *Tenino* was going to lift off the reef any minute, if it hadn't already, and Tom was there and he was alive, I knew that, at least.

It was not a wise decision, only a lucky outcome. To tell the truth, it was no decision at all. I didn't have an intelligent thought pass through my brain after Tom yelled, "Mom's over."

Why did she do it? Trauma and horror stories in her past, a guilt trip laid on her like a death sentence—was that enough to die for?

I tried to imagine what I would feel if all that had happened to me. Like, what if Mom thought I'd caused the *Defiant* to sink? Or thought I'd left my dad to drown and saved myself, or something like that. Even then, would I ever choose to die?

For one thing, how could you leave people? I mean, how would I ever leave Sara? And another, how could you ever stand not to know what came next? That was the whole thing. I mean, I'd always want to know what came next. It'd be like finding the last pages of a book ripped out, just when you're getting to find out what happened.

When we got out of this goddamned mess—when we got home—I would just ask her straight out, why. Say, "I don't get it, Mom. How could you choose that? What would make a person choose death?"

And when she said, "Because of dah de dah dah," I'd say, "Yeah, OK, I get it, but Mom, listen. *You* gotta tell Tom. He's not a little kid. No kidding, you tell him yourself. Not me, not ever again."

■   ■   ■

WHEN WE GOT out of Chatham into Icy Strait, something new. Snow. It looked like bedsheets blowing on the line—down to the water, lifting up over us so we could see again, then back to the water, mostly closing out everything ahead of us. The worst wind dropped, though, which made the going a little easier. It gets funneled straight down the cuts between the mountains. We'd been heading right into it going north up Chatham Strait.

Toby started hollering and whining.

"She's hungry," Tom said.

"So am I," Mom said. "I'll see what there is. Time we all ate, especially since we're going to get into some weather." She looked at me to see if I got her meaning—let's go, mister, no hanging back, is what she meant.

She fixed sandwiches, bracing herself against the table because of the rolling. Tom started bouncing Toby up and down on the orange fender he'd brought in off the deck for her to play with. She sat on top of it, where it tied on to the line, and he bounced it like a ball, hanging on to her with one hand so she wouldn't roll off.

All of a sudden I heard a thud, and then a shriek from Toby. I heard Tom say, "Look at this, Mom. Ever see a fender like this? Like it has a plug or something, holding it on the line. Why would it have something inside like that?"

I knew right off. "That's how they hide the crack, or whatever," I shouted at him. "Let me see it."

Tom brought it out to me, and I said, "See, they keep the stuff inside, and screw this into the fender. I bet all the fenders are like this."

Tom nodded and poked his hand around inside it. "Remember Don yelling at me and Toby for playing with the fender on the *AnaCat* in Ketchikan?"

"Likely place, you think of it. Yeah. I got it. See, when the Coast Guard comes along with their little boarding party, you just hang the fenders over the side so they can tie up their boat easy, welcome aboard. No problem, nice and polite."

We both laughed. It was kind of exciting, actually, like we'd made a huge drug bust? We had them now—hard evidence, Buster.

All of a sudden the radio started spouting at us.

"*Tenino*. Calling *Tenino*. We have your position. You'll have to pass us to get to Tern Bay. We're waiting for you, suckers."

"Yeah, sure," I said. "Right ahead of us. Probably run right over them in the snow."

"If they think we're going back to Tern Bay, why wouldn't they just go there and wait for us?" Tom said.

"No way they could have tailed us all this way, and if they did, how come they didn't overtake us? We haven't exactly been going full bore, you know."

"Well, like you said, maybe they got their buddies to call us, and they've been sitting up here waiting for us."

"Closing with you, *Tenino*. Keep looking, bastards."

"This is United States Coast Guard Juneau Communications Center. Channel Sixteen is for calling and distress only. Please switch to a working channel."

"Maybe we should call the Coast Guard and tell them the *AnaCat* needs assistance," I said. " 'What color is your vessel, how many aboard . . .' jam up the *AnaCat*'s radio talking to the Coast Guard. I'm tired of hearing those shitheads threaten us."

"I think they've figured out where we are," Tom said. "They

know we're almost home. Maybe I should go up on the bridge and watch."

"Sure. Great idea. You couldn't see your own hands in this snow."

I FINALLY LET Tom take over awhile. I was so tired I just flopped down on the bench in the galley to sleep, didn't even bother to go below. And of course, as soon as I closed my eyes, there they were, the mummies wrapped in kelp.

I couldn't sleep—my mind seemed to be stuck permanently in the On position, everything whirling around inside—drugs in fenders, radio calls, round-trip tickets, Sara. Finally I gave up and took over the wheel again. Tom went back to the galley to lie down. The snow stopped for a little while, and I could see the mountains up behind Hoonah.

All of a sudden I realized the radio was calling, "Mayday" over and over, the static making it very hard to hear. I adjusted the squelch knob, trying to pick it up better.

"Mayday, Mayday. Fishing vessel *AnaCat*. No engine. South Inian Pass. Going on rocks."

"Tom," I yelled. "Tom, come here. Listen to this a second."

Tom came in and stood there listening to nothing. "Yeah?" he said. "What's up?"

"A Mayday. The *Anacat*'s in South Inian Pass. Listen. The Coast Guard ought to pick them up."

We stood there listening for the Coast Guard or a repeat call. The snow had started again, so it seemed like we were traveling through outer space. Nothing from the radio.

"You sure?" he said.

"Certain. 'Mayday, no engine, going on the rocks in South Inian Pass,' he said."

South Inian Pass was actually west of Tern Bay. I thought about it. So that was it. When the storm subsided, they'd decided to try to cut us off. They'd gone through Peril Strait to the outside, come up around Yakobi Island into Cross Sound, and then tried to get through South Inian without realizing that the currents there can run as fierce as any passage in Southeast. And if you get ocean swells rolling in and the tide going out—you've got a scene, man. Dumb asses—why didn't they look at those charts?

Usually Maydays get picked up by the Coast Guard before the guy finishes talking, but this time, nothing. I knew I'd heard it, though. Unless hearing nonexistent voices was catching!

I kept trying to see through the snow, expecting the *AnaCat* to come bursting right out of it, dead ahead, even though the radar wasn't showing anything.

After several minutes, the voice and static came again.

"Mayday, Mayday. Fishing vessel *AnaCat*. On the rocks, South Inian Pass, taking on water. Mayday. Can anyone hear me?"

I shouted at Tom again. When he came out, I repeated what I'd heard.

"Maybe we ought to call the Coast Guard," he said. "They aren't answering him. Maybe they aren't picking him up."

"Oh, right," I said. "We get a radio relay going with the Coast Guard and who comes charging over the hill? It's a trap, I bet. The *AnaCat*'s sitting right out here somewhere, waiting for us, hollering 'Mayday' so they can find us in the snow."

"So why doesn't the Coast Guard answer?"

"Who knows? Maybe they're on some low wattage, or hiding out somewhere close so the Coast Guard isn't receiving it."

"They were trying to head us off, weren't they? They must have come around from Sitka. Maybe they came through Inian to wait for us to turn into Kialik Strait."

"Yeah," I said. I was a little surprised Tom could figure that out. I mean, he hadn't spent a lot of time on the charts, or fishing offshore the way I had.

"Sam and I go through South Inian pretty often," he said. "But Sam watches out for the current so we go through at slack, or we sometimes don't even go if it's blowing up too much in Cross Sound."

Right then it came again.

"Mayday. *AnaCat*. Can somebody help us? We need a pump. Boat's filling. South Inian."

All of a sudden Mom jumped through the door, grabbed the transmitter and shoved it at me. "Call them. Tell them we're on our way, maybe an hour and a half ETA, two hours? Then get on that horn to the Coast Guard. We can relay."

She shoved me away from the wheel and pushed the throttle up. The boat jumped forward.

"This is no joke, Bo Rohlik. Those guys are in trouble."

"Listen, Mom, even if they are in trouble, somebody'll get to them out of Pelican or Elfin Cove. Once we start relaying, they'll get our position. Next thing we know, bammo! They mean business. We'll never make it if we tell them where we are."

"You listen to me, Bo! No more dying. Nothing broken anymore. Never again. No way are we going to let another boat go down. We're on our way. Get on that horn and tell him. Right now."

She pushed the throttle up again. "We're winning," she shouted. She started singing, then. *"Joy to the fishes in the deep blue sea. Joy to you and me."*

Even though she sounded totally wild, in a way I felt better when Mom took over the wheel. Like she was going to be the boss again. Well, I mean, I didn't want a crazy woman skippering that boat. But all of sudden I was tired. I mean like, exhausted? I could have dropped on the floor and slept a hundred years. She could run the damned boat to China for all I cared.

I answered the Mayday without giving the name of our boat. "Mayday relay, *AnaCat*. Mayday relay, *AnaCat*. We are proceeding in your direction at eight knots. ETA two hours. Contacting Coast Guard. Standing by on One Six with Mayday relay. Out."

Then I called the Coast Guard. "Mayday relay, Mayday relay, Mayday relay. Fishing vessel *AnaCat* on the rocks in South Inian Pass, taking on water, requesting pump and assistance. Do you copy? Over."

"Seelonce, Mayday. This is United States Coast Guard Juneau Communication Center. We copy Mayday relay. Vessel relaying, give your call numbers and position. Over."

I looked at Mom. She nodded at me to go ahead, but I didn't want to. I still thought it might be a trick to get our position.

"Roger, Coast Guard, Juneau. We are proceeding at eight knots with ETA of two hours, standing by for further relay. Do you copy Mayday transmission direct? Over."

"Mayday. This is United States Coast Guard Juneau Com Center, calling vessel relaying Mayday. We are not receiving Mayday transmission. Please give your name and call numbers and stand by to relay. Over."

"See? It's a trick," I said. "Why can't the Coast Guard hear them if they're really in trouble?"

Mom shouted, "Do it, goddammit. What the hell difference does it make? If they're around, they'll find us anyway."

"Mayday relay. This is the fishing vessel *Tenino,* WYP4577, east of Point Adolphus, position 58 degrees 21.2 minutes North, 135 degrees 43.0 minutes West. This is *Tenino,* standing by on Mayday relay. Over."

"Mayday, *Tenino,* can you get a description of the vessel requiring assistance, how many on board, medical status of crew, and survival equipment available? Over."

"What did I tell you," I said. "What color is your vessel?" I pushed the Transmit button again.

"Mayday relay. *Tenino* to *AnaCat, Tenino* to *AnaCat.* Come in, *AnaCat. Tenino,* standing by on One Six. Over."

We waited and waited, not saying anything in case they answered. It seemed so long—maybe they couldn't hear us anymore, or maybe they'd sunk already. We were rolling badly ourselves, every wave crashing green over the bow. I kept thinking what it must be like in the Pass, the boat smashing against the rocks, all that roar of the water and surf.

Nothing over the radio. Maybe they were out on deck trying to see if they could do anything.

Then we heard a call, very faint, a lot of static, and a lot of words we couldn't catch.

"Call . . . *Teni* . . . pump . . ."

I was holding my breath. We all were, actually.

"This is *Tenino,* standing by on One Six. You are breaking up, *AnaCat.* Repeat your message. Over."

They came right back then.

"Pump . . . filling . . . last maybe two . . . *Teni* . . ."

"*Tenino* to *AnaCat, Tenino* to *AnaCat.* Coast Guard asks number aboard, survival equipment. Do you need medical assistance? *Tenino* standing by on One Six, over."

"Three   ab . . . raft . . . bat . . . low . . . suits . . . outbo . . .
no med . . . one, two ssss . . ."

"*Tenino* to *AnaCat*. Three aboard, life raft with outboard, survival suits, no medical assistance, batteries low for transmit. One,
two, query, hours? This is *Tenino* standing by on One Six, over."

"Two hours . . . no outbo . . . roger . . ."

"Roger, *AnaCat*. Two hours, no outboard. Stand by. This is
Tenino standing by on One Six. Out."

Toby started to whine and fuss in the bunk, so Tom got
some crackers and the jar of peanut butter and sat in the corner
of the wheelhouse with Toby on his lap. Mom kept jogging up
the throttle till I grabbed her hand. We were slamming into those
seas so hard I thought we'd crack apart. I made her turn the
wheel to quarter a little more. I called the Coast Guard and then
the *AnaCat*.

"*Tenino* to *AnaCat, Tenino* to *AnaCat*. Coast Guard Sitka
Air Unit contacted. ETA seventy minutes. They will drop a
pump, and evacuate crew as needed. Sitka Air Unit. Do you copy?
Tenino standing by on One Six. Over."

We watched the radio as though somebody might appear in
it. Once there was some crackling like somebody might be trying to call, but nobody said anything. I repeated the information
on the helicopter. Still nothing.

"We're getting pretty close ourselves," Mom said.

"Right over there is the entrance to Kialik Strait," I told her,
pointing at nothing in the snow. "We could be home in an hour."

"You want to go home?" Mom asked.

I turned my head so I didn't have to look at her. "How do
you know it isn't a trick? They could be right on top of us, any
minute. Bam, bam, bam, it's all over."

"You want to go home?"

I shrugged. No more dying? What about no more guilt trips, Mom? But I didn't say it out loud. "Go for it, I guess."

Mom nudged the throttle up. "Try them again," she said. "Tell them *Tenino*'s on the way!"

TOM

"Joy to you and meeee!" Mom kept shouting, and even Bo was laughing a little, but he shouted her down. "'*Join* the fishes in the deep blue sea' is more like it, Mom."

I thought everybody was crazy, a little, jiving around and singing just because probably the *Anacat* was going to catch up with us or else we had to try to help them out, and we didn't even really know which. But Mom and Bo seemed revved about it, so I guessed it would be OK.

You know what I was doing, anyway. Taking care of Toby. Even Bo wouldn't ever have to do that, I knew that. Mom would never make Bo take care of Toby, not in one million zillion years. Only me. I knew she was retarded, but I was super tired of taking care of her. Bo and Mom would get to do everything at the sinking boat, throw out the life preservers, lines, stuff like that, maybe get to haul the guys out of the water, and I'd get to change Toby's diaper.

I sat there, getting all mad, and sort of poking at her, not very nice, and she got mad and started crying, so Mom said, "Tom, take her somewhere else, can't you? We might not hear if the *AnaCat* calls."

Good. Why did we have to save them when they were such jerks, anyway? I didn't say it out loud, just under my breath like I'm not supposed to, and Mom looked at me mad, so I dragged Toby back to the bunk and brought her some spoons and stuff from the galley, but she didn't want to play, only hang on Mom. I shut the door to the wheelhouse so she couldn't go in, and she really yelled then, so I just let her. I was pretty mad at everybody.

After a while she got tired from yelling and fell asleep crosswise on the bunk. I just lay there thinking about Mom and Toby when I was trying to drag them over the rail and Bo was trying to keep the Zodiac from getting pulled away by the current. I thought they were gone about a million times because it was so hard to hold them with the water screaming past, Bo yelling at me, "Help me, you gotta hold her, goddammit, Tom, lift!"

All at once I thought that Mom must have wanted to jump in. She must have not wanted to go home with me and Bo and Toby. But maybe she thought, "Well, we're aground now, so I can swim to shore with Toby and come back and get Tom and Bo." She probably was thinking that.

Why would anyone jump in, that water just screaming past, and too dark to see where to go? But she must have thought that. She probably was trying to save us. Nobody could ever take us away from her, like she said, and so she had to save us from the *AnaCat* and from being aground, in case the boat had a hole in it, or something.

It was so dark, she probably didn't know the water was going so fast around us. She thought she could swim to shore with Toby. And leave Toby and come back for us. But you couldn't leave Toby on shore by herself. She might not have thought of that. Probably she just didn't think about that.

But then, I thought I'd never really known what Mom was thinking. Not till she talked about her dad getting killed. Even a kid two years old would have understood that.

It seemed like there were all sorts of dangerous things inside people's heads that you couldn't see. Like the reef in Rocky Pass. "Hazards to navigation," like the Coast Guard was always saying. "Mariners should use caution in transiting the area." Only not just mariners, I thought. Me.

SUDDENLY I HEARD Mom shout out something in the wheelhouse. I jumped up, trying not to wake Toby, and opened the door. Mom was pointing and stamping up and down, and Bo was staring through the window with his nose practically on the glass.

"Rockets," Mom shouted. "Bombs bursting in air. It's war, it's war." She made a machine gun noise, atatata atatata atatata, and started yelling, *"Praise the Lord, and pass the ammunition . . ."*

I looked at her—it seemed so weird a thing to be doing, singing about war and shooting a machine gun while you're trying to steer a boat. She was crying, tears running down her face and her nose running and her eyes squinched up, and she kept trying to wipe her face on the sleeve of her sweater, not letting go of the wheel. Bo maybe didn't notice she was crying because he was trying to see out through the snow.

Then I heard this boom, even through all that noise from the waves and engine, and in a minute there was a flash, orange turning to black smoke and then disappearing in the snow.

Bo said, real excited, "Yeah, yeah, there—look at it— they've set off another flare."

Mom was shouting, *". . . and we'll alllllll be free."*

She stopped crying and started laughing and singing the words louder, and going atatata atatata in between. "It's blowing away, man, blowing in the wind," she shouted. It seemed like that set her off again, and she started singing, *"How many times must the cannonballs fly . . ."*

"Easy," Bo said. "Take her in slow now. The current's with us, and it's way too fast—you know Inian Pass. We'll be all the way through to Cross Sound if you don't take it easy."

Mom reached for the throttle and pulled it back so we dropped way down, and the current started throwing us around sideways.

"We're gonna roll right on top of her in a minute," Bo said, "unless you jog this boat up and go straight through the Pass."

"No way," Mom said. "Did you see those flares? That's our destination. A dust-off. We're going to pick those guys up."

"Helicopters do dust-offs, Mom, not boats. The helicopter ought to be here by now."

Bo was trying to see through the snow again. He pressed his face to the glass. "Can't see it," he said, "too much snow."

"Well, maybe it's too much for the helicopter," Mom said. "They probably can't see to come in."

"They'll come along the water, not over the mountains," Bo said. "They'll make it. We could duck in along the north edge, or go through and down to Pelican, or . . ."

Mom stopped him. "Swim for it, kid, we're going to get those guys off that boat. Another flare. See it? You can just see the smoke now. Right off there to port. We'll be there in five minutes."

She took one hand off the wheel and waved her arm, then grabbed the wheel again when we rolled. "Get the lines out, Bo. Tom, get those life rings off the bulkhead and tie some lines on them for throwing. Wait a second—shut the door so Toby can't get out here if she wakes up."

Bo was trying to watch through the windshield, the wipers going a mile a minute, but only little holes that they could make in the ice. "I'm going up on the bridge," he said.

He headed out before he fastened his jacket even, trying to get his gloves out of his pocket and at the same time shove the door open onto the deck.

I shut the door to the stateroom where Toby was, grabbed a jacket and went out on deck. I turned around and got up on the gearbox and got hold of one of the life rings. The life ring finally came loose, and I got one more, but that was all I could reach.

Bo had hauled a bunch of lines out of the lazerette, and we fastened a couple of them to the life rings for throwing over. He opened the door again and then turned and hollered back at me, "Get in here."

Mom pulled the throttle back so we were washing around every way in the current, not even going ahead. Then she turned the wheel over hard, and we rolled so bad I thought we were going down. I was lying on one wall looking up at the other, then up again, starting over the other way.

Bo started screaming, "Turn, turn," and Mom tried to fight

the wheel back, but she wasn't strong enough to hold it, I guess, because the next wave caught us and we rolled again. Mom was shouting, "They're right there, right beside us," and Bo was grabbing at the wheel trying to drag us around. I was just trying not to get thrown over upside down again.

All three of us dragged on the wheel, finally, and we got pretty straight on with the waves, at least quartering. The wind wasn't bad, but the current was running full bore against it, so all the swells coming in off Cross Sound were just piling up in front of us. Mom let Bo take it. She grabbed a jacket and headed out. I could hear Toby crying but I couldn't let her out there in the wheelhouse, and anyway I thought I'd have to help Bo hang on that wheel if we got turned again.

All of a sudden a bright light shone across the bow, and sort of moved around. "Mom," Bo said. "She's got the spotlight. That's great. Gives them a perfect target. It's probably nothing but a fucking trap!"

The spotlight moved around on the bow and then off over the water to port, and there was the *AnaCat,* tipped sideways so most of what we could see was the bottom of her hull and rudder, every wave breaking over her. I didn't see how she could still be afloat, except she must have been held up by the rocks. One of the guys crawled out onto the deck to signal us when they saw the spotlight. Right that second we saw him raise his head, and when I looked up, there was the helicopter.

It came over low, a bright light under it, and tilted sideways, probably so the pilot and everyone could see what was happening. The downdraft from the rotors churned spray off the waves and the wind blew it in sheets across the *Anacat.* The helicopter turned and disappeared in the snow.

Bo reached up, grabbed the transmitter and handed it to me. "Call them," he said. "Find out what they want us to do."

"Mayday relay," I said, like I'd heard him. "This is *Tenino*. Over."

"Coast Guard Sitka Air Unit, *Tenino*. Tell the crew they'll have to go in the water. We can't pick them off the deck. Over."

"How can we do that?" I asked Bo. "If they can hear us, they can hear the helicopter."

"Get that loud-hailer bullhorn thing out of the locker and get up on the bridge."

I shoved around in the locker and found the bullhorn, went out on deck and clawed my way up the ladder. Mom was up there, hanging on to the aft edge of the bridge, trying to aim the spotlight. I stood right next to her and shouted at the *Anacat* but I knew they couldn't hear. The helicopter came in again right over us. The noise was so terrible I could hardly hold the horn because of trying to cover my ears, and the downdraft sucked our breath away.

When they'd made another pass, and disappeared again, I waved the horn so that the guys on the *AnaCat* maybe would see it and know we were trying to talk to them. That worked, too, because they crawled out, trying to hang on to the deck rail to keep toward our side of the boat.

"Water pickup," I yelled as loud as I could, and tried to point so they'd get it even if they couldn't hear me. Watching them, I knew I'd never be able to jump off the boat into that huge sea. Not a chance. I'd rather stay right there, even if it was sinking.

The helicopter came in closer this time; the draft from the rotors about knocked me and Mom onto the floor of the bridge.

They had the hatch open, and I could see people inside, pushing stuff around, getting it ready to drop. The people on the deck of the *AnaCat* looked like orange astronauts in their survival suits. One of them probably was Lanny, but you couldn't tell who anybody was in those suits.

The helicopter circled low and dropped a ladder with a basket on it. It looked like the people on the deck were arguing, and one of them turned around and went back toward the cabin. One of the others tried to drag him toward the stern, but the person grabbed on to the rail and kicked at him. Finally two of them jumped over.

The helicopter hovered right over one of them and he grabbed hold of the basket, hauled himself into it, and right away the basket started going up. When that guy was up they dropped it again for the other one. The third person was teetering on the boat rail, waiting to go over, I guess, after the others were up, but looking like maybe he wasn't going to jump. I knew how he felt. I'd never be able to make myself jump in that water.

Mom gave me a shove and said, "Get inside. Tell Bo to stand by till the other one goes over, and then move off of here fast. We're way too close in."

I was halfway down the ladder, watching over my shoulder the helicopter, when this huge wave out of nowhere hit us. We were lifting up like on an elevator and dropping down, twisting like the whole world had tipped over. I was lying on the deck trying to hang on to something, anything I could get my hand on, and everything on the deck was sliding around, banging and smashing against the rails. I could hear the helicopter rotor ratatat right on top of us, and I knew for sure we were all going down.

JESS

The surge hits—I can't think, only grab. Not now—jesus god—*not now!*

Finally we level out a little. I have to crawl back and hang off the bridge to see if Tom's still on board. He's lying flat out, hanging on to the boom support with one hand—thank god's he's there. I inch onto the ladder and drop to the deck. We wrestle the door open and reel through the cabin to the wheelhouse.

Bo is clinging like death to the wheel, static sparking from the radio, now and then a word, then a few together.

"Missed . . . surge . . . no   sight . . . can   you . . . over . . ."

I take the transmitter and call them. "*Tenino*. You're breaking up. *AnaCat* crewman missing? Confirm. Over."

"Roger, *Tenino*." They come in clearer, this time. "We have no sighting. Continuing search. Over . . ."

"Roger, Coast Guard. We'll assist if possible. This is *Tenino*. Over and out."

Bo turns the wheel hard, nudges the throttle up and says, "Take her, Tom. Keep her away from shore. I'm going out."

I help Tom keep the wheel over so we can quarter again, when Bo starts thumping on the ceiling and hollering down the tube, "Turn, turn to port, I see him, portside, hard dammit, turn!"

We can't see anything at all, but when we start coming up I do see an object floating, high above our heads. Then it's down in the trough. I can't see it anymore. But that indecipherable shape, visible one instant, then gone is a man about to drown.

And now we have one of those choices that isn't a choice— every answer's wrong. A little girl holds a gun aimed at your buddy. Who dies? Who knows? My mother knows. I forgive you, Mom.

Here's the choice: get that man, whoever he is, out of the water, or . . . what choice? There isn't any choice. A man is going to drown and we can save him.

Where have all the soldiers gone . . . gone to graveyards . . . every . . . one . . .

A survival suit rolled in the locker—put your feet into it, unroll it to the waist, grope around for the zipper—hate these things—can't move in them, can't do anything useful once your hands are inside—the gloves are stiff—hope you can hold him, tie him up, whatever . . .

I waddle to the door and yell at Bo to get me a line. When he sees the suit, he comes barging through the door. "No way, no way you're going back in that water. Shit, we've already pulled you out once!"

I finish zipping up, push him off and get out on deck before I blow up the collar. "This one isn't your choice, soldier," I tell him. "Tie this into my harness."

Bo is furious with fright, I can see, but he fastens the line to my harness, and cleats the other end down on the rail. Tom's trying to hold the boat where we saw the man floating, but I can't see him anymore. Tom must have seen him again, though, because the boat veers to port and we roll into the trough, the next wave lifting us. From the top, I can just see a shape in the next trough, and then we're sliding down the mountainside toward it.

I lie on the rail and get my huge legs lifted and stretched out behind me. We're in the trough again, lying over so that all I can see is sky and snow streaking past.

Now the iron mountain is rising next to us, lifting me when I slide from the rail . . . I'm looking down on the boat, looking down on Bo clinging to the rail, now Tom's there next to him, slow motion, slow motion . . . I can reach him now . . .

. . . a man is swimming in this pool—the bottom of this pool is Never . . . I have him in my arms—I have him I have him . . .

. . . get the line around—can't reach can't reach—yes—I have him.

. . . rising again—can't see . . . can't see the bottom . . . pull this line . . . Bo, Bo—pull on this line . . .

. . . this man swimming and swimming and not swimming . . .

. . . they have him they have him—I can see him up on the rail . . . I am

PART FIVE

TOM

Bo told me to get going, get headed back toward Tern Bay. Bo was crying, so I got going.

The snow was still coming down too hard to see anything, so I didn't dare put the throttle up very much, but I could see on the radar where the shore was, and I headed out more toward the center of the Pass, even though the current is harder out there, but I didn't want to wind up on the rocks like the *AnaCat*. I was still trying to stop myself shaking, but I thought probably I never would.

I had started shaking when I knew that Mom was going back in that water, but I made myself keep thinking what to do. I tried to keep the bow where I'd seen something floating, but all I could see were waves waves waves coming every way.

Mom was out on the bow pointing, or more flopping her arm, because of that suit. I tried to turn the bow toward where she was flopping. In a second she sort of pushed her arm back at me, like slow now, ease up, so I pulled the throttle back, and of course we got turned sideways again, roll, roll, no way on at all.

Then Bo came up to the window and pointed in the water, and when we rolled again I saw the man right next to the starboard bow. Bo started yelling at Mom and trying to hold her back, not wanting her to go, but she pushed him off her and lay out flat on the rail. Then she turned over and disappeared over the side. The line she was tied to zipped over the rail until it was mostly pulled out, but still slack a little, so Mom must have been still close to the boat.

Bo hung over watching, and it seemed like about twenty hours before he moved. Then he took the line Mom was fastened on, and started walking the slack in it back toward the stern until I couldn't see him anymore. I tried to hold the boat steady but it was hard because we didn't have much way on.

I couldn't stand it that I didn't know what was happening or where anybody was, so I set the steering on auto and the engine forward just enough to hold against the current. When the autopilot took over, I went out on deck. Bo was hanging over the rail.

I hung over next to Bo, and there was Mom practically in my face. She was trying to get her arm around the man's head, but it seemed like he was fighting her and pushing her under, and she was also trying to keep from smashing into the boat.

Bo shouted at me, "Pull her in. He's so panicked he'll drown them both."

We hauled on the line, pulling them both toward us because the guy was hanging on to Mom and shoving her clear under. On the next roll, the guy came slamming right up at me, Mom under him. Only it wasn't a guy, it was Lanny. Right that second when I could see her face, I thought, no way, no way I'm pulling her out of that water. I hated her all over again. She wasn't even a keeper—how could Mom go in there to save her? Bo said, "Shit—not her" when he saw who it was.

I tried to keep the line tight while Bo got a line from one of the pulleys under her arms. We hauled together on the line and Bo threw himself down on the deck so his weight under the pulley would get her up over the edge. Finally, with us both hauling, she came over right on top of me.

Just when I got out from under her, there was another surge like the one that hit when the helicopter was there. A huge wave broke right over the whole boat. When we came up, nobody. Mom was gone. Empty water. Nightmare time again.

Bo screamed, "Not the prop, not the prop!" He hauled on the line Mom was tied to, and it seemed like the line was caught under the stern. I could see she could've got dragged into the propeller. I ran and hung over the stern and there she was, floating right below me. She hadn't gone in the prop, but she must have gotten slammed against the hull, she wasn't moving at all, not trying to swim or anything, and she had blood all over her face.

I reached over and tried to get some slack in the line, and hold her away from the boat while Bo pulled her around to the side, but the way we were rolling, I could only see her sometimes, sometimes no.

When Bo got her around at the side, he turned the line around a winch on the boom. When we went down again, I got my fingers on her suit and hung there till the boat went over the other way. Then Bo winched in on the line, and she came slamming up over the rail.

Bo was panting away, "Help me . . . drag . . . carry her . . . help me . . . she's in shock . . ."

Mom was like nowhere, not talking, not moving, blood pouring down all over her face. We got her on the bed, unzipped her suit, and rolled her in the sleeping bag, just like in Rocky Pass. It seemed to me like we hadn't ever gotten out of Rocky Pass. It seemed to me like all the bad stuff in the whole world just kept happening over and over.

"Get going, Tom," Bo said. "Get us out of here." I don't think he knew he was crying. Or maybe he didn't even care if I saw that he was crying. Maybe it's OK to sometimes screw up a little, even with your brother.

BO

patched my mother's forehead. It would take some stitching, later—she'd have a scar. She'd hit the side of the boat hard enough to split her forehead open, maybe it had split her skull in half? I tried to open her eye and look at the pupil, but I couldn't tell anything in what little light there was. Her pulse seemed regular but fast, maybe almost as fast as mine. "Mom," I said, "Mom, wake up."

I didn't like to move her, and I kept having to pick Toby up, because she wanted her mother. So did I. After struggling with Toby for a while, I went through to the galley, got her some crackers, and poured milk in her bottle. I dragged a cushion off the galley bench and put it on the floor of the wheelhouse, practically under Tom's feet, put Toby down on it, and shut the door so she wouldn't get in and climb on Mom. Then I went down the ladder to check on Lanny.

She was moving a little, now and then opening her eyes and squinting up at the ceiling. I knew she didn't have a clue about what happened to her—she'd gotten a pretty hard hit somewhere along the line, but she was looking good compared to Mom. I asked her how she was feeling and she croaked something I didn't get, but at least she was conscious. I thought I should try to get something hot into her—tea with sugar or something, so I went up and put the kettle on.

Mom hadn't moved. I stood looking down at her, and all at once I was totally angry. How could one person demand so much? I kept wondering why she would risk everything, her life and ours, too, for that ugly bitch lying down below. I mean, what was the trade-off? I felt like shaking her and shouting at her—"What were you trading, Mom?" She hadn't even asked us. I mean, she just assumed we could do it. That we'd be there. Like one of those stupid "trust" games, where you hurl yourself blindfolded off a cliff or something because you have total faith in your friends to catch you.

What infuriated me the most, though, was thinking she wasn't even crazy. She'd tried to fit herself to a world where she couldn't like, lock in. So finally she'd just fallen back on herself and right away set a standard I'd never live up to.

I started to cry. Sheeh! I really needed that. I don't even know what I was crying about, for pete's sake, but I sure made the most of it, like really bawling? It was like everything that had happened had turned to saltwater inside me.

■   ■   ■

ALL MY FURY finally ran down like a clock running down and I wasn't mad anymore, only I wanted it to be over. I wanted to know what came next, *now.* I wanted Sara.

I started worrying that something had happened to her—she'd moved away, she'd fallen in love with some geek from Seattle, she'd been buried in an avalanche. You know how you start worrying when you've been away and you're almost home—the house burned down, the dog died, your mom went crazy . . .

I made a picture of Sara, waiting for us on the dock, standing there waiting for me to throw her the lines, her long legs pressed tight in the cold, her hair blowing back in the wind leaving those little curls clinging around her face, her eyes meeting mine when I threw the stern line over. No smile, she wouldn't smile yet when our eyes met, because we had to say things first, the things we said when we looked at each other like that. She'd bend over and cleat the spring line, then the stern, straighten up, look again. Then the smile. Sara, be there.

Mom started working her mouth back and forth like she was trying to get it loosened up. I watched her, then reached into the sleeping bag and took her hand and squeezed it. In a second, she squeezed back, then opened her eyes.

"Did we do it?" she said.

"We got her."

"Alive?"

"She's alive," I said. "Are you?"

"I didn't have to die this time," she said. "Because I always can."

Sheeeh!

I could hear Tom calling from the wheelhouse. I opened the door.

"Is she OK?" he asked. He turned to look at me a second and it seemed like his whole face was eyes.

"Yeah," I said. "I think she'll make it. Her head seems to be all right. On the outside, anyway."

"Inside, too," Mom said, "inside, too, you guys."

She turned her head very carefully so she could see Tom at the wheel. She said, "You be the tree, Tom. I'll be the rock."

"Huunh," Tom said. He leaned back to look in at her and then at me. He shrugged, a sort of "what next" shrug.

Her eyes closed, and she slept for a while.

I went back down with the tea. Lanny sat up and tried to take the cup, but her hands were too stiff to hold it. I held it so she could sip a little. She seemed puzzled over who I was, finally said, "Don?"

"The helicopter got him," I said.

She shook her head and repeated, "helicopter, helicopter," as though she was trying to place it. Her eyes closed right there while she was sitting up and she slumped down sound asleep. I think she was mostly exhausted, not really injured. I straightened her out and went back up to Mom.

Toby had gone to sleep on the cushion at Tom's feet. "Leave the door open," Tom said.

"Aye, aye, Captain," I said, and he laughed.

Mom opened her eyes again. "Bo," she said, rolling her eyes over to look at me. "Answer me. Tell me the truth. Would a man actually take an assault weapon and kill someone just because he'd been fired? Could a man even own such a weapon?" She rubbed her hands across her mouth. "And those social workers. Would anyone actually take children away from a mother who loves them?"

Her voice rose and she raised her head to stare at me. "Could a man lean on a Dumpster behind a restaurant and die of *starvation?* Please!"

I could have drowned in those green-water eyes. I needed to tell her, "No, none of those things could ever happen. You invented them, Mom—you've been dreaming."

"Mom," I said, "it happens. But not to us anymore. Not now. Not to us."

She reached for my hand, and here it came, one of her talk numbers, a whole crowd speaking through her mouth. I mean, ice water shock cure? I don't think so.

"I keep hearing those words marching to war." Her voice sank to a whisper. *Tenino, die, Tenino, die. He's mean, Gus— you have to get rid of him. Go then, Boone, see if I care.* All those voices—there isn't any place to think anymore."

She raised her arms straight toward the ceiling. "Wait—I have a question. May we have a drumroll, please . . ."

She looked at me and actually laughed. "Do I have to listen to them?"

"Let's listen to our audience reaction, Audrey Bickle.

"Let's not, Jess Rohlik."

I think Tom and I got it at the exact same second. We looked through the door at each other and then we were laughing so hard I don't know why he didn't steer us straight up on shore. When we could catch our breath, Tom said, "Hey, sounds like she's back to normal."

I mean like, depend on it?

TOM

When Bo came out to put water on the stove for hot water bottles, I thought he was going to tell me where we should go and how to do everything. But he didn't. He didn't even say one single word. Like he thought I'd know without him telling me. Like he honestly did think I wasn't a little kid anymore.

We were getting out of the Pass and I could see the flasher in the middle that's opposite Idaho Inlet. The water was a lot calmer, even though it was still snowing hard. I started thinking about what Lanny would do when she found out she was on the boat we'd stolen. Lanny didn't know where she was, Bo said—probably she'd got bashed into the *AnaCat*. I thought she probably was about scared to death, too, losing the helicopter, and all that crazy booming water everywhere. I hoped she was about scared to death. I kept thinking how I'd planned to sink their boat and them, too. I didn't feel sorry for her one tiniest small amount, getting that scared. Maybe it was all right we'd saved her, if Mom was OK. But it seemed like almost we'd traded Mom for Lanny. Yeeech!

Then I all of a sudden thought we hadn't told the Coast Guard we'd found her and maybe the helicopter might still be looking. So I reached over and got the transmitter and called them: "Calling United States Coast Guard. Fishing vessel, *Tenino, Tenino, Tenino,* WYP4577. Over."

In just a second they answered, it was a woman now, and she said, "This is United States Coast Guard Juneau Communication Center. Come in, *Tenino*. Over."

"This is *Tenino,* Coast Guard. We found Lanny, the one that got lost off of the *AnaCat.* Over."

"Coast Guard Juneau Com Center, confirming you have missing crewman aboard, *Tenino?* Over."

"Roger, Coast Guard, we have her. Over."

"Roger, *Tenino,*" the Coast Guard woman said. "Do you need medical assistance at this time? Over."

"This is *Tenino*. I don't think we actually need medical assistance right this second, because my brother knows pretty much first aid, and we're almost home. Over."

I waited for her to answer, but really listening to Mom talking to Bo. All at once I got so excited that Mom was going to be OK and we were almost home that I just shouted it right out on the transmitter, "My mom's alive!"

Then I remembered and said, "Oh, I mean, this is *Tenino*—my mom got her head cut and she got knocked out, I guess, hitting the boat, because she went in the water to try to get lines on

Lanny which was actually very brave if you ask me, but she's talking now so she's OK. Over."

"Roger, *Tenino,* confirming no need for immediate medical assistance. Please switch and answer Channel Twenty-two alpha. Over."

I switched channels and called her back.

"Roger, *Tenino,* what is your present position, destination and expected time of arrival? Over."

"This is *Tenino.* We're a little ways east of South Inian Pass. I can see the flasher by Idaho Inlet ahead, a little to port. We are heading for Tern Bay. That's where we live. I don't know time of arrival exactly because I don't know how to do the LORAN like Bo does, but probably I'd say two hours, or one, even. Over."

"*Tenino,* may we have the names, ages, and addresses of those aboard. Over."

"This is *Tenino.* Well, I don't know how old Lanny is, but she lives in Ketchikan on Reynolds Street, but I don't remember the number, only it's a brown house, pretty big. My mom's name is Jess Rohlik and she's thirty-five and my brother is Bo Rohlik and he's fifteen, and my sister is October Rain and she's three. And our address is Tern Bay, Alaska, 99945. Over."

"Roger, *Tenino,* May we have your name and age, please? Over."

"Oh yeah, I forgot. My name is Tom Rohlik and my age is ten years old. Over. No, wait, not yet over, because actually, we stole this boat from that guy, Kozloff, that the helicopter picked up, because we had to get away from them and get our mom away from them because they do drugs and carry it around to other boats, and we found out how they do it. And they can have the *Tenino* back the second we get to Tern Bay, but I hope we don't have to go to kids' jail or anything, because we just wanted to get my mom away from them. Anyway my mom was really brave and saved one of them even though they do drugs. Now over."

It seemed like the lady at the Coast Guard was really a long time coming back, but probably they got a call on another channel or something.

But after a while she came back on.

"This is Coast Guard Juneau Com Center, *Tenino* We have checked with the helicopter and they will hold Mr. Kozloff and Mr. Lockwood, pending your report. Please proceed to Tern Bay as planned. Medical personnel will meet you at the dock."

She sort of laughed, and it sounded like she said something to somebody else. Then she came back and said, "We're making a notation of your assistance to the *AnaCat,* and your mother's bravery. No kids' jail, skipper. Over and out."

Skipper? Me, she meant? Hooeee.

We were getting up Kialik Strait pretty far, and it had almost stopped snowing. I could see the shore a little, and a couple of times the light flash at Kialik Point. Then I all of a sudden saw something else in the water ahead of us, off to starboard. A skiff. Not going anywhere, just slapping around in the water, tossing up and down. When we got closer, I could see someone in an orange life jacket, waving an oar. Somebody with a broken-down engine, caught by the tide. You can't row very far up the Strait when the tide's going out.

I didn't know what to do. It seemed like we already had enough troubles, stealing a boat, Mom with her head bashed up, Lanny not in too great shape, either. But I remembered being in the skiff in Ketchikan, those creepy water voices, waiting for that Santa to get me. Whoever was out in that skiff, they were probably cold and scared, too, waiting out there in the snow for someone to get them.

I started thinking, what can I do all by myself, Mom hurt, and Bo having to take care of everyone? Nothing, is all. Nothing I can do, all by myself.

But then I thought, yes I can. It seems like you can always do something, right? Maybe only throw a line, but something. And that Coast Guard lady meant me: Tom Rohlik, skipper of the F/V *Tenino*. So when we got closer, I headed over.

Marcia Simpson lives on Lopez Island in the San Juans. *Rogue's Yarn* is her third novel.